PRAISE FOR SANDRA HILL'S CAJUN NOVELS

"The action is fast, and the love scenes are wonderful...Do yourself a favor and pick up this very funny book. Then write to Sandra Hill and demand sequels."
—All About Romance on *The Love Potion*

"If you like your romances hot and spicy and your men the same way, then you will like *Tall, Dark, and Cajun*...Eccentric characters, witty dialogue, humorous situations...and hot romance...[Hill] perfectly captures the bayou's mystique and makes it come to life."
—RomRevToday.com on *Tall, Dark, and Cajun*, a *USA Today* bestseller and named as one of the Top 10 Romances of 2004 by Amazon and *Booklist*

"Hill will tickle readers' funny bones yet again as she writes in her trademark sexy style. A real crowd-pleaser, guar-an-teed."
—*Booklist* (starred review, on *The Cajun Cowboy*)

"Hill's thigh-slapping humor and thoughtful look at the endangered Louisiana bayou ecosystem turn this into an engaging read."
—*Publishers Weekly*, on *The Red-Hot Cajun*

"4 Stars! A hoot and a half! Snappy dialogue and outrageous characters keep the tempo lively and the humor infectious in this crazy adventure story. Hill is a master at taking outlandish situations and making them laugh-out-loud funny."
—*Romantic Times BOOKreviews Magazine* on *Pink Jinx*, a *USA Today* bestseller

BAYOU ANGEL

CAJUN SERIES, BOOK 8

SANDRA HILL

SH
BOOKS

This book is dedicated to all those hurricane and environmental disaster survivors who struggle to regain their old lives. Tante Lulu recognized your bravery and needs in this book by establishing a new foundation. While her charity is a fictitious one, there are plenty of good ones out there.

And this book is dedicated to my husband Robert C. Hill who has led and aided many a charitable endeavor in our region. His generous spirit inspires us all.

CHAPTER 1

The angel was wild tonight...

*A*ngel Sabato stood at the edge of the dance floor like a dunce, shaking in his thousand-dollar Tres Outlaws boots as he watched the redhead shake her booty to the beat of "Wild Thing." For an ex-nun, she sure had moves.

Ironically, he was the one feeling wild. His hands were clammy, his heart was thumping—*da dump, da dump, da dump*—and, truth to tell, he was scared spitless. Tonight was going to be the night. Do-or-die time.

It was ridiculous, really. He was thirty-four years old. He'd been around the block so many times there were probably street signs named after him. At the least, his "tread marks" were notorious. Shyness wasn't even in his vocabulary. After all, he was the dick-for-brains who'd once bared it all for *Playgirl* magazine.

Just then the redhead in question, Grace O'Brien, noticed him and smiled widely, crooking a forefinger for him to come out and join her.

Not a chance.

It wasn't dancing he had on his mind.

She said something to her partner, one of the young LeDeuxs...a freshman at LSU. Then she left the kid behind and snaked a slow, sensuous boogie toward him, her twinkling green eyes holding his the entire time, her arms held out in front of her, fingers beckoning. She must be half plastered or, more likely, in a teasing mood.

He was not in the mood for teasing.

"Yo, matey," she drawled at him.

This was the tail end of the Pirate Ball. It was being held here in Houma, Louisiana, to celebrate the successful search by Jinx, Inc., a treasure-hunting company, for Jean Lafitte's hidden gold. Thus the silly pirate talk. Not to mention silly pirate costumes.

He and Grace had worked on the Jinx team's Pirate Project these past weeks. Before that they'd been professional poker players. And before that, Grace had been a nun, and he had been in the navy, then construction, and...well, a lot of things.

She was dancing around him now, dressed in a saucy tavern-wench costume with a jagged knee-length hem, while he was in a puffy shirt tied with a red sash. *Jerry Seinfeld would be so proud of me.*

When he pretended to ignore her sexy dancing, she grabbed his upper arm and attempted to tug him forward. Being about seventy-five pounds heavier at six-foot-one to her measly five-foot-five, he was pretty much immovable.

She put her hands on her hips and glared at him. "Come out here and shake a peg leg, you randy buccaneer."

He had to grin at that. "Who says I'm randy?"

"You're always randy."

"And you know this...how?"

"All the satisfied smiles I've seen on women exiting your revolving bedroom door the past ten years."

"You noticed?"

"Stop changing the subject. I wanna dance."

"Are you blitzed?" he asked with a laugh.

2

"Just a little," she slurred.

Luckily, the DJ changed the music to a different pace. Now Mariah Carey was urging "Touch My Body."

He opened his arms to Grace and adjusted her so that her arms were around his neck and his hands were linked behind her waist, just above her butt. And yes, Mariah, he had touching in mind. Touching Grace.

"I'm flying back to Jersey early tomorrow morning. I need to talk to you," he said into her hair, which smelled like apples, or was it peaches? Some kind of frickin' fruit, anyway.

"Uh-huh. I'm listening," she replied, definitely not listening as she nuzzled her face into the crook of his neck, inadvertently pressing her belly against the crotch of his tights.

Yeah, he was wearing XXX-sized tights. With testosterone-induced hysterical irrelevance, he mused that the guys back in his old gang in Newark would get a kick out of him in latex, unless it were of the prophylactic kind. Or was that spandex? Spandex, latex, whatever! That was beside the point. *Call me crazy, but did she just lick my ear?*

Blood drained from his head and slam-dunked into sex central. For a second, he thought his knees might give out.

"Not here," he gurgled. "Let's go outside for a walk, down by the bayou. Better yet, I'll take you back to your hotel room."

"I already checked out. I'll be staying with Tante Lulu from now on." She leaned her head back to look at him. "You sound serious."

"I am serious, babe." He wondered if she was aware that when she arched back like that it caused his erection to rub against her belly button, which was exposed by her low-riding wench skirt. And that was damn serious.

"You can drive me to the cottage. Let's go tell Tante Lulu that I'm leaving."

"So, you're staying with that Cajun dingbat, huh?" he asked, arm looped over her shoulder as they walked to the other side of the hall, where Tante Lulu was chattering away to some guy in a frock coat and tricorne hat. At least he wasn't wearing tights.

Louise Rivard, better known as Tante Lulu, was the craziest old woman he'd ever met. But she was a noted *traiteur*, or folk healer, and Grace had decided to apprentice herself to the fruit-cake in hopes of learning more about the healing arts. Really, Grace's life was like a pendulum swinging from one extreme to the other. Nun to poker player to treasure hunter to healer. He couldn't wait to see where she landed next, as long as she took him along for the ride.

"Don't call her a dingbat." Grace turned slightly and swatted him on the chest, then grinned. "Even if she is a dingbat."

"Grace...Angel...hope y'all had a good time t'night." Tante Lulu was dressed as a senior citizen pirate gal. A scary sight, to be sure —she was ninety years old, give or take. No one knew for sure. She eyed them suspiciously when Grace told her she would be leaving with him. Grace was oblivious to that pointed look, which took in his arm on Grace's shoulder, but he could practically see the matchmaking wheels churning in Tante Lulu's little brain. "That full moon t'night, she is purty enough to make a cat smooch a hound dog."

"Huh?" Grace said.

"Welcome to TanteLuluville," he muttered under his breath, then smiled.

"Ya got a hope chest?" Tante Lulu asked Angel just before they walked away. Tante Lulu had a tradition of making hope chests for the men in her family, or male friends of the family, just before the "thunderbolt of love" hit them.

Hah! He had news for the Louisiana love bug. That thund-erbolt had done its business with him a long time ago.

"So, what did you want to talk to me about?" Grace asked, once they were sitting in his rental car back in Tante Lulu's cottage driveway. She didn't seem so tipsy anymore.

A full moon allowed him to see Grace's face. She was

concerned. For him.

"I want you to come back with me, sweetheart." Well, that was laying his cards on the table from the get-go.

She frowned. "Back to your motel room?"

"No. I mean, yeah, that would be great, but I meant, fly back to the East Coast with me in the morning. Come with me and the Jinx team to Germany for our next project." He gulped. "Just come with me, that's all."

"I don't understand. You know I quit treasure hunting. It was never intended to be more than a one-shot deal for me. I've already explained why I'm staying here." She moved closer and accidentally put a hand on his thigh.

Big mistake, that.

He picked her up by the waist and laid her across his lap, her head cradled over his left elbow. "This isn't about treasure hunting, or folk healing, or any other damn profession. It's about you and me." He leaned down, kissed her lightly on the lips, and whispered against her gaping mouth, "I love you, Grace."

She squirmed into a sitting position on his lap. "I love you, too, sweetie. You're my best friend."

"Dammit! That's not what I'm talking about. I'm *in love* with you, have been for a long time."

A stunned silence was not what he was looking for here.

"You're kidding, right? What's the punch line? You gonna tell some lame nun joke?" She nipped at his lower lip with her teeth as punishment.

Angel jerked backward, though he didn't release her from his embrace. It was true, he had been teasing Grace with nun jokes for ages, even though she hadn't been a nun for ages, but not now. "This is not a joke, Grace."

She stared at him for a long moment. "Sex. All this forced celibacy while trapped out in the bayou must have turned you horny. You want to have sex with me." Grinning, she taunted him with that last accusation.

"No! I mean, yes. Here's the deal: I don't want sex for sex's sake, as in any ol' female would do. I want to *make love* with you. But that's not all I want. C'mon," he said, opening the car door and hauling her outside. *Oh, God! I'm blowing it. What the hell is wrong with me?* "Let's walk."

"You're scaring me, Angel."

"I'm scaring myself," he muttered as he linked his hand with hers and led her onto Tante Lulu's back porch facing the bayou. Once they were leaning against the rail, he raised their linked hands and kissed her knuckles.

"Oooh, you are smooth."

"You have no idea." Something occurred to him then, related to her mentioning going back to his motel room. *"Would* you have sex with me? Just like that?" He snapped his fingers. "Friends with benefits?"

"I don't know. Maybe."

Angel was both angry and intrigued.

"Actually, I probably wouldn't. Even half drunk. You and I have been friends for a long time. I wouldn't want to do anything to ruin that."

He shook his head. "Not anymore."

She frowned. "What do you mean?"

"I mean, friendship isn't enough anymore. Haven't you felt it, too, Gracie, these weeks we've been here in Louisiana? Those LeDeuxs are crazy as coots, but they're a close-knit family. They would do anything for each other. And you can just see the passion between the husbands and wives. Luc and Sylvie. Remy and Rachel. René and Val. Rusty and Charmaine. John and Celine. That's what I want."

"Passion?"

"Passion, yeah, but more than that."

"Family?" she said with an oddly sad sigh.

"Bingo. I want a woman to love who will love me back. And a home...a real home, not some luxury condo. And kids."

The more he explained himself, the stiffer she got. Then she started biting on her thumbnail, a nervous habit she'd been trying to break ever since he'd first met her. Angel sensed he was losing her bit by bit, but he didn't know how to fix it.

"You and I have no close family ties," she reminded him, pulling her hand out of his grasp and walking to the other end of the porch. He followed after her. "The LeDeuxs have family out the wazoo."

"We can make our own family. I love you, honey. That's what people in love do."

"Where is all this coming from?" Her voice was shrill with panic. "You never mentioned love before."

"It's been there for a long time. I just haven't had the nerve to say anything."

"You? Lacking nerve?"

He nodded. "But I had to say something now. This Amber Project—Jinx's next job—is going to take months, maybe even a year, and it'll be mostly on-site in Germany. We're searching for that famous Amber Room that the Nazis supposedly dismantled and hid. Definitely Jinx's most ambitious treasure hunt yet, and I want you to be there with me. As my wife. Doesn't a honeymoon in Europe sound great?" His heart was racing so fast it felt as if it might explode. Deep down, he sensed he was fighting a losing battle. How could he have misread her so badly?

"This is insane. You've never even kissed me...that way. You can't ask someone to marry you without even a proper kiss."

That was his cue. "I thought you'd never ask."

When she saw his slow grin and his equally slow approach, she stuttered, "That's not what—oh, good grief, what are you doing?"

"About to kiss you properly." Before she could blink, or tell him to get lost, he backed her up against the wall of the cottage, cupped her butt cheeks, raising her to just the right height on her tiptoes, spread her legs with his knees, anchored her with his belly against her belly, combed his fingers through her hair to hold her

7

in place, then kissed her with all the love he'd been holding in for so long.

It should have been a gentle kiss, coaxing. An introduction. Something that said, "Hi! We've known each other forever, as friends, but this is how I really feel. I love you. Do you love me?"

Instead, his sex drive shot from zero to the speed of light in a nanosecond, and the gentle, coaxing kiss was anything but. It was hungry and demanding and said, "Oh, baby, I want you so bad. I can't wait, I can't wait, I can't wait—"

Just then, a loud bellow echoed behind them.

"*What* was that?" he asked, his head jerking back.

"An alligator, I think. Probably Remy's pet Useless. It's harmless."

An alligator? Close by? Harmless? He pressed his forehead against hers, both of them panting for breath.

"This is not the way I want to make love to you the first time, sweetheart. Come back to my motel room with me, and we can talk."

She tried to laugh but it came out choked. "I think we've done enough *talking*." Ducking under his arm, she stepped away.

Immediately, Angel sensed the tension in the air, and it wasn't a good tension. She put up a halting hand when he moved a step closer.

"Angel, I am not going to marry you, and we are not going to have a family together. It is just not going to happen. Ever."

"Why?"

"Because I'm not in love with you."

Angel had been playing poker for too many years not to read her "tells." He'd like to think she was lying through her teeth. She wasn't. How could he have interpreted her signals so wrong? "You don't mean that, Gracie." *Please, God, don't let her mean it.*

"Angel! Come on. I've seen you puking your guts out when you've drunk too much. That's a friend, not a lover."

8

He shrugged. "I've gone out and bought you tampons when you had an accident in white slacks. Didn't make me go 'eew!'"

"I saw you clipping your gross toenails in the kitchen."

He grinned. "You have funny-looking toes. The pinkies are crooked."

"You told me my toes were cute."

"They are cute. Crooked cute."

All this was just blowing smoke, in his opinion. Of no importance. Once again, he tried to move closer.

Once again, she put up a halting hand. "You've been the best friend I've ever had, but I don't feel *that way* about you. Really, I had no idea—"

"Your kiss," he said, indicating with a wave of his hand the section of porch they'd just left, "your kiss said something else."

There were tears in her eyes. "Sexual attraction fueled by too much alcohol."

"I'm not buyin' it."

"You have to. Besides, there are things in my past...things you don't know about me."

"Hell, I have secrets in my past, too. Big deal!" He waited a moment, then asked, "What things?"

"I can't say. Just know that I have good reasons for saying that you and I will never be a family, aside from my just thinking of you as a friend—my best friend."

"Well, we're sure as hell not gonna continue being friends with this between us now."

"Oh, Angel."

"I'm leaving, Gracie. Are you coming with me?"

She shook her head, unable to speak.

"So be it. I doubt we'll be seeing each other again. I don't do begging very well." He stared at her, then added, "I love you, babe. I really do."

~

Two weeks later, and the news heard 'round the world, or at least, down the bayou...

GRACE WAS IN THE PANTRY, using a mortar and pestle to grind dried herbs for Tante Lulu's amazing medicinal potions.

Pennyroyal, horehound, sassafras, and catnip, which could be brewed into a tea and used for coughs.

Yarrow and jimsonweed to go in poultices.

Sumac for arthritis.

So many healing uses for nature's bounty. And any one of them could have varying uses, depending on the stage of development—seed, root, flower, or full-grown plant.

Dust motes danced on the stream of sunlight coming from the lone window. Through the screen she could hear a hundred bayou birds join together, celebrating their unique habitat. As she worked, she glanced over at the floor-to-ceiling shelves, neatly lined with dozens of glass bottles. Some of them were baby food jars. Some jelly jars. Even old green mason jars with lead lids. Each had its own label. Each followed specific ingredients for one of the noted *traiteur's* remedies—983, at last count—that were outlined, longhand, in numerous journals that had their own shelf. No computer software for her boss. *No-siree,* as Tante Lulu would say.

The pungent odors in the room, the feeling of history, the warmth of Tante Lulu's essence: all these things contributed to Grace's sense of well-being. She was at peace. Not happy, precisely, but finally she was where she belonged.

A psychiatrist would have a field day with her history. From promiscuous teenager to nun. Nun to poker player. Poker player to treasure hunter. Treasure hunter to folk healer. Still, she'd found a place that felt safe and promising to her.

The only thing interfering with her happiness was Angel. Her heart grieved at the hole her former friend had created in her life by his absence. The louse hadn't called her. Probably his pride had kicked in. And she wasn't going to call him. That would give him false expectations. Even if she was in love—and she wasn't—there were other reasons why a future with him would be out of the question.

"Yoo-hoo!"

Tante Lulu must be back from her trip to Boudreaux's General Store. Her nephew John LeDeux had picked her up an hour ago.

Grace finished bottling her concoction, dusted her hands off, and walked into the kitchen, where Tante Lulu and John were unloading armfuls of overflowing paper bags. Both of them glanced at her. And said nothing.

"What?" It was obvious by the way they avoided direct eye contact that something was wrong.

"Ah, Gracie, bless yer heart," Tante Lulu said, reaching up to pat her cheek.

Now Grace was really frightened. "Tell me."

"Tee-John was talkin' ta Ronnie this mornin'," Tante Lulu started to explain, then stopped, turning to her nephew for help.

Tee-John, or Little John, was the nickname that had been given to John LeDeux when he was a kid, and much smaller than his six foot or so in height now.Ronnie was Veronica Jinkowsky, owner of Jinx, Inc., the treasure hunting company.

"Oh, my God! Is it Angel? Has something happened to him?"

"You could say that," John drawled out. The sympathy in his dark Cajun eyes caused alarm bells to go off in her head and her heart rate to accelerate alarmingly.

"He got married yesterday," John told her. "To an airline stewardess he met on the way to Germany. Talk about!"

Grace plopped down into the kitchen chair, stunned. *So much for true love!* She tried her best not to be hurt. After all, she was the one who'd sent him away, but the tears came anyway.

They would never Renew their friendship now.

She tried to tell herself it was best this way.

CHAPTER 2

One year later, on the road to Munchkinville...

Grace O'Brien drove her eight-year-old BMW, a gift to herself after placing first in the 2000 World Poker Tour, down the rutted dirt road near the other end of Bayou Black.

She was doing her best not to run over any snakes or armadillos, which were in abundance. A difficult task when she was also trying to tune out the ancient Cajun lady riding shotgun, giving her advice on every blessed thing in the universe.

Grace had been working with Tante Lulu for the past year and had grown to love the old lady, who had become like a mother to her, as well as a teacher. But there was no question she was an unabashed interfering busybody.

And eccentric. Like today: she was wearing a black Dorothy Hamill-style wedge-cut wig, a denim miniskirt that came down to the knees on her five-foot frame, a red T-shirt with the slogan "Proud to be a Cajun," and neon pink flip-flops that exposed red-painted toenails. Sex kitten for the over-eighty crowd.

It had probably been a mistake to buy the little house on Bayou

Black next door to Tante Lulu's, even though the proximity made her apprenticeship to the noted healer so much easier. Privacy was no longer an option.

"We need ta stop by Lester Sonnier's place on the way home t'day. He's got poison oak on his privates. Prob'ly from doin' the hanky-panky with Maybelle Foucet in her back yard. Ever'one knows ya shouldn't shuck yer britches in a poison oak patch, but not that Lester. Dumb as duckweed, I do declare. Didja remember ta bring the aloe and gator-snot salve?"

"Yes, but—"

"No buts, sweetie. Sometimes the icky stuff works best, thass what I allus say. And if it burns Lester's noodle a bit, well, mebbe he'll learn a lesson. Lawdy, Lawdy, it's hotter'n a two-dollar whore on the Fourth of July." She waved an accordion-pleated fan in front of her face...a fan sporting a collage of Richard Simmons pictures; Tante Lulu had a longtime crush on the exercise guru— thought he was, in her words, hotter than a goat's behind in a pepper garden. "This heat mus' be why yer hair is curly as a pig's tail, bless yer heart. No oomph. Why dontcha make an appointment with Charmaine? She has some new goop what kin take out the frizzies."

Charmaine, Tante Lulu's "niece" and a self-proclaimed "bimbo with class," owned several beauty salons, along with a spa on her husband's ranch. With Grace's red, naturally curly hair, Charmaine would probably turn her into a sexy Howdy Doody-ette.

"Uh, thanks, but I really don't have the time."

"Okeydokey. Ya kin use my special conditioner, then. And I ain't gonna tell ya what's in it, either." She grinned impishly.

"Maybe I have time for an appointment, after all."

The wily old hen's grin was now one of satisfaction. Goal accomplished. "Aaron and Daniel are comin' fer dinner on Sunday," Tante Lulu informed her, jumping to yet another subject without warning. Her conversations were like verbal popcorn. All over the place.

Grace groaned inwardly. These twin LeDeux nephews were on Tante Lulu's thunderbolt-of-love list. The fact that she was telling Grace about her plans did not bode well...for them, or for Grace.

"I'm thinkin' it's 'bout time I made them boys hope chests."

Them boys are at least thirty years old. This time Grace's groan was out loud.

Tante Lulu had this convoluted theory on love. It involved thunderbolts of love, hope chests *for men*, and St. Jude, the patron saint of hopeless causes. Usually, people ran for the hills, or just avoided her, when she started eyeing them in a particular way.

But there were no hills in sight now, and Grace had to work with Tante Lulu. "I'm not interested. I've told you that a hundred times."

"Ain't ya got yearnin's? Lawd's sake, I'm eighty-three, and my wild oats turned ta bran flakes long ago, but I still got yearnin's."

Way too much information. And the last time she saw eight-three, I was still a nun.

"Mebbe you could go on one of them singles cruises. I heard 'bout this gal from over Baton Rouge way who met a rich feller on the way ta Bermuda. They married up, right on the ship."

"I can't afford any cruises right now." *And I'm not looking for a "rich feller."*

"Huh? Ya mus' be loaded, what with yer poker and treasure huntin' loot."

Grace felt her face heat up. "I've had...expenses."

"Oh, ya mean all those charities ya donate to? Teenage Crisis Pregnancy Centers of America. Birthright. Babies in Peril. National Adoption Hotline."

"Tante Lulu! How would you know that?"

The old lady shrugged. "I was lookin' fer a pen one day at yer cottage and went into yer desk. Yer checkbook flipped open, and I jist happened ta notice all those charities, and, whoo-boy, yer sure generous."

14

"I can't believe you invaded my privacy like that."

"What? Is it a big secret or sumpin'? Coo! Ain't nothin' wrong with helpin' babies and teenage mothers. But gol-ly, I'm sorry if I upset you."

An apology from Tante Lulu was something unusual, and really, no harm had been done.

"That's okay." She smiled at the old lady, whose brow was furrowed even more than usual. "Tell me again, where are we going?" she asked, changing the subject. She hoped.

"I ain't zackly sure."

"It's a young girl we're looking for, right?"

"Yep, Lena Duval. She's a waitress at the diner where one of my great-great-nephews works as a busboy on the weekends."

"And all we know is that she's tired all the time?" Tante Lulu nodded. "Tired as a one-legged nun in a butt-kickin' contest, all day long." She put her gnarled fingertips to her mouth in an *oops* fashion and gave Grace an apologetic look for the mention of nuns. People just couldn't seem to disassociate Grace from the good sisters. "And sickly. Chugs down them energy drinks like crazy durin' the day and that nighttime cold medicine at night. They ain't helpin' none. The girl's only nineteen years old, bless her heart, but she feels rotten all the time. Leastways, thass what I heard."

"Isn't this the kind of thing she should see a doctor about?"

"Mebbe. But word is she won't go ta no doctor."

"Why? It can't be lack of medical insurance. There's always the free clinic."

"Fer some reason, she refuses ta go. Thass why I'm fixin' ta look inta matters. Turn left, up ahead. That mus' be it."

Grace went down what was little more than a wide dirt path off the road, then stopped in a clearing before a rusted-out structure that was falling down on itself. It had probably started out as a small single-wide trailer, like fifty years ago, with haphazard additions made as needed. Grass hadn't grown within thirty yards

15

of this place in ages, if ever. It must be a mud hazard when it rained. Surely no one lived here.

But wait, a young, dark-skinned boy was on the roof pounding on some shingles. A roof that was a mismatch of different-colored roofing materials, including black tar paper. Out back, a scowling young black girl was hanging clothes on a line. If Grace hadn't already guessed she was a tween, she would have figured it out, because the girl wore flip-flops, a Hannah Montana long-sleeved T-shirt proclaiming "Girls Rock," and cropped denim pants with a hanging chain belt, a Hannah Montana fashion accessory. She wouldn't have been surprised if her underwear had Hannah Montana printed on the butt.

Before they had a chance to register all this Hannah Montana paraphernalia, a handpainted red bike careened around the side of their car and came to a screeching halt by the trailer's front door. On its handlebars was an empty newspaper delivery bag. On its seat was a startled African-American kid of about ten, gazing at them with alarm.

"How many munchkins are there in this place?" Grace asked. "So far, I've seen three kids, not counting the young woman we're coming to see."

"Somethin's not right here," Tante Lulu said.

"No kidding."

"I got the creepy-crawlies and heebie-jeebies all t'gether. And I swear, St. Jude's tappin' me on the shoulder."

Grace didn't know about saints, but hairs were standing out on the back of her neck, too. "I think I'll stay in the car."

"Huh?"

"I signed on to learn alternative medicine. This looks like way more than folk healing to me."

"Girl—" Tante Lulu said with disgust.

Girl. I'm thirty-five years old and she calls me girl.

"Haven't you learned yet? Healin' is fer more than the body. Sometimes we need ta work on the heart…or the soul."

16

I wish someone would heal me.

"I'm workin' on it, sweetie."

Grace's head shot up. Had she spoken aloud, or was the old lady reading minds now, too?

Tante Lulu just smiled at her. "First things first, *chère.* Yer right at the top of my list."

Grace bit her tongue to restrain herself from telling the Cajun fruitcake to butt out. But she wanted to.

~

When trouble comes knock, knock, knocking on your door...

WITH A DEEP SIGH OF EXHAUSTION, and it only ten a.m., Lena Duval finished tying the apron of her waitress uniform and left the trailer bedroom she shared with her younger sister Ella. Lionel and Miles shared the other, even smaller bedroom.

"Has anyone seen the aspirin?" she called out. "I need it bad." That, along with twenty-four hours of sleep. Lena couldn't remember the last time she'd felt good. At least two weeks. Maybe a month. She had the symptoms of the flu, all-over achy, bone-deep tired, sore throat, swollen glands, fever, but none of the over-the-counter remedies helped.

She couldn't afford to be sick.

And it didn't help that Lionel was up on the roof, pounding away, trying to fix yet another leak. *Bam, Bam, Bam!* Any minute now her head was going to explode. Lionel was fifteen, a sophomore in high school, old enough to do that kind of work. The problem was, he could hardly tell a hammer from a hoe. Computers, on the other hand, that was a different story. He'd fixed up that ten-year-old Mac that she'd bought at Goodwill for a dollar with so many bells and whistles it did everything except make gumbo.

Lionel was going through a phase right now where he was

trying to find himself. That meant a leather jacket she'd bought at a yard sale, which he wore all the time; dreadlocks; tongue, nose, eyebrow, and ear piercings, which he'd had done without her permission; and a tattoo reading S-E-X on the back of his neck but was, thank God, not permanent. Not that Lionel had engaged in sex yet. At least that's what he'd told her last month when she'd tried to talk to him about condoms, much to his embarrassment.

Miles was her biggest concern, though. Sweet, quiet, introverted ten-year-old Miles, who had been only five when their mother died, and six at the time of Katrina. He never talked about it, but Lena knew he held a lot of pain inside.

Well, they all did, actually.

Going into the bathroom, she found the aspirin, popped three in her mouth, washed them down with a plastic cup of water. Looking into the medicine cabinet mirror, she was alarmed at how awful she looked. Her mocha-colored Creole skin was pale as café au lait, and not in a nice way. She'd lost weight; her fitted waitress uniform hung loose, its belt on the last notch. Oh, well. A pity party didn't pay the bills.

Just then, she realized that the trailer was awfully quiet, except for Lionel's pounding. *Bam, bam, bam!* Miles should be back from his paper route by now, with the Saturday-morning cartoons blaring. Not that he didn't have other chores to do.

Instead, the back door slammed and twelve-year-old Ella, who had been hanging laundry, came to stand in the doorway. Their parents, Max and Ruby Duval, had been French Quarter jazz musicians, and they'd named their kids after jazz greats, Lena Horne, Lionel Hampton, Ella Fitzgerald, and Miles Davis.

Ella, not quite a child, not quite an adolescent, was no problem in the "finding herself" department. She already knew what she was. A Hannah Montana clone. Thank God for thrift shops, which they scavenged every Saturday, because everything Ella did was according to the bible of Billy Ray Cyrus's precocious daughter. There was a dress code at Ella's school that skirts could be no shorter than the tips of the fingers when arms were held straight at the sides. It was a constant fight to meet that standard.

But right now Ella looked worried.

"What?"

"We got visitors."

"Visitors?" She put a hand to her chest. "Hurry, go hide."

"They already saw us."

"They?"

"Two ladies," Ella told her.

Oh, God! Not Child Protective Services again!

"Miles just got home."

"Did they see him?"

Ella nodded, twirling one of her shoulder-length curls nervously. She was trying to grow her hair longer and straighter to emulate the achy-breaky you-know-who.

Lionel and Miles came in the back door, looking to her for direction.

"Okay, plan B. Straighten up this place real quick, everyone, and take your places." She had to admit that the combination kitchen, dining room and living room already looked neat. Because there were so many of them in such a small trailer, a storage space was required for everything. Plus, she had her siblings trained to pick up after themselves. Everyone worked.

"And remember, Daddy is off working on one of the oil rigs." *Hah! The closest Max Duval ever got to an oil rig was the time he fell off a fishing boat in the Gulf. Drunk as a sailor, of course.* Truth to tell, their father was dead, buried during the post-Hurricane Katrina chaos, but these women, whoever they were, didn't need to know that. In fact, they couldn't know that. Especially if they were from CPS, which was always snooping around.

Before the first knock came on the door, the kids were in their assigned places. Ella stood at the kitchen sink, washing the breakfast dishes. Miles sat on the floor in the corner, watching cartoons on the small TV. Lionel was pecking away at the computer.

"Yoo-hoo!" someone said, knocking again. "Anyone home?"

Taking a deep breath, Lena opened the door, barely a crack. "Yes?"

"Hi there, sweetie. I'm Louise Rivard from up the bayou, but you kin call me Tante Lulu. I'm Michael LeDeux's great-auntie. Kin we come in?"

She frowned, then realized the lady—Tante Lulu—was referring to Mike, the busboy at the diner. A nice kid, but what he had to do with her she had no idea. In fact, he and Lionel were in the same high school. Although Lionel was a year or two younger than Michael, they'd played football together this year. She glanced over at Lionel, who just shrugged inside his leather jacket. Really, that jacket was going to start walking by itself if he didn't take it off once in a while, if only to air it out. She reminded herself to check tonight to see if he slept in the blasted thing.

"Uh, we're busy right now. What do you want?" She didn't care if she sounded rude.

"We's here to help ya, honey. But first, I gotta pee." Pushing Lena aside, the old woman—and she was *really* old—walked straight inside, without invitation, and into the bathroom, shutting the door behind her. She was dressed weird, for an old person.

The other woman, lots younger but still old, at least thirty, grimaced with embarrassment, but then she walked past her, too. "I'm Grace O'Brien," she said. She was dressed more normal than the old bat, wearing jeans and a pretty pink tapered-waist blouse. "I'm Tante Lulu's assistant."

Lena was stunned. How had these two strangers managed to get inside the trailer? Her fevered, fuzzy brain must be worse off than she'd thought. "Assistant to what?"

"We're folk healers."

"*Like hoodoos?*" *Oh, God! That's all I need. A bunch of nutty holy rollers! Or whatever those people call themselves.*

The lady, who had bouncy red curls and pale green eyes, smiled. "Not really. We're more into herbs than magic."

"Do you use snakes and stuff?" Lionel asked from behind them. "There's a boy at school whose grandma cures people with snakes. She has a whole bushel basket of 'em in her cellar."

"Eeew," Ella said from the sink, where she still stood with her back to them.

"Lionel Duke Duval! You better not have been touchin' any snakes," Lena warned.

Lionel ducked his head and went back to his computer. "I just looked. Jeesh!"

"Don't you backtalk."

"All I said was Jeesh. Jeesh!"

Lena gave him a look that said they would talk about this later. Her brothers and sister knew better than to speak up like that in front of strangers.

"Actually, I have a degree in alternative medicine," the woman, who'd said her name was Grace, explained. "And Tante Lulu has more than fifty years' experience as a *traiteur*. That's a Cajun folk healer. Mostly she deals with potions made from herbs or animal products indigenous to the bayou. No snakes...at least, not live snakes." She smiled some more.

Lionel was gazing up at Grace with interest. "I wanna be a doctor someday. Or a computer software engineer."

"That's great. What are you doing?" Already the woman was peering over Lionel's shoulder. "The history of Louisiana Indians? That sounds interesting."

"I'm reading it for extra credit."

Lena was about to tell this woman that what Lionel read was none of her business when they all heard the toilet flush and the water run, and then the old lady with about a gazillion wrinkles and a lopsided black wig walked out. Lena was still bug-eyed at Tante Lulu's oddball attire, but she had to admit that the lady had a kindly face.

21

Lena wasn't fooled by that, though. They'd been tricked too many times by well-meaning folks who just wanted to break up their family and put them in foster care.

"Yer toilet flushes kinda sluggish, Lena. Ya needs a plumber."

Yeah, like she could afford a plumber. Not this month. She still owed on the used hot-water heater she'd bought six months ago.

"Is that an earring in yer nose?" Tante Lulu asked as she passed Lionel, narrowing her eyes to see better. "Doan the snot get caught in it? Holy smokes! Ya got more holes in yer skin than a sieve. It's a wonder ya doan pee out yer eyebrow."

Lena almost smiled. She'd made similar remarks to her brother in the past, to no avail.

Lionel ducked his head with embarrassment and refused to reply.

"Now, ain't this nice?" Tante Lulu said, walking into the living room, big as you please, and plopping down on the couch, near where Miles was sitting on the floor. She patted him on the head.

Lena was too stunned by anyone saying their trailer was nice to speak at first. Then she was further stunned by the woman's next question.

"Where's yer momma?"

"Our mother died a long time ago. Of cancer."

"Oh, thass too bad. How old was you? Are you the oldest?"

"Yes, I'm the oldest. I was fourteen at the time, five years ago." She crossed her arms over her chest and glared. "What do you want here?"

Ignoring her question, the busybody continued, "And where's yer daddy?"

Lena felt her face heat up, even hotter than it already was. The other kids looked away studiously. "He's out working on the oil rigs."

"Is that so? What's his name?"

"Max Duval," she replied before she had a chance to bite her tongue.

"The jazz player? I usta go to the Pelican Club in the French Quarter to hear him and yer mama play. Didja say he's workin' the rigs now?" Tante Lulu was clearly suspicious.

Lena nodded.

"Ain'tcha got no other family?"

She shook her head, then leaned back against the closed front door, light-headed. Much as she hated to give up a day of tips, maybe she would call in sick. She really, really needed to lie down.

She must have blacked out then, or had one of her dizzy spells, because she had no idea how she ended up on the couch, with Tante Lulu and the other woman leaning over her, doing something with a thermometer and damp cloths on her forehead. Her brothers and sister stood behind them, scared to death and not knowing what to do without her directing them. She tried to tell the women to leave, and she tried to tell her family to settle down, that everything would be okay if she could just crawl into bed for a few hours. But no words would come out.

Instead, she heard the old lady whisper in her ear. "Doan you be worryin' none, sweetie. St. Jude sent me."

I thought she said Mike LeDeux sent her. Now it's Jude. An alarming thought entered her head. She put a hand on the age-spotted arm. "You can't call a doctor, and you can't take me to the clinic. You just can't. They'll find out."

Tante Lulu stared at her for a long moment, then nodded.

"I'll take care of ya, honey. Me and St. Jude. I promise."

CHAPTER 3

You could say they were Cajun angels...

$\mathcal{S}$he was waking up.

Finally! Grace sat down on the edge of the mattress in her guest bedroom, one of three in the little cottage, helping Lena Duval to sit up.

Grace did not want to be here. In fact, she was having trouble breathing, so tense was she. But she'd been unable to explain why when Tante Lulu had asked her to take over while she went on an errand.

This young girl, Lena, was nineteen years old, only a year or so older than Grace's own daughter, who would be eighteen on December 10. Sarah...that was the way Grace always thought of the baby she'd given away when she was sixteen, although she had no idea if she'd birthed a boy or girl. She hadn't wanted to know at the time, and not out of any grief, either. Self-centered, like most teenagers, she'd just wanted the problem to go away.

If that wasn't bad enough, she'd had an abortion when she was fifteen.

Not one, but two horrendous mistakes!

Afterward, the first few years, she'd awakened often during the night, hearing a baby cry. Which was ridiculous in a convent.

Now, in the presence of Lena, she wasn't able to keep herself from thinking of her child, which would not be African-American, like Lena, but a combination of Irish and Greek. What would she look like now? Tall, like her father, or average height, like Grace? Would she have red hair or black? Curly or straight as a poker? Green eyes or twinkling blue?

And she couldn't bear to think of the baby that had never been born, either. That one would have been a girl, too, she'd been convinced, with surfer good looks and white-blonde hair like her daddy. Anne Marie...she'd named the fetus Anne Marie. Sometimes she imagined Anne Marie as a little impish angel who floated about her shoulders.

Questions, questions, questions. Painful questions for which there would never be answers. Questions she was mostly able to bury by keeping busy.

But this young girl was a harsh, unavoidable reminder of her past sins.

Grace sighed deeply and said, "Are you awake, Lena?"

It was barely eleven a.m. in late May, and already the temperature was up to eighty-five, warm air being swirled around by the ceiling fan. The air conditioner would need to be turned on soon, but right now the sounds and smells of the bayou coming through the open screened window were refreshing. To Grace, anyhow. She was still new enough to this rather tropical paradise to appreciate the scent of bougainvillea bushes and fig tree blossoms, the warbling of myriad birds, the almost celestial essence of the bayou itself with its cathedral-like oak trees arching across the waters. Natives were more likely to complain about the humidity, bugs, and pesty birds.

The girl blinked with confusion, just before tears began to stream down her face. It was the first time in two days—since she and Tante Lulu had visited the trailer—that Lena had been strong enough to do anything other than lie flat on her back, but she still looked like death warmed over.

"Where am I?" the girl choked out.

Grace held a straw to her mouth and let her drink a bit of the herbal tea Tante Lulu swore would help restore her strength. Lena had to be thirsty, despite the intravenous line into her right arm, giving her fluids. "My cottage. I live next door to Tante Lulu."

Lena tried, unsuccessfully, to slide her legs over the side, then flopped back down with weakness. Panicked, her eyes went wild. "My brothers and sister?"

Grace gently arranged the light cover around her and fluffed the pillows propping her up. "They're in school right now. I stayed with them the past two nights."

"Oh, my God! Two nights! Miles must be frantic. He's never away from me. I have to get up."

"No, sweetheart, what you have to do is stay down. You've got a bad case of Epstein-Barr virus—mononucleosis."

"Mono? I've got the kissing disease? No way!" The girl's body stiffened with outrage. "I haven't been kissin' nobody."

Grace had to smile. "You can get mono other ways, Lena. The most important thing is rest, and I mean weeks of rest."

"I can't. I need to work. I need to take care of my brothers and sister."

"It's out of your hands. For the time being, you are not to worry. Tante Lulu and I will take care of everything."

Lena shook her head, hard, then groaned, putting a hand to her head. "No, you don't understand. If they find out...I mean—"

"I know exactly what you mean. You're afraid Child Protective Services will be on your case." In fact, she was pretty sure that the man and woman who'd been walking around the outside of the trailer yesterday, taking notes, were from CPS. Grace had declined to answer their knocks on the door, not sure what she would have said. Luckily, the children had been in school. The frowns on the visitors' faces had not been a good sign. Grace wouldn't be surprised if the trailer would be classified inappropriate housing for the family, even if there were a live father. Newspapers had carried headlines recently about the HUD trailers given out after Hurricane Katrina now being deemed health hazards. Something about poisonous insulation. Who knew what was in this ancient trailer?

She wondered how they'd fared with Hurricane Ike last year. Although this section of the state had been spared major damage, the winds had to have shaken the old trailer like a rag doll.

"How...who...oh, no! Who talked to you? My brothers and sister know better."

"They all talked, Lena. They had to. Do you have any idea how scared they were? You've always been there for them. It took a lot of convincing to get them to settle for me over the next two weeks...'til school lets out for summer vacation. Then they can stay here at my house all the time while you continue to recuperate."

Lena frowned. "Why?"

"Why what?"

"Why would you help us?"

"Oh, sweetie! Because it's the right thing to do." *And, truth to tell, because Tante Lulu guilted me into it.*

It about broke Grace's heart that the girl would even ask that question, though. Had help been that scarce for them over the past four years, since Katrina? Probably. Lena's siblings had explained that they never applied for government or charity assistance that required a name and address. That meant no welfare or food stamps. As for school records, they lied and said their father worked on the oil rigs. The only way they'd managed to get the money to buy the trailer and its lot was through emergency funding given in the chaos immediately following the hurricane.

In the midst of all this pondering, a little niggling worry in the back of Grace's mind caused her to wonder if her little girl, not so little now, had led a safe, happy life or been forced to struggle like this brave young woman here. She would never know.

"I feel like we've been rescued by angels," Lena said.

"Hardly angels." At least not me, and there are people who would say Tante Lulu hardly qualifies, either.

"I'm afraid that all the lies I've told are going to come back and bite me in the butt. They could put me in jail." She probably referred to the housing money she'd accepted, pretending her father was alive.

"At the least, they'll take away my brothers and sister. They'll say I'm not old enough or fit enough to care for them."

"Tante Lulu and I are going to help you. That's all you need to think about, for now. Okay?"

Lena sighed deeply, too tired to argue. "Did you take me to a hospital?"

"No. One of Tante Lulu's nephews is a doctor. He checked you out here." And ranted and raved the whole time. Daniel LeDeux had moved from Alaska to Louisiana, burned out as a pediatric oncologist, and still had not applied for a Louisiana medical license. He was not a happy camper over Tante Lulu pulling him into a situation that posed both legal and ethical complications. When he'd told all this to Tante Lulu—yelled, actually—she'd had the nerve to say, "Thass all well an' good, boy, but not to worry. St. Jude's on our side." To which the good doctor had said something rude about St. Jude. For which Tante Lulu had smacked him on the arm with a soup ladle and threatened, "Keep it up, buster, and I'll whomp you so hard yer granchillen will be born with knots on their head the size of goose eggs."

Lena's eyes were fluttering, a precursor to falling asleep once again. But before she did, she reached out one hand to clasp one of Grace's. "Thank you" was all she said.

For Grace, it was enough. In fact, it was everything. The scary thing was, Grace was beginning to understand Tante Lulu and her interfering in everybody's lives.

And, in some warped way, by helping this girl, it felt as if she was helping her own child.

~

Greasing the wheels of the law, Tante Lulu style...

"I WANNA SET up one of those foundation thingees."

Lucien LeDeux stared, unblinking, at his great-aunt across the desk of his Houma law office. He wasn't surprised by her request. Hell, it was mild compared to other stuff she'd asked him to do over the years. "Why?"

"Why not?" Tante Lulu shrugged her little shoulders, and it tugged at his heart to see her getting even smaller with age. She was wearing a floral muumuu—or whatever you called one of those Hawaiian kind of dresses that probably went out of fashion about fifty years ago—but, loose as it was, it couldn't hide her diminishing height and bony frame. She wore her hair in its natural gray today, a helmet style that hugged her head, but that was offset by bright red lipstick with matching fake fingernails, thanks, no doubt, to his half sister Charmaine, a beautician.

He had to wonder how many years they would have the old bird around. *Forever, I hope.*

"Luc, I have plenty of money, and I'm thinkin' it's 'bout time I put it ta better use than earnin' interest in some bank, or molderin' away under my mattress."

"You keep money under your mattress?"

"Some."

"How much?"

She mentioned a sum so alarming he had to clutch the arms of his chair to keep from leaping over the desk and shaking her.

"It takes a lot of money to set up a foundation, then people to run it, campaigns to continue funding, that kind of stuff. How much, total, are you thinking of donating for seed money?"

"One, mebbe two million."

"Dollars?"

"No. Apples. Of course I meant dollars. Jeesh!"

He would have swallowed his teeth, if he had false teeth. "Son of a bi...gun! Where did you get so much money?"

"Dontcha be usin' that kinda language 'round me, boy."

I'm a grown man with three kids, and she still calls me "boy." How amazing is that? He grinned.

"It's not funny. I'll tell ya where I got the money. I've been around since the Gold Rush, practic'ly. Mebbe I never made much with my *traiteur* work, but I still managed ta save. I dint have no mortgage or big bills or chillen of my own. Then there was the Jinx treasure-huntin' project. I was one of the biggest investors. When they found that pirate loot, whoo-boy, it was more money in the bank fer me. Plus, I own part of Charmaine's beauty spas. And I bought stock in Micro-somethin' or other when they first started making those gadgets."

"Whoa, whoa, whoa! Are the gadgets you're referring to computers? And could you possibly have bought Microsoft stock before the industry exploded?"

"Ain't that what I jist said? I knowed this lady down in N'awleans who was second cousin to a young'un called Bill Bates who tol' me I oughta buy the stock."

Unbelievable! "Do you mean Bill Gates?"

"You are such an idjit sometimes, Luc. Do ya honestly think I doan know what a computer is? An' Bill Gates is almos' as famous as Richard Simmons. Holy crawfish! I'm old, but I ain't stoopid."

Okay, she sucked me in with that one. "You've got a lot of great-nephews and -nieces," he pointed out. "Gifting them might be a good idea."

She waved a hand airily. "I've already taken care of them."

He raised his brows at that news. He was the only lawyer in the family, except for his sister-in-law Val, who specialized in more high-powered cases. How come Tante Lulu hadn't consulted him? "Is this about that sick girl you took in last week? And the kids you and Grace are caring for?"

"Partly. It breaks my heart ta see what that girl's been through. Lena Duval is her name. She's only nineteen years old, but she's been takin' care of her whole family since Hurrycane Katrina, bless her heart—two younger brothers and a younger sister. An' she's had ta do it all, secret-like, 'cause, sure as shootin', if Child Protective Services had known 'bout them, they woulda put 'em in foster homes. *Separate* foster homes. She was only fifteen at the time."

He didn't want to hear about any of this tug-your-heart bull-shit. What it amounted to was Tante Lulu butting into other people's lives again. "Where are the parents?"

"Her mother died of cancer a year before Katrina, and her daddy died durin' the hurrycane. Prob'ly got drunk and drowned. But Lena and the kids been tellin' anyone what asks that their daddy is workin' out on the oil rigs."

He frowned. "Who's supporting them? Welfare?"

She shook her head. "Nope. If they'da asked fer help, them nosy social workers woulda been out ta their home, sniffin' around. In fact, Grace sez they mighta been there yesterday. Ya gotta know, those youngens are livin' in practic'ly a tin shack up the bayou. Sad, it is! Thass one of the things I wanna do with this foundation. Help build homes, or renovate homes, fer folks what been hurt by Katrina. And I wanna help families stay t'gether."

"So what're they livin' on?"

"Waitressin'. Lawn work. Newspaper delivery. Baby-sittin'."

Mind-boggling! And not just kids being able to survive on so little. How his aunt got involved in other people's business, and dragged the rest of the family in, was beyond belief. But he had to admire her kind heart.

"Can't you just give this group of kids money—I mean, not give it to them, but buy them a home and help them manage?"

SANDRA HILL

"I could...and I will, but I wonder how many other families out there are still sufferin' from that damn hurrycane."

Tante Lulu hardly ever swore. It was an indication of her distress that she did now. Hell, it had been four years since Katrina, and everyone knew that hundreds, maybe thousands, of families still hadn't recovered.

"Okay, how about donating a large amount of money to an existing foundation?"

"Nope. I want my foundation ta be different. Families, thass what mine will be about. There's lotsa charities that helps sick kids. Me, I wanna help *families*."

He tapped a forefinger to his closed lips, thinking. "I know this woman, Samantha Starr. She runs the Starr Wish Foundation in N'awleans. How 'bout I set up a meeting? Maybe she can give you some advice."

"Thass a start." Tante Lulu frowned, as if something just occurred to her. "Starr, you say? Is she from the Starr Foods family, the one that has that chain of supermarkets?"

"Yes."

"Doan that beat all? I know ol' man Starr. Crazy as a loony bird."

Luc had to laugh, inside. It was like the dingbat criticizing the loony bird.

"Stan founded Starr Foods after World War II in a little French Quarter grocery store. Now there's prob'ly a hundred supermarkets in the Starr chain across the South."

Was there anyone his aunt didn't know?

"And do somethin' legal-like ta make sure this Duval family doan get separated."

"Huh? What do you expect me to do?"

"Yer the expert. I jist doan want no state do-gooders on the trailer doorstep sayin' Lena cain't be the guardian of her family."

"She's only nineteen? I don't know many judges who would think this is a good idea. Every agency in the state is going to jump on this case, wondering what kind of care they'd gotten from a fifteen-year-old after the disaster."

"You kin do it," his aunt said. "Yer the best."

"Stop buttering me up."

"It's the truth, sugar. Mebbe I should go ta the newspapers. Ooh, I know. Celine's a newspaper reporter. Bet she knows people." Celine was his half brother Tee-John's wife. A smart lady, Celine made herself scarce every time she saw Tante Lulu head her way.

"Don't you dare go publicizing this—at least not 'til we know where we stand." *We? Did I say "we"? Man, I am so screwed. She's roped me in again.*

Tante Lulu stood and picked up her purse, a purse that was about the size of a Yankee carpetbag. "I gotta get started on a house fer these young'uns right away. And I gotta do it secret-like 'til we got all this legal nonsense straightened out."

Oooh, he didn't like the sound of "legal nonsense." But then he figured "Don't ask, don't tell" might be the best policy for him at the moment.

"Too bad Angel Sabato got married. He usta work in construction. We coulda had him come here and put up a fine little cottage, lickety-split. Then when the social workers come ta call, they kin see the kids got a good home. Us LeDeuxs could help, but we doan know snake spit 'bout drawin' up plans."

"Angel isn't married."

"What?"

"His marriage was annulled almost a year ago—a month after the ceremony, actually."

"How come no one tol' me?"

"Maybe no one thought you would care."

She stood, leaned across the desk, and swatted him a good one with her Richard Simmons fan. "Sometimes you are dumber'n a gator on roller skates, Luc. 'Course I care. Now gimme some sugar."

He walked around the desk and leaned down, way down, to kiss her cheek.

As she walked out the door, telling him to call her when he'd set up the meeting with Samantha Starr, he heard her say to his secretary, "Do you hear thunder?"

And Luc just knew that someone better duck quick.

~

It ain't that hard to lasso an angel...

"HULLO! WHO'S THIS?"

"Angel...Angel Sabato."

"Well, how are ya, *cher*?"

"Who is...whoa! Is that you, Tante Lulu?"

"Yep. Whatcha up to, boy? Still treasure huntin'?"

"Yeah. Sort of. I just got back from Germany. The Amber Project was a bust."

"Sometimes thass the way things go."

His suspicious mind went on red alert. The old bat wouldn't be calling him for no reason. "Why are you calling me, Tante Lulu? Oh, no! Did something happen to Grace?"

"Grace is fine. That one, she be learnin' ta be a *traiteur* real good. The only thing she has trouble with is milkin' snakes fer snake-pee ointment."

"Are you kidding?"

"'Course I'm kidding. *Mon Dieu!* Are all men idjits? Anyways, I'm glad ta hear ya still care what happens ta Grace."

Note to self: Keep your frickin' mouth shut, Sabato. Do not mention she-who-shall-remain-on-my-shit-list. He bit his bottom lip into silence, but he noticed that his hands were fisted with tension. It had taken him a long time to stop thinking about Grace 24/7. Did he want to open a vein again?

Hell, no!

"So, yer between jobs, then?"

I should end this conversation right now. Talking to this wily old bird is like jump roping in a minefield. "Yeeeesss," he said hesitantly.

"I have a job fer you."

"No." Whew! I thought she was going to say something about thunderbolts...or Grace.

"Ya cain't say no before ya even know what the job is."

Wanna bet? "Yes, I can. Because there is no way in hell that I'm coming back to Louisiana." *There! I took a stand. Man, I am so proud of myself.*

"Why not?"

She's like a puppy on a pants leg. "Ask Grace why not." *Damn! I can't believe I said that. Pathetic, pathetic, pathetic.*

"This ain't about Grace."

I sincerely doubt that. "What's the problem?"

"We need ta put up a little house fer some orphans, and we need ta do it fast and secret-like."

"Tante Lulu, as noble as your project sounds, I am not coming back to Louisiana. No way."

"No way?"

If there was such a thing as mental Teflon, Tante Lulu had it in spades. He shouldn't say anything. He really shouldn't.

Did he listen to himself?

Nope.

"You're trying to set me up, aren't you? Well, you're not going to rope me in that easy. I have my pride."

"Pooyie! Pride doan make the gumbo boil."

"What?"

"We're desperate here, Angel. We need a builder. There's plenty of people ta do the grunt work, if only they had blueprints and directions. And you can name yer price. Hello...are ya still there?"

"I'm here."

"Besides, I have a feelin' about you and Grace."

"That door closed a long time ago."

"Didja ever think ya mighta given up too easy?"

Only every other day. "What makes you say that? Does she talk about me?"

"Heck, no. This news'll jar yer preserves, boy: Grace thinks yer still married."

Oh, that's just dandy. She must think I'm a one-hundred-proof slimeball. "I'd like to help you, but I just can't."

"I'm disappointed in ya, boy. Instead of pitchin' a hissy fit and runnin' off ta marry the first gal ya met, mebbe ya shoulda stayed here and fought fer what ya wanted."

She hung up before he could answer.

Long after the connection was broken and he was still listening to the dial tone, Angel sat with a puzzled expression on his face. Then the oddest thing happened.

He found himself saying a little prayer to St. Jude.

CHAPTER 4

The cast gets bigger, and bigger...

ante Lulu arrived late for her meeting with the Starr Wish Foundation folks. It was all Daniel LeDeux's fault.

It had taken her and Luc more than an hour to convince Daniel to accompany them and possibly serve on the board of directors of the new foundation she was forming, if that actually happened. Grace was back at her cottage, keeping a watch on Lena. After all this time in bed, the girl was antsy to get up and about, which could set her back a ways, if she wasn't careful.

"I swear, old lady. Drag me into any more of your schemes and I'm going to throttle you," Daniel said under his breath as they walked down the hallway toward the conference room at the Starr Foods headquarters in New Orleans.

"Someone's shoelaces are tied too tight." She might be old, but her hearing was still good.

Daniel glowered some more. "First you have me practicing medicine in a state where I have no license. Then you try to get me to prescribe Viagra for a friend of yours. Then you try to redecorate my apartment—with a circular bed and a mirrored ceiling. Then you sign me up for Cajun dance lessons, as if I don't already know how to dance. Now this!"

"Shut yer trap, boy. Dontcha know how ta show respect fer yer elders?"

"Listen up! You may be the Queen Bee of Cajun Busybodies, but I'm tired to death of you involving me in your peccadilloes."

"What pickles?"

"Not pickles. Peccadilloes. Little offensive acts."

"Well, I declare! Mus' be an Eskimo word. But me, I ain't never been offensive in all my life."

"And you only being as old as God's toothbrush."

At his sarcasm, Tante Lulu just smiled and said, "Personally, I'm thinkin' yer ornery ways are jist signs of yer bein' horned up."

"She means horny," Luc interpreted with a grin. Daniel pulled at his hair with both hands and gritted out, "Aaarrgh!"

Luc looped an arm over Daniel's shoulder. "It's better to just go along with her, *cher*. If you're not careful, she'll sic the thunderbolt on you."

"The what?"

"Never mind. Now's not the time," Tante Lulu told them both. "How do I look?" She'd put on her la-de-da business outfit today, to impress the Starr folks. A suit and pumps with little high heels. Even nylons. Okay, the suit was pink, and her hair was bright blonde, but a lady still needed to look like a lady.

"You look great," Luc said.

Daniel's eyes held a different opinion, but then, he was from Alaska, and them Eskimos up there wouldn't know style if it hit them in the head with a glacier.

"I'm thinkin' 'bout gettin' plastic surgery. I have a few wrinkles on my face that need a lift. My powder gets clogged in the furrows."

"A few wrinkles?" Daniel scoffed. "Hey, don't be thinking I'll give you a face-lift. I'm not that kind of doctor."

"A doctor's a doctor. By the way, ya coulda wore a suit, like

Luc," she complained. Daniel actually looked fine in khaki slacks, a golf shirt, and loafers, but he needed to have his ego deflated a bit. All the LeDeux men were too good-looking for their own good, thought they were all that and a bowl of grits.

"You could have left me at home."

"You been hibernatin' too long. Time ya got out and socialized. Do ya even have a girlfriend?" She narrowed her eyes at him.

"Oh, no! Don't you dare. You are not getting involved in my personal life. Whether I have a girlfriend or not is none of your business."

"Are ya gay?"

Daniel sputtered, "You...you...no! I am not gay." Luckily, the conference room door opened just then and a woman stood there, waiting to greet them. She was tall, about five-ten, and nearing thirty, if not over that hump. Her auburn hair was held back off her face in a French braid. Freckles covered her face and arms, exposed by the short-sleeved, belted jade green dress she wore. The freckles gave a clue as to her identity. All the Starr family were covered with freckles. They were Yankee carpetbaggers who'd moved South from Boston after World War II but came from Scotland generations back.

"Hey, Sam!" Luc shook the lady's hand, then turned to Tante Lulu. "This is Samantha Starr. Sam, this is my great-aunt, Louise Rivard, or Tante Lulu, as she prefers." Luc waved a hand at Daniel, who was scowling like a nitwit. "Sam, this is my half brother, Dr. Daniel LeDeux."

Daniel nodded at Samantha but continued to scowl.

"He's not gay," Tante Lulu told her, just in case she was interested. "And he's got a butt tighter than the bark on a cypress tree." Tante Lulu ducked behind Luc as she spoke, just in case Daniel had his hands in throttle position; really, she was smarter than folks gave her credit for.

Samantha favored Daniel with a good once-over. "A doctor, huh? A non-gay doctor with a nice ass? Be still, my heart! My ex-husband Nick was a doctor. Nick the Prick, I like to call him."

Daniel bared his teeth at her.

Tante Lulu kinda liked the girl. Oh, she was so stuck up she'd probably drown in a rainstorm. Still, she reminded her of Charmaine, except prissy, and not enough va-va-voom in her clothes and makeup. *I kin take care of that va-va-voom in no time. Betcha I have a potion ta wipe out those freckle spots, too.*

There was only one other person in the conference room. A dapper, gray-haired gentleman with a neatly trimmed goatee, wearing a pretty sky-blue shirt, darker blue bow tie, and white plantation suit. And freckles. *Well, shut my mouth!* Tante Lulu would know him anywhere. Stanley Starr.

She sucked in her tummy and stood straighter. In the old days, that would have caused her bosoms to arch out, but she'd lost her bosoms about twenty years ago, along with her hiney. If she'd known Stan was going to be here today, though, she would have worn her padded panties and inflatable bra, 'ceptin' last time she had to lie down for an hour, she was so winded from all that blowin'.

"Stan," she said, cool as could be.

"Louise!" Stan got up and came up to her, giving her a quick kiss on both cheeks. She could swear he pinched her butt, too, but maybe she was mistaken about that. It mighta been her panty hose up in her crotch again. "You are a sight for sore eyes." He took her by the shoulders and held her several feet away from him, examining her closely. "Pretty as ever."

"Oh, good Lord!" she heard Daniel say behind her.

"Ditto," Samantha said, equally disgusted.

Young folks thought that just because a person got old their juices all dried up. She could tell them a thing or two.

"I didn't invite the rest of the board today," Samantha said. "I figured we would have some preliminary discussions first."

Everyone was pulling out chairs, and Samantha went over to a silver coffee service on a sideboard. She raised her eyes at each of them before pouring.

"You still inta Elvis lak ya usta be, Stan?" Tante Lulu asked, noticing a bunch of Elvis stuff on the walls.

"Oh, yeah! None of that Muzak crap in our supermarkets. Elvis all the way."

Samantha rolled her eyes and set cups of strong Creole coffee before them all before sitting down across from her, next to her grandfather. Luc and Daniel bracketed her on the other side.

Stanley took off his suit jacket, hanging it on the back of his chair. Tante Lulu about melted when she noticed his red suspenders and sleeve garters. Whoo-boy, she did love a sharp-dressed man in suspenders and garters.

"Let's get down to business," Luc said. "My aunt wants to start a foundation centered on families—keeping families together. Can you help us?"

Samantha spent the next fifteen minutes explaining how the Starr Wish Foundation started after Hurricane Katrina, its mission, funding, and everyday operation. Turns out Samantha worked in the accounting department of Starr Foods but was also chairman of the foundation board.

"Sounds daunting," Luc said with a long sigh.

"It is...or at least it was. Took us more than a year to just get set up."

"I cain't wait that long."

Everyone turned to look at her.

"What's the hurry?" Samantha asked.

"I'm eighty-somethin'. I might be dead t'morrow."

Luc and Daniel gave her slanty-eyed looks. Luc knew enough not to say anything, but that dumb cluck Daniel said, "Eighty-something? You wish!"

"Give or take."

"There might be an alternative," Samantha said. "I've had a chance to think about this since Luc called me last week, and I've discussed various ideas with my grandfather and the foundation board. What would you think about partnering with us on a foundation?"

"Oh, I doan know—" Tante Lulu started to say.

"Now, hear me out," Samantha urged. "I could take over full-time with the foundation. The two foundations could work under one umbrella. One dealing with wishes, as we've been doing. The other with family, as you've indicated. There would be savings in cost of administration and cooperative funding. Really, it could be a win-win situation."

"What would you gain from it?" Daniel asked.

Samantha shot him a glare, then addressed her comments to her and Luc. "Money, for one thing."

Daniel snickered.

Samantha ignored him and continued. "Fresh ideas. Serving more people. Let me give you one example where working together could be a good idea. Suppose you have a family where the mother and father die in a car accident, leaving behind their little adopted son, who is still in foster care. The little boy wishes they could find his *real* mom. So, it's granting wishes and reuniting families."

"Some of them charities Grace supports fer pregnant teenagers might even get involved," Tante Lulu mused. "Like tracin' lost parents and kids. Would it be any faster than us settin' up our own charity?"

"Lots faster," Samantha answered. "A matter of weeks, or more likely months, I would think. If you go out on your own—and you have a perfect right to do so—I guarantee it will take at least a year before you can do any business. Plus, we already have offices."

"Why don't you give us a complete proposal, with ideas, costs, the whole works, and we'll meet again...let's say, one week from today." Luc looked to Tante Lulu for approval.

She nodded. "One thing, though. I was kinda hopin' ta name

my charity Cajun Knights. You know, like knights in shining armor."

Daniel's mouth dropped open, but Luc preempted him. "Uh-uh. That would imply only males being the rescuers."

"Ya got a point there."

"You can name your foundation anything you want...within reason," Samantha said. "Maybe we could call the umbrella organization something like Louisiana Hope Foundation. Our division would be Starr Wishes, and yours could be...whatever?"

"Sounds good to me," Luc said. "What do you think, Tante Lulu? What would yours be named? LeDeux Dreams? Or Lulu's Dream?" He grinned at his own suggestions.

"Nope." She didn't even hesitate. "Jude's Angels."

∾

Even angels need a little help from above...

ANGEL SABATO SURVEYED the crowded room at the Swamp Tavern, then cracked his knuckles. He was hot tonight.

Hot and determined.

It had been three weeks since Tante Lulu's call, but he'd had business matters to tie up in Jersey before heading south. The green-eyed witch might have given him the big kiss-off a year ago, but she wouldn't escape him this time.

As he eased his way into the tavern, more than a few women eyed him with interest. Nothing new there. He might be thirty-four years old, but he filled out his six-foot-one frame nicely, thank you very much. Good genes from his Mexican mother—and that was about all she'd given him before overdosing on her favorite addiction du jour—and his absentee-from-birth Italian father. Thank God for the navy, which he'd entered at sixteen, lying about his age. The military managed to straighten him out when nothing else had and gave him an education, too.

Appearance aside, he wasn't looking for action tonight; hadn't been for a long time, truth to tell. Nope, there was only one woman in his carnal crosshairs.

But there was no rush. He had a plan this time. No shock-and-awe declaration of love. No hasty wedding proposal. In fact, he planned to pretty much ignore her, at first, or pretend to ignore her. His pride demanded a little retribution. He'd been a player in the dating wars for too many years to have been so clumsy last year. This time would be different. He didn't intend to chase his tail forever, but if he was giving it one more shot, he was damn sure going to be a sharpshooter.

With loud Cajun music piercing his eardrums, something about Louisiana men being hot stuff, it took him ten minutes to weave his way over to the bar. "Excuse me."

"Oops!"

"Sorry."

"Ouch!" Once there, he waved a hand to the bartender, indicating he would have whatever was on tap. After slapping a couple of bills down with a nod of thanks, he turned, took a long draw on the foamy brew, and leaned back, bracing his elbows against the bar.

He saw now that it was the Swamp Rats onstage playing their usual rowdy music, having now segued into "Big Mamou." The tiny dance floor and all the empty spaces between tables were filled with laughing couples doing an energetic Cajun two-step. Above the stage was a wide banner proclaiming, "Louisiana Hope Foundation: Starr Wishes and Jude's Angels." There had been a hefty fifty-dollar cover charge to get in tonight, and by the size of the crowd he figured they were raking in the cash, for a good cause.

The song ended, and René LeDeux stepped up to the microphone. Angel had met René and the rest of the crazy LeDeux clan when on a project here last year with Jinx.

"We're not going to have our usual LeDeux Cajun Village People act tonight, folks," René said.

Groans and boos and hisses resounded through the room.

"Now, now, we got somethin' even better. And don't forget, all door receipts will go to this new foundation about to be formed, which will grant wishes to people *and families* in need right here in Loo-zee-anna."

While he'd been speaking, a group of about three dozen men and women lined up behind him, having come from back stage. The men were in varied, sometimes outrageous, attire...cop, cowboy, construction worker, football player, soldier, firefighter, even a pirate, while some of the women were dressed in short, tight sheath dresses and kickass high heels, but there was also a Miss Louisiana runner-up in a strapless gown and tiara, a beach bunny in bikini and see-through sarong cover-up, a cowgirl, and a female bodybuilder who could probably bench-press a bus. He recognized Grace right away, at the back, wearing a shimmery black knee-length sleeveless dress and strappy gold stilettos. Her red curls were a bit longer than a year ago, and she seemed to be wearing makeup—not her usual style—but other than that, she was the same. Just right.

"We're gonna have us an auction here, folks. You've heard of penny a dance, right? How 'bout dollar a dance—lots of dollars?"

The crowd hooted and hollered.

"Here's the rules. You are bidding on two dances with these fine folks behind me. Dances only! I leave it up to you to fast-talk your way into anything more than a dance." René winked meaningfully. "Once you're declared the winner, the partner you've chosen will come down and accept the cash or check, made out to Louisiana Hope Foundation. No credit cards, please. You'll all wait 'til the auction is over to begin dancing. Any questions? Okay, folks, let's have us some fun...Loo-zee-anna style." Wild cheering took place 'til the first victim—uh, auction offering—stepped forth.

"Ooooh, baby, lookee who's number one on the block. Lafayette's very own Skip Dupree, 2001 National Rodeo Champion. Ladies, all I can say is, if Skip dances as well as he rides, well, whoo-ee!"

Skip flashed René a glower that could cut ice, not that René gave a damn. Clearly, someone—probably Tante Lulu—had talked the mini-celebrity into this nonsense, which he was now regretting.

"Okay, let's start at a hundred. Who'll give me a hundred? Got one hundred. Now two? And three? Don't slow down. Four, four, four...four from a new bidder on the left. Lilly Belle Ginot, don't you be hidin' over there in the corner. I heard you're a Skip Dupree fan from way back. Are ya really gonna let these other ladies beat you out?"

Although he was no professional auctioneer, René had the rapid-fire chant down pat, all complemented by his slick Cajun shtick.

The young lady, Lilly Belle, ducked her head and tried to blend into the crowd, to no avail. Finally, she gave in and yelled, "Six hundred!"

"Thank you very much, but, ladies, let's be serious. You know that song 'Save a Horse, Ride a Cowboy'? Well, I'm not sayin' it was written about good ol' Skip here, but..."

Skip shot a glance of disbelief at René. All the other folks behind them on the stage started to fidget, wondering what the outrageous Cajun would do to them when their turns came up.

The bidding soon ended with René yelling out, "Going...going...sold! For fifteen hundred dollars. To the pretty lady from up N'awleans way. Sorry, Lilly Belle. Maybe you could try for the Houma construction worker comin' up soon. I hear he has a hot...hammer."

Skip swaggered down off the stage on his bowlegs to connect with his dancing partner. Angel didn't have to be able to read lips to know what he muttered to René before he left. Two words. Began with F and ended with U.

A NASCAR driver, Boots Larson, got this introduction: "I hear tell his sponsor is DieHard, and it's not just his auto parts that earned that title." Boots was young enough and dumb enough to think he'd been given a compliment. He topped off at nine hundred dollars.

A New Orleans Saints player brought the bidding up higher again, to eleven hundred. René got a lot of mileage over teasing, "I guess us guys have learned a lesson here. Women love rodeo more than football," which garnered much laughter, until said football player, not to be outdone, tugged off his jersey and did a bump and grind around the stage to a couple bars of that *Monday Night Football* song from the band. That little act brought the bidding up to thirteen hundred dollars.

Police Lieutenant John LeDeux's partner, Tank Woodrow, wearing a cop uniform, which he probably hadn't worn in years, seemed to stall at a measly three hundred dollars, which René tried to imply meant that rodeo riders and football players were sexier than cops. But Tank wasn't buying. No way was he taking off his shirt, even when René reminded him that this was for a good cause. "And don't you dare pull that DieHard/cowboy crap on me," Tank was heard to mutter at René.

Of course, that just caused René to say, "I'm not sayin' Tank here has buns of steel, but a little birdie tol' me that he sets off the metal detectors at the N'awleans airport." Tank gave up with a disgusted shake of his head as the bidding went up quickly to five hundred dollars.

The beauty queen garnered three hundred dollars, while the bathing beauty got five hundred. The owner of a belly-dancing school, a friend of Charmaine LeDeux, wearing an honest-to-God hottie harem outfit, got a rise from the crowd, pun intended, by giving a demonstration of her talents. She brought in six hundred dollars.

SANDRA HILL

On and on the auction went until customers were starting to get restless and thirsty, with only three people left to be auctioned. A stunning brunette from Baton Rouge, who was a weather girl for one of the TV stations; Grace; and an air force top-gun pilot who looked like Tom Cruise, but taller.

He would have liked to place a bid on Grace, a really big bid, then stroll through the cheering crowd up to the stage, where he would pick her up in his arms, carry her off to a corner, let her slide down his body, and then say, "Honey, I'm home."

But no, the direct MO hadn't worked the last time.

On the other hand, he could bid on the brunette. That would be in-your-face, take-*that*-Grace. Nope. Too suspicious and in some ways downright mean.

Timing was everything. In poker. In life. In love.

So, with a deep sigh, he set his half-empty bottle on the bar and walked toward the exit. He wouldn't stick around to watch another man dancing with Grace. But he gave one last glance up at her and murmured, "Tomorrow is another day, Scarlett."

Chuckling, he added, "And frankly, my dear, I don't give a damn if you resist or not. You. Are. Mine!"

The strangest thing happened then. As he opened the door of his rental pickup, he could swear he heard a thunderbolt in the distance, and there, sitting on the driver's seat, was a small St. Jude statue.

CHAPTER 5

Beware of old ladies with friends in high places...

"That was fun," Grace told Tante Lulu as she drove them back to their respective cottages.

"If it was so much fun, how come ya dint go home with that lawyer what bought two dances with you?"

"He couldn't keep his hands to himself—even dancing."

"I knowed a man like that once. His name was Octavius, but we called him Octy-puss. 'Course, iffen it's the right man, a woman doan mind a little wanderin' fingers." Grace smiled, not about to ask if she'd experienced a man handling her that way. Knowing Tante Lulu, she would tell her. In detail.

After a year of living next to and working with the old lady, she was coming to love her and her outspokenness, almost as much as her LeDeux family did. In fact, she treated Grace like family. Something Grace hadn't had for many years.

As she went down the two-lane road, not a streetlight for miles, she relished the starlit sky and the heady smell of tropical flowers wafting through their open windows. In many ways, traveling through southern Louisiana was like going back a half

SANDRA HILL

century or more to the days of roadside advertising signs and small general stores that sold everything from bait to bread.

"I bet the auction brought in plenty of money for the foundation," Grace remarked.

"Yep. I never did think it would take so much, though, even with the cash I put in. And it's movin' so slow; a three-legged turtle could make faster progress, I do declare." She sighed deeply. "Guess it's like cookin'. Cain't rush a good gumbo."

"Well, at least we can start on the house for the Duvals, right?" Lena and her siblings were still living in Grace's three-bedroom cottage now that school was out for the summer, with Tante Lulu, Grace, and other family members sharing responsibility. That was the easy part. Ducking Child Protective Services was the hard part.

"I'm hopin' it can be done in a month. If they're settled in proper and have a monthly income ta help out, we kin invite all the government do-gooders ta come see."

"I left some college brochures for Lena to look over. Maybe she'll take us up on the offer to further her education. She might even be entitled to some grants, as well, if she gets her GED first."

Conditions were very cramped in her little cottage, but Grace didn't mind too much. Except for all the reminders Lena posed about—well, things she would rather forget. Like, was her own seventeen-year-old daughter about to start college, or was she a late starter about to enter her senior year? Or was she struggling somewhere, in need of help? Was she pretty, like Lena? Tall? Thin or curvy? Smart? Did she have a boyfriend? Or was she married, God forbid?

At one time, Grace had considered doing an Internet search, but Catholic guilt was a powerful thing. She really didn't believe she deserved a reunion with her child, if that was even possible. Besides, she would need to start by talking with her parents, and that she was not prepared to do.

50

Grace shook her head from side to side to rid herself of unwelcome thoughts, ones that got her nowhere.

"What'sa matter?"

"Nothing. Just bad memories."

Tante Lulu nodded. "I gets those, too, but no use dwellin' over burnt roux. A body's just gotta move on, and trust in God."

"And St. Jude," Grace offered with a smile.

"Guar-an-teed!"

"Changing the subject, you know, it was the oddest thing. I could swear I saw Angel in the back of the tavern tonight."

"Hmmmm."

The way Tante Lulu said, "Hmmmm," and her subsequent silence caused red flags to rise in Grace's head. "It couldn't have been him, could it?"

The old lady yawned loudly, then murmured, "Mebbe it was."

Uh-oh! "Why would he be here?"

"Mebbe someone invited him."

Those red flags were practically doing the hula now. "Okay, what's going on?"

"Nuthin'."

Grace pulled over to the side of the road and stared at Tante Lulu.

"What?"

"Spill."

"Doan go havin' a conniption. We needed someone ta come help us construct a house fer the Duvals real quick. Angel agreed ta supervise as long as the rest of the family, and some of them Starrs, do the hard labor."

"Why would he do that?"

"'Cause I asked. 'Cause he's a good person. 'Cause he saw the need. Jeesh!"

"Why wouldn't he have let me know he was coming?" Grace was confused and hurt at the same time.

"Why should he...after ya clipped his tail?"

"We were friends for a long time before I—well, before that last night. Friends don't just sever all ties."

"Sweetie, ya cain't be friends when one of the parties is in love. It's like tryin' ta put the crawfish back in the shell once ya sucked it out."

"What about his wife? Did she come, too?"

"What wife?"

Grace groaned at Tante Lulu's deliberate obtuseness. "You know very well what wife."

"Guess you'll hafta ask him 'bout that."

"Where's he staying?"

"I dunno. Wait. I think I heard Remy offer ta let him stay in his houseboat. Ya gonna go talk ta him?"

"Of course I am."

"Tomorrow?"

"No. I promised to take the kids to the beach. Grand Isle. Lena is still so weak. Being out in the sun might energize her a bit."

"Good idea. Give her more of that lemon-balm tea with St. John's wort, too."

A companionable silence followed as Grace mused on Angel and how she still missed him...as a friend. She was going to give him a piece of her mind. Yes, she was. True friends were hard to find, and he had been unfair cutting her off the way he had. Besides that, she was curious about this woman he had married so quickly after leaving Louisiana.

"Think I'll start a hope chest fer Angel."

"Why would you do that if he's already married?"

"Ya never know what St. Jude has in the works, honey."

That's what Grace was afraid of.

~

The best-laid plans of mice and clueless men...

52

TWO DAYS LATER, Angel was sitting at the built-in corner kitchen booth of his temporary abode—a houseboat, of all things—drinking a cup of coffee and studying rough drafts for the Duval house spread out on the table before him. The design was one of those standard plans that could be purchased, then modified to fit specific needs.

He'd spent all day yesterday going over the site with several of the LeDeux men, Tante Lulu, and some woman from the foundation, Samantha Starr. Today he hoped to order supplies, then get started on demolishing the trailer and hauling away the debris. That ought to get rid of some of his excess energy. Cold showers weren't doing the trick anymore, now that he was back within Grace's radar. Actually, he was looking forward to this project. A hands-on, instant-gratification kind of thing, he supposed. Especially since he wasn't getting gratification in any other way.

And he couldn't ask for better digs than this glorified houseboat. Once a rich man's plaything, the fancy vessel had been permanently anchored on Bayou Black, down a ways in front of Remy's home, several miles away from Tante Lulu and Grace's cottages.

Surprisingly large, it had a great room that combined a salon, galley kitchen, and office alcove. A skylight brightened the fine brass trim and the rich patina of old cypress wood paneling. Plush cushions sat on the window seats, and a red-field Persian rug covered the floor. The small bathroom sported a high-tech shower, the kind with water jets hitting you from every angle. Very sexy.

Added to the boat's attractions was the lapping of water outside, accompanied by birdsong and that particular floral scent he associated with the bayous. A guy could get used to swamp living.

Just then, his cell phone rang. He checked the caller ID and smiled. Tante Lulu.

"How's my favorite adopted aunt?"

"Grace is on her way."

"Here?"

"Yep."

"What does she know?"

"Nuthin'. 'Ceptin that I invited ya here ta build the first foundation house."

"Okay...oh, here she is. Hold on."

Grace stood on the other side of the screen door, tapping lightly. His heart began racing at just one glance her way. Her red hair was shoulder length now and flipped up lightly on the ends, kind of like Meg Ryan used to wear.

It was probably still curly as all get-out when it was wet, though.

She wore a watermelon-colored strappy sundress, with a white belt that matched her sandals, where cotton-candy-pink toes peeked out. Cherry lip gloss completed the look.

He stood and waved for Grace to enter. Putting his hand over the phone, he said, "C'mon in. I just need to finish this call."

To Tante Lulu, he said, "Sorry. A visitor just stopped by."

He saw Grace's head shoot up at his referring to her as a visitor, but then she began to amble about the room, studying the furnishings.

"Is that Grace?" Tante Lulu whispered.

"Yes, sweetheart, I had a good time last night, too. What did you say the name of that wine was?"

"Huh?" Tante Lulu replied. "Oh, right. I get it. Tee-hee-hee!"

"No, I can't make it tonight. Maybe tomorrow. Yes, I like jazz. That sounds great. What time should I pick you up?" He murmured something low and husky then—a bunch of gibberish that probably sounded like flirty talk to Grace.

Once he clicked off, Grace started toward him. He could tell she was going to give him a hug.

I don't think so!

Instead, he held out a hand for her to shake. Formally. Like strangers.

She looked at it as if he'd offered her a snake, then glanced up at him in question. Hurt blurred her eyes.

For a second he softened, but, no, he had to be strong.

The plan...he had to keep to the plan. "Hi, Grace. Long time no see."

"Too long, Angel. I've missed you."

He arched his eyebrows.

"As a friend."

Shit!

When he didn't respond, she asked, "Was that your wife on the phone?"

"No," was all he said. *Dammit, does she have to appear so blasé at the mention of my having a wife?*

Her face flushed with color. She must have thought he was cheating on his wife by what she'd overheard of his phone call. In the old days, she would have berated him up one side and down the other for his tomcatting. Little did she know how long it had been since he'd done any...tomcatting.

"I'm surprised that you didn't call to let me know you were coming back to Louisiana."

"I've been busy."

More hurt shone in her green eyes, but she soon pulled herself together and sank down on one of the window-seat cushions. "What's been going on in your life?"

Oh, super! Now we're going to chitchat. If she mentions the weather, I just might puke. He sat down, as well, across the room in an armchair, just outside the desk alcove. "Well, for one thing, the Amber Project was a bust for Jinx."

"That happens sometimes. Win some, lose some."

He nodded. "Still, it was almost a year wasted."

"And next?"

"I don't know. Ronnie has a lot of projects lined up for her company. I'm just not sure I want to continue with the treasure hunting. I probably will, but this job here will give me a break to think things over."

"So that's why you're really here? Not just because Tante Lulu asked you to help with building the house?"

"Why else would I be here, Grace?" he asked, looking her directly in the eye. "Are you thinking I'm still in love with you, and I've come back with my tail between my legs, hoping you'll give me a pet or two?"

By the quick blush on her face he could tell that's exactly what she'd thought. "Of course not. It's been a year. And you got..."

When she didn't finish, he did it for her. "Married?"

"Well, yes."

"Don't you want to ask me about that?"

"It's none of my business," she said, which was such a total crock that they both burst out laughing at the same time. They had always butted into each other's business. "Okay, who is she? Is she beautiful? Was it love at first sight? Where is she now? Do you have any"—she gulped in the oddest way—"children?"

"Gracie, Gracie, Gracie." He shook his head at her. "Her name is Gloria Stewart. Yes, she is beautiful—more than beautiful. No, there are no children, thank God! Love at first sight? You've got to be kidding! More like love on the rebound, for both of us. She'd recently been jilted, practically at the altar. Wounded pride makes men and women do dumb things." He paused and exhaled loudly with self-disgust. "Gloria is a very nice girl...woman, I mean, but that's about it."

Grace cocked her head to the side, still blushing. "I don't understand."

"We were divorced one month after the wedding. An annulment, actually. She got a job with a European airline; that's where she is now. France. In the end, though, biiiig mistake!"

"The marriage or the divorce?"

"What do you think?"

56

"Oh, Angel!"

"No pity here, baby! If you're thinking I'm still in love with you, rest assured. I got over that sickness long ago," he lied.

She jerked back as if he'd slapped her. Probably because he'd referred to love as sickness. Well, hell's bells, what does she want me to say? Something flowery and gag-me sweet? Yeah, right!

"We can be friends again then, okay?"

What alien world are you living in, cupcake? "Sure, but I'm going to be really busy for the next few weeks. Maybe we can get together for a drink some time before I finish the job." He was making it clear that there would be no same-old buddy-buddy friendship resuming here.

She stood and began to walk toward the door. "Well, I just wanted to stop by and wish you welcome."

He tipped his chair back, hands linked behind his neck, ankles crossed. Casual was the look he was going for. Meanwhile, it felt as if his lungs were about to burst.

And then, her shoulders drooping with disappointment, she went out the door.

Dammit, he couldn't be a shit like this, not to Grace. He hesitantly unfolded himself from the chair, then, with a curse, decisively walked out on the deck and caught up with her just before she got into her car. Taking her into his arms, he gave a squeeze and kissed her on the top of her head. She felt so right in his embrace. Why couldn't she see that?

For just a second, she wrapped her arms around his waist and squeezed, too.

Blood rushed to his head, and his knees almost buckled. Putting her away from him, he saw her eyes brimming with tears —tears he had caused. "It *is* good seeing you again, Gracie."

"Same for me," she whispered.

He opened her car door for her.

Just before she left, she opened her window. "Just so you know, Angel, if I was ever free to love any man, it would be you."

With those ominous words, she was off, crushed shells from the driveway spinning in her wake.

He stared after her, mouth agape. *What the hell does that mean?*

A strange voice in his head replied, *Dumb twit! Why not ask her?* Two days back in the South and already Tante Lulu's bizarre St. Jude voices were erupting in his head.

If ever I was free, he repeated her words in his head and frowned with confusion. Could she be...?

He recalled a conversation he'd had with her soon after they'd met years ago:

"Are you married?"

"No."

"Ever?"

"No."

Well, another theory shot down. In that instant he realized that for as many years as he'd known Grace, he really didn't know much about her. She'd always been close-mouthed about her past, not just the time she'd been in a convent, but before that, too. He didn't even know if she had any family...parents, siblings. Maybe that was the key to breaking down her defenses.

Well, at least he'd gotten through his first meeting with Grace, relatively unscathed. The question was: What next?

What next was a loud roar at his feet that about caused him to jump out of his skin. "Sonofabitch!" It was Useless, that dumbass pet alligator of Remy's.

"Give me a minute, and I'll go get you some Cheez Doodles," he promised, as if the dumb beast-that-should-be-shoes could understand him.

Useless opened his mouth wide, flashing his big I-could-bite-your-numbskull-noggin-off teeth. The message was clear: "Hurry!"

And in his head, once again, Angel heard, *Dumb twit!*

Temperatures rising...

GRACE COULD TELL that Angel was annoyed when the whole lot of them showed up at the Duval trailer later that day to help him.

Hands on hips, he glared at her car, which was unloading Lena, Lionel, Miles, and Ella. They were going to box any things still left in the trailer that they wanted to keep. Then he aimed his glare at the next two vehicles, which carried Luc, René, Remy, and John LeDeux, along with some of their sons, who planned— unasked, of course—to help Angel demolish the trailer and put the parts in the commercial Dumpster that had already been delivered. In the last car, a lavender convertible, driven by Charmaine LeDeux Lanier, came its owner, Tante Lulu, who considered any event an opportunity to feast. That meant folding tables and chairs, baskets of food, and coolers full of beer and soda pop.

She was dressed for the part today in bibbed carpenter pants with loops holding a hammer, screwdriver, drill, and various other tools that no one in their right mind would ever let her use; child-sized leather work boots; and a baseball cap with the message "Wanna Get Nailed?" She probably didn't know what it meant. On the other hand, she probably did.

"Damn!" Angel muttered. "This is supposed to be a job, not a party."

Tante Lulu, overhearing him, said, "Stuff it."

John LeDeux, who was one of Tante Lulu's youngest "nephews" at twenty-nine years old, grinned at Angel. *"Cher,* we gotta Cajunize you. You need to get a little *joie de vivre.* Joy of life."

Angel told him he was the one who needed to get a life, in graphic terms.

But John wasn't listening. He'd just noticed that his six-year-old son, Etienne, had somehow managed to climb up onto the top of the trailer and was doing a Snoopy dance of victory.

"Hey, y'all, watch this!"

Everyone knew that when a southern male called that out, he

was about to do something stupid, like stick a hand in a gator's mouth, or jump off a tall tree in a shallow bayou stream. Even if that male happened to be only six years old. Usually beer was involved, though Etienne of course could be high only on Kool-Aid.

"Aye-tee-ann! Don't you dare jump!" John yelled. "Get your butt down here right now!"

Etienne looked at his dad and just grinned.

Cursing under his breath, John climbed up after him.

Word was that John LeDeux had been the most mischievous little devil the bayou had ever known. It appeared that he was getting his payback bigtime with his son.

Meanwhile, Angel was talking—rather, arguing—with the men about who should do what job, giving Grace a chance to study him—something she hadn't had a chance to do when she'd gone to the houseboat earlier that day.

The once long ponytail was clipped short. Low-riding faded jeans, highlighting the cutest belly button—and, yes, she had noticed it was a slight outie—led down to heavy work boots. He wore no shirt, and, since the temperature was almost ninety and humid, he was sweating like a pig. But oh, my, the boy—uh, pig—did look smokin' hot good.

Grace could swear her own temperature shot through the roof. How odd! She'd never felt that kind of attraction to Angel before.

Just then, his eyes caught hers...and held.

It was the worst kind of cliché, but honestly, it felt as if the universe stopped and they were the only two people in the world. Probably no more than a second passed, but what a second!

This must be how all of Angel's women felt. Their IQs dropped down to about their bust sizes, and their hormones went dirty dancing. Not her, though. Nope, this was just an aberration, caused by the heat, no doubt.

Besides, Angel obviously hadn't been as affected as she,

because he had already turned away and was talking softly to Lena, who pointed to some items she wanted to take with her. His hand was on Lena's shoulder...long fingers with short, trimmed nails. Fingers that she knew were talented in dealing cards at poker or digging for treasure but would probably be equally talented at other things. *Whaaat? Where did that thought come from? Holy Moly! Am I going off the deep end here?*

She watched Angel and Lena as they examined a battered boy's bike. A clothesline. And a water heater, of all things, which she insisted on taking because it still wasn't paid for and she didn't want to waste the money. Maybe she could sell it in one of those weekly circulars, Lena said.

John sidled up to Grace and whispered in her ear, "You're droolin', darlin'."

"Drop dead!"

He laughed. "Tsk, tsk, tsk! Is that any way for a nun to talk?"

"I haven't been a nun for ages, so don't you start with the nun jokes, either." In the old days, when she'd thought she and Angel were best friends, he used to tease her constantly with hokey nun jokes. Who ever thought she would miss *that*?

John put up his hands in surrender. "Sorry," he said, then negated his apology by calling out to Tante Lulu, "Did you hear thunder, Auntie?"

Grace sighed. A perfect beginning to another day down the bayou.

CHAPTER 6

Bad girls don't cry...

$\mathcal{L}$ ater, Grace sank down into a folding lawn chair next to Lena, who had been ordered by Angel to "freakin' sit down and freakin' rest" after almost fainting in the midday heat.

To which Grace had told him not to take his bad mood out on the girl.

For which he had scowled at Grace, then mumbled an apology to Lena.

Under her breath, Tante Lulu, who had overheard, warned him, "Cool yer engines, boy, or yer train is gonna crash."

Angel, a rascal just like the old lady's nephews, grinned. "My engine is just fine, thank you very much."

Meanwhile, the usually shy Miles had taken a fancy to Angel and was following him around like a shadow. She had to give Angel credit. Instead of telling the kid to get lost, even in a nice way, he was giving him small jobs and hunkering down to his level at times to explain how to do certain things the correct way.

Ella, in her full Hannah Montana regalia right down to a

temporary tattoo of her favorite star on her upper arm, was flicking through some fashion magazines that Charmaine had given her. Lionel, with all his myriad piercings, had finally taken off his leather jacket, only to reveal, to Lena's horror, a sleeveless black T-shirt with the saying, "Coed Naked Gator Wrestling Team." On the other hand, Tee-John's son, Etienne, was fascinated by the piercings, as well as the shirt, and asked his father if he could get some, to which Tee-John had replied, "Yeah. When you're thirty."

Charmaine, who today wore skintight black capri pants; a leopard-print shell with the glittery sequined hair stylist message "Let Me Do You"; high-heeled wedgie shoes; and big teased hair, based on a Texas principle of "Higher the hair, closer to God," handed Grace and Lena glasses of cold sweet tea. "I swear, it's hot enough to make a southern gal glisten," she said, exhaling on a long whoosh. Presumably southern girls didn't ever sweat. They were too refined. Instead, they "glistened."

Then Charmaine was off to help Tante Lulu put away the left-over food, of which there wasn't much. Gone were the fried chicken and fried green tomatoes, a mess of collard greens, potato salad, seafood étouffée, lazy bread, banana and vanilla wafer pudding, and Peachy Praline Cobbler cake.

"Miles, you come over here," Lena yelled at her brother, who was tagging after Angel like a puppy. "You're getting in the way."

Angel waved a hand at her. "That's okay. Miles is my apprentice."

Miles beamed as if Angel had just handed him the moon...or an Xbox game.

With a wink, Angel smiled at Lena in understanding.

And Lena said, "Oh, my God!" waving a hand in front of her face.

"Ditto," Grace agreed.

The two of them then took long drinks of the deliciously cool beverage and set their half-empty glasses on the ground beside them. Lena sighed deeply. "Why am I still so weak?" she asked tearfully.

"Honey, you've been very sick. It takes time. Speaking of which, we should head back to the cottage soon. You overdid it yesterday at the beach and working here today. Really—"

"No!" Lena protested with surprising vehemence.

Grace tilted her head in question, putting a hand on the girl's jeans-clad knee.

"I don't want to leave 'til it's"—she hiccoughed on a small sob —"all gone."

"Why?"

"This trailer is the only thing we've had for sure these past four years. Once it's gone...I'm scared."

"But we've promised everything will be all right."

She shook her head hard. "No. You can't be certain. Even if you build the house, that doesn't mean the authorities will let me keep the kids with me."

Actually, Grace had some of the same reservations about them being able to defeat the authorities. Look what they did to those Mormon kids in Texas. Not that she condoned polygamy or marrying off young girls to old men, but CPS swooped in without any proof of abuse, taking hundreds of children from their parents. Sort of like guilt by accusation.

"I mean, what kind of job would I be able to get to support a new house—even a small one?" Lena continued. "I had trouble taking care of the trailer."

"We're hoping you'll go to college."

"Hah! Like that would help! Even less money coming in."

"I understand how you're feeling. I really do. It's hard to trust people when you've been...hurt."

Lena raised her eyebrows in question.

"Tell me about your mother," Grace said, not about to speak about herself and her own hurts.

Lena's face brightened. She was a very pretty girl, resembling a young Halle Berry. It wasn't surprising that Remy's twenty-four-year-old son, Andy LeDeux, a New Orleans Saints football player, kept eyeing her when she wasn't looking. Adopted from a Romanian orphanage as a child, his nickname was Candy Andy because he was, well, eye candy. To his chagrin, Lena didn't even notice him.   *

"Mama was so pretty, and she sang like an angel. Everyone said so. I have some tapes she made one time. Would you like to hear them?"

"I'd love to."

"Daddy always drank a lot, but it got worse after Mama got sick. Way worse. She lingered for two years. He'd be gone for days, even weeks at a time. He said he had gigs in other towns, but...you know. We lost our little house outside N'awleans and rented an apartment that was in a bad part of the city. Couldn't even go out after dark. Then, after Mama died..." She shivered and couldn't seem to finish.

Grace got the picture. Lena had been acting the little mother even before her mother's death. "Oh, sweetie, you've been carrying a heavy burden for such a long time. Maybe it's time to let someone help."

"No! It's not a burden. It's—" She deliberately stopped herself, then said with an uncustomary bitterness, "Bet you never had any problems growing up. Bet you were a cheerleader, and your mother baked cookies for the PTA, and you were Daddy's little girl."

"Hardly," Grace said. "My father was a rigid, sanctimonious bastard, and my mother read the Bible three times a day but didn't have a maternal bone in her body. They treated me like crap. Bad girl, bad girl, bad girl, that's what they always called me. Even when I was only two years old." Grace clapped a hand over her mouth, tears welling in her eyes. She never revealed information about herself like that. Never. And she certainly didn't cry over a long-buried past. She swiped the back of her hand over both eyes.

Only then—*dammit!*—did she see Angel standing in front of them with a photograph he must have found in the trailer. He'd been about to hand it to Lena. The expression on his face could only be described as stunned.

Other than her loose tongue, the worst thing was the voice in her head, which said, *Now we're getting somewhere.*

"Grace?" Angel said, folding himself down onto his haunches in front of her. "You never said—"

"No!" She swatted away his hands, which were reaching for her. "I don't want to talk about it. And would you please go put on a shirt."

"Huh?" He looked down at himself. His chest, with dark hair leading down in a vee toward his navel, and the Never-Never Land accentuated by his jeans strained over muscular thighs and a package that was as impressive as it had been years ago when he'd posed for *Playgirl* magazine. And, yes, she'd checked it out. What woman, or girl, over fifteen hadn't? "My chest bothers you?"

She tried to laugh, but it came out as a gurgle. "Not your chest, you idiot. Your belly button."

"There's a problem with my belly button?"

"No, there's no problem with your belly button. That's the problem."

Lena giggled.

One of the LeDeux men chortled.

Tante Lulu pulled out a mini St. Jude statue.

A slow grin crept over Angel's lips. "You like my belly button," he accused. Then, "Oh, no, we're not changing the subject. I want to talk with you." He rose in one graceful motion, tugging her to her feet. Then, to her consternation, and everyone else's amusement, he frog-marched her off toward the woods.

~

I'll show you mine if you show me yours...

ANGEL PUSHED Grace forward with hands clamped on both of her upper arms. He was so angry. At those people who had hurt Grace. At Grace for holding it in all these years. At himself for never making the effort to really know her.

But now he was damn sure going to find out everything she'd been hiding. He sensed it was an important key to understanding Grace...and maybe to his winning her love.

"Stop shoving me. I can walk on my own."

"Maybe I can't."

"Huh?" She turned abruptly and he ran into her, almost knocking them both down. To steady himself, he put his arms around her and held on tight, his legs outspread. It was amazing how well they fit together, despite their differences in height. Even after they were both steady, he still held on.

A thousand different emotions pelted him as the scent of Grace enveloped him, and he didn't mean perfume. Most important, love. He loved her so frickin' much and was frustrated that he couldn't express himself without her running for the hills. Not that there were many hills in southern Louisiana.

The encouraging thing was that Grace embraced him back. Only for a moment, but hell, he took his perks wherever he could.

Stepping back, he studied her in a long, slow sweep of her body, presumably to make sure he hadn't hurt her, but really because he liked looking at her. A true redhead, she had hair that often took on the highlights of her surroundings. Today, flame-colored in the sunshine. Another day, orangish, like rust. She had a few freckles, but mostly her skin was that creamy white that failed to tan, a stunning contrast to those pale green crystal eyes. She was of average height and build but gave the appearance of being fine-boned and fragile, which she was not. He liked her curves, including a most tempting heart-shaped ass. Today she wore a white Swamp Rats T-shirt, tucked into black jeans with a braided belt.

"Stop looking at me like that."

"Huh?" He shook his head to wipe away his forbidden thoughts...forbidden for now, anyhow. "I was just checking to see if I hurt you," he lied, although he noticed his finger marks on the easily bruised skin of her upper arms. Then he motioned to a dead log lying in a small clearing up ahead. "Let's sit down there."

"Check for snakes first."

Yeech! Reptiles were a natural part of the tropical environment here. He wasn't afraid of them, but that didn't mean he liked the buggers. Carefully, he kicked the log in several places. Since nothing slithered out, he figured they were safe.

He sat down.

When Grace sat next to him, he noticed that she put about three feet of distance between them. *Back to step one, are we, babe?*

"What was all that about back there...what you said to Lena?"

"Nothing."

"It was not nothing, dammit."

"It's none of your business."

"I'm making it my business."

"Why?"

"We have a history, Grace. Yeah, yeah, I know. As friends. But I can't believe you kept such important stuff from me." He rubbed his nape wearily.

She bristled. "I don't know everything about you, either."

"Ask away. I'm an open book."

She sighed. "I shouldn't have said anything. I never do. And I don't want to start now."

"If you don't tell me, I'll find out on my own."

She turned slowly, inch by inch, to glare at him. "What do you mean?"

He shrugged. "I'll hire a private investigator. And I won't stop at your family history, either. I'll uncover all your secrets."

She looked as if she was about to throw up.

Which made him really, really curious. What secrets did she hide?

"LeDeux—John, I mean—is a cop. Bet he could recommend someone." He watched her closely, to see her reaction.

There was fear in her green eyes. Another puzzle. Soon replaced by anger. "I'll never forgive you if you start digging in my past."

"What do I have to lose?"

"You told me that you were over me—that you didn't, uh, love me anymore. And you implied we couldn't even be friends."

"So?"

"So, stop meddling."

"Meddle, meddle, meddle."

"That was immature."

"It's one of my better attributes."

She said something vulgar.

Which only made him grin.

"I don't need your pity, Angel."

"Agreed. And I don't need any sugarcoating."

"I had a lousy childhood, okay?"

"So did I."

"Oh, great, now we're going to play the one-upmanship game...over bad history. Look. It's no big deal. I was an only child, born to older parents. My mother was forty-two when I was born, my dad was fifty. They were really strict, religious people. Very judgmental. The least little thing was considered a sin, including my red hair—a sign of the devil. In fact, my mother believed she got pregnant so late in life as punishment for some sin or other she had committed..."

Oh, my God! They considered her a penance to bear. What a burden to put on a kid!

"... though God knows, the worst thing I ever saw her do was gossip about a fellow parishioner." Grace was still talking, not having noticed his angry reaction: tight fists, thinned mouth, blood boiling. "They were Catholic, but a small sect that broke off from the modern church. Very conservative."

He closed his eyes on a painful thought. "Were you abused?"

She shook her head. "Not physically...or at least not much. But the stricter they became, the more I rebelled. Until I finally left home at sixteen."

"And went where?"

"The convent."

He frowned. "Why would you choose that? I suspect that's exactly what your parents wanted."

"They did, but you know, joining a nunnery wasn't a bad thing for me. I finished high school, then college and grad school. I wasn't unhappy there."

"Why did you leave?"

"I was playing poker online and had entered a few tournaments—this while I was getting a master's at NYU. I discovered that I was good."

"Don't tell me. When I first met you, you were a nun?"

"Yep!"

He laughed. "Son of a gun! I never would have guessed. As I recall, you were wearing a plain gray shift dress and sandals, and you smelled like vanilla. You wore no makeup and your hair was like a cap of tight red curls."

Now it was her turn to laugh. "Nuns aren't very fashion conscious. We had been baking vanilla butter cookies for a church sale all afternoon the day of the tournament. I guess we went a little overboard on the vanilla."

Something occurred to him then. "Oh, my God, I hit on a nun."

"Yes, you did." She smiled at him, and, man, she had the sweetest smile. It reached all the way up and encompassed her whole face, especially her dancing eyes. "Actually, I was flattered."

"And you shot me down. Zap! I don't get shot down very often, so I was crushed."

She smiled some more. "Liar! You just moved on to the other females in the casino that day."

"Hey, it was about that time that I posed for *Playgirl*. Did you know about it?"

"Oh, yeah." She grinned at him. "You were already a name in poker, and the title of your feature was 'His Poker Is Hot.'"

His face heated up. That stupid stunt was going to follow him to the grave. "So, did you look at the picture?"

A wider grin, accompanied by twinkling green eyes. "What do you think?"

"A nun ogling soft porn. Tsk, tsk!"

"What makes you think I was ogling?"

He pretended to be hurt "You didn't like my...uh, attributes?"

She leaned over and smacked him on the arm. "You are such a wuss, fishing for X-rated compliments."

"So, is that why you left the convent?"

She laughed. "Because I was checking out naked guy pictures?"

"No. Because of the card playing?"

"Uh-huh. I won a tournament, and my picture was in the newspaper. I was politely told to resign or get booted out." Grace stood and brushed some pieces of bark off her rear end.

Angel uncoiled his body and stood, too. "Were you upset about that?"

"No. I wasn't meant for the religious life, though there were good people there. Religious, yeah, but way different from my parents."

"When was the last time you saw your parents? Oh," he quickly added, having forgotten how old they were at her birth, "are they still alive?"

"I have no idea. And that is the end of confession for today, Father Sabato."

Angel started to ask more, then stopped himself. He suspected there was a whole lot Grace hadn't told him, but he could wait. He'd learned more about her today than he had in the past ten years. And he needed to think over everything she had disclosed to find the missing pieces of her puzzle.

"I'm glad we can at least talk to each other like this—like old times," Grace said as they walked side by side back to the trailer site.

If she says we can still be friends, I am going to throttle her...or kiss her senseless.

~

Lawyers and poker players know how to fake it...

MOST EVERYONE HAD LEFT by the time they returned, except for Tante Lulu, Luc, and a new arrival Grace recognized as Samantha Starr, who would be running the joint Hope Foundation once it got under way officially.

"C'mere, Angel," Tante Lulu said. "I cain't explain these drawings to Samantha nohow."

He walked over without giving Grace another look. Which was fine. Really. And she wasn't jealous of the appreciative once-over Samantha gave Angel, even if it was obvious that she liked his belly button, too. The show-off hadn't put a shirt back on yet.

Besides, there was no contest in comparing herself to the stunning auburn-haired beauty. Samantha was tall, and Grace had always wished she was taller, and even though her hair was red, it wasn't brassy red like Grace's but a deep mahogany. Of course, she had a ton of freckles; Grace didn't envy those.

"What's up?" she asked Luc.

"Everyone had dates or commitments. Charmaine took the kids back to your cottage. She'll stay until you bring Tante Lulu."

Grace nodded. "Well, we got a lot done here today, didn't we?"

They both scanned the clearing, which really was a clearing now. No more trailer. The Dumpster was full, and sheets of metal siding lay in a huge pile.

"If Tante Lulu and Samantha approve those drawings," Luc said, pointing to the picnic table where the three were studying what appeared to be blueprints, "Angel will order the supplies today and get started tomorrow laying a foundation."

"So quick!"

"Yep, but that's what they need. The house will be up in two weeks. Lots of inside finishing to be done after that, but the kids would be able to move in within a month. If everything goes smoothly, that is."

"Are you as worried as I am that this is not going to work?"

"Yes. Well, no. Somehow, even the most outrageous of Tante Lulu's schemes always work out in the end."

"Of course they do. She's got St. Jude on her side."

"Ain't that the truth?"

They smiled at each other. Luc was a very handsome man. A very handsome *married* man with three teenage daughters.

Just then, they heard a car approaching. Someone must be returning.

But no, it was a strange vehicle. A strange vehicle with a logo on the side.

"Uh-oh," she and Luc said at the same time.

A man and a woman got out of the car and walked toward them. They wore serious business suits and serious expressions on their faces.

A sideways glance showed that Tante Lulu, Angel, and Samantha had also noticed the new arrivals and were coming up to stand beside her and Luc.

"What are you people doing here?" the man asked. He was about forty with horseshoe hair, bald on top, bushy on the sides. Lines bracketed his eyes and lips, but they probably weren't due to smiles. Even as he spoke, he pulled a pack of antacids from his pocket and popped one into his mouth.

"What are *you* doing here?" Luc countered.

That didn't go over big.

Mr. Tums was already unfolding a wallet and showing them a CPS identification card. "I'm Merrill Olsen from Child Protective

73

Services, and this is my assistant, Jancie Pitot." Jancie was thirty-something, a very plain, almost homely woman, who weighed at least two hundred pounds, and by her pinched lips, she looked as if she could use a stomach settler, too.

Tante Lulu, never one to mince words, whispered, "That feller 'pears as ornery as a bee-stung dog, and that gal has a four-pocket behind if I ever saw one."

"I'm Luc—Lucien LeDeux, representing the Hope Foundation. This is my aunt, Louise Rivard, and that is Samantha Starr, cochairman of the foundation. And these two are Angel Sabato and Grace O'Brien. What can we do for you folks?"

"What are you people doing here? And where the hell's the trailer that was standing here yesterday?"

"Gone, gone, gone," Angel quipped.

Neither Mr. Tums nor Ms. Pitot was amused.

In fact, Tante Lulu muttered under her breath again, "Those two have hearts as cold as a cast-iron commode."

"Who tore it down?" Ms. Pitot asked.

"We did," Angel replied for all of them.

"What right did you have to do that?" Mr. Turns wanted to know.

"Right of ownership. The legal papers are on file in the parish courthouse, in case you're interested," Luc said in a lawyerly voice.

Face reddening, Ms. Pitot said, "Where are the kids who were living here? Did you buy the place from them? Because, believe me, you might be Lawyer McDreamy, but you're in big trouble if you did."

Everyone looked at Luc at the mention of Lawyer McDreamy.

Lips twitching with suppressed mirth, Luc told them, "This plot was a long-abandoned railroad right-of-way with an old trailer on it. It was legally purchased four years ago."

"By whom?" Mr. Tums' eyes widened as he seemed to notice for the first time the pile of rubble that once was a trailer. He sputtered, "Something fishy's going on here. I demand some answers."

Luc shrugged. "Sue me."

"Don't you people have something better to do? Like reform the foster-care system? Or take care of kids who are in abusive homes? Or help families stay together?" Grace's outburst surprised not only the CPS workers, but everyone else there, including herself.

Ignoring her, Mr. Tums and Ms. Pitot were about to turn on their heels, but first Mr. Tums warned them, "We'll be back. With the police. You won't be such smartasses then."

"Jancie Pitot," Tante Lulu said suddenly. "I know you. Yer the one what peed yer pants on the Our Lady of the Bayou quilt at the church bazaar when you was a chile."

Jancie's face bloomed pink with embarrassment.

"How's yer mama, *chère*? She still got the gout?"

Jancie muttered something about her mother being okay, and the two stomped toward their car.

Once they left the area, Luc sighed.

"What?" the rest of them asked.

"We've got trouble."

They all turned to him, waiting for an explanation.

"Minors can't buy property in Louisiana."

CHAPTER 7

And then he invited the green-eyed cat to stop by...

Once they had discussed the problems they would be facing with CPS and how to speed up the building project, Angel said, "I'm outta here."

Luc slapped an arm over his shoulder. "Hot date?"

"We shall see. Whether it turns out to be hot or not." Angel cast a quick glance at Grace to check if she was listening.

She was.

"Who you datin'?" Leave it to Tante Lulu. Blunt as usual.

Angel didn't suppose she would appreciate him telling her it was none of her business. "Larise Dupree. Charmaine introduced us."

Tante Lulu muttered something about him being a dumb doodle and Charmaine needing to be whacked upside the head.

"Hey, I know Larise," Samantha said. "We went to school together. Isn't she a model? In fact, I heard she posed nude for *Playboy* last year."

"That figures," Grace mumbled under her breath. "Birds of a feather."

"What did you say?" Angel inquired sweetly.

She pretended not to hear him.

"I like models," Luc said. "Especially nude ones."

"Remind me ta tell that ta yer wife," Tante Lulu said. Luc just hugged his aunt.

"Hey, Samantha. I got a good idea. Mebbe you could double-date with Angel. I could fix ya up with my nephew Daniel. You met him. Remember? The doctor who ain't gay."

"Don't. You. Dare. I don't need to be fixed up with anyone, and certainly not with a sarcastic Doctor McDreamy."

"Ya doan hafta shout." Tante Lulu had her head tilted to the side and was hitting the side of her head with the heel of one hand. "And ain't it cool that we got a Lawyer McDreamy and a Doctor McDreamy in our family?"

"How about you, Grace?" Angel gave her another of his sweet, innocent looks, which she wasn't buying one bit. "Do you want to double date?"

"What do you think?"

"Hey, if you don't have anyone special, there's this bartender over in the French Quarter I met yesterday. He used to be a navy SEAL...about twenty years ago. Of course, he's bald, but some women like that. And you know what they say about navy SEALs. Staying power out the ying-yang. I told him about you, and he was really, really interested in doing—I mean, meeting an ex-nun. What do you say?"

Grace folded her arms over her chest and flashed him the cutest glower. "Do you have a death wish?"

"Okay, maybe some other time? How about you, Sam? You interested in the SEAL?"

"Get a life!"

Angel just smiled to himself. A good day's work. He couldn't wait to get back to the houseboat, take a shower, then lie down with a cold beer and watch a Braves baseball game on TV. Alone. "Can I give anyone a lift?" he offered.

He thought he heard Grace say something crude about a part of his anatomy that had done way too much lifting already.

Tante Lulu winked at him.

His plan was progressing very nicely, if he did say so himself.

∼

Was she (going to be) in the jailhouse now?...

THERE WERE EIGHTEEN BLEEPIN' people seated at the long conference table in the new Hope Foundation headquarters in New Orleans: nine on the LeDeux side, including himself, and nine on the Starr family side. This was the first official meeting of the board of directors of the new charity.

With that number, they would never get anything done, but apparently there had been nine Starrs on the previous board, who weren't about to give up their seats. Therefore, Tante Lulu insisted on matching that number.

In the background, Elvis music played. It had been louder when they'd first entered, Stanley Starr being a huge Elvis fan—in fact, the walls were covered with Elvis memorabilia, even a pair of Elvis socks, suitably framed—but Samantha had insisted he at least turn down the volume. He'd grumbled something about them all being hound dogs with no taste in music.

Angel smiled to himself. The guys back in the Newark slums would be amazed at his being on the board of directors of anything. Too highfalutin, as Tante Lulu would say. In fact, they'd be more inclined to predict him being in jail by now, or dead.

To the left of him was Grace, who kept trying to cozy up to him as if they were now going to be best buds. *Not in this lifetime!* She'd whispered to him earlier, on first plopping down next to him, that this was the least of the things the old lady had talked her into. Like the time she'd gone on a rattle hunt, as in the rattles of shedded snake-skins, which apparently had some healing property—*Who knew*!—and ran into a humongous ol' slitherer that had been in the process of doing nature's bump and grind, i.e, stripping, and was not happy about being interrupted.

Speaking of stripping, if Grace only knew what he was thinking as he looked her over while she chatted about this and that. Like how much fun would it be to undo, slowly, all fourteen buttons on the front of her fitted white blouse? And yes, he'd counted them. Several times. Her perfume wasn't overpowering, that same enticing citrusy smell. Which of course prompted him to think about a program he'd watched on the History Channel last night about the history of birth control. It appeared that Casanova had done some interesting things with lemons. Whooee! No wonder the ol' boy had been considered a great lover!

He shook his head to clear it before Grace suspected that he'd lied when he said he had no romantic feelings for her anymore.

Scanning the table, he saw Luc, Remy, René, John, and Charmaine, as expected, along with another "What the hell am I doing here" person, Daniel LeDeux, a physician. Daniel seemed to have a permanent bug up his ass, which wasn't helped by Tante Lulu, who kept telling everyone that he wasn't gay, as if there were some question about his sexual preference.

Holding court in the center of their side was Tante Lulu, who today wore wobbly high heels, enough makeup to plaster a wall, a floaty multicolored dress that Grace told him in an aside came from the Mary Kate and Ashley collection, whatever that meant, sunglasses, and a wide-brimmed black straw hat with a big honkin' rose and a little veil. Greta Garbo for the oldsters!

And if that didn't beat all, the old codger across the table—Stanley Starr—resembled a thinner, shorter version of Colonel Sanders of Kentucky Fried Chicken fame, goatee, white suit, and all. And about a gazillion freckles, or were they age spots? He was staring at Tante Lulu as if she were an old-guy wet dream. *Eeeew!*

In fact, the Starr family would give the LeDeux family a run for the money in the wacky department:

Aunt Dot, who was about seventy and butch as they came in her man haircut and husky voice—clearly a lesbian.

Douglas—pronounced in a Scots dialect as Doog-lass—was a fifty-year-old, hair-dyed, Drakkar-reeking, Armani-clad ladies' man; in fact, he'd been giving Grace the eye ever since they walked in. If his chances weren't so ludicrous, Angel would have been over the table by now to clean his clock.

Angus—yeah, he was named like a cow—was a barely twenty-year-old geek to the max, complete with a superiority attitude, as if the rest of them were idiots. A bunch of gee-whiz techno toys were spread before him, like a cell phone that could probably launch a rocket, a constantly beeping pager, and a mini-laptop at which he kept clicking away. *Is he taking minutes? Or visiting Internet porn sites? Or just bored?*

Maire, spelled M-A-I-R-E, she was quick to point out, had to be a Mary Kay rep, or else she'd swallowed a gallon of Pepto-Bismol; she wore a pink suit, pink shoes, pink lipstick and rouge, and a pink diamond ring the size of a golf ball, and she even had pink-tinted blonde hair.

Wallace, Samantha's brother, about twenty-five, who was off to the races. Literally. Apparently, he was responsible for Starr Foods owning a thoroughbred farm, and one of the horses was racing this weekend.

Bruce, Samantha's father, took his Scottish heritage seriously. Thus the kilt, the knee socks, and something called a *sporran*, which resembled a furry fanny pack, except it hung down his stomach.

Lilith, Bruce's wife and Samantha's stepmother, had some kind of turban on her head with a matching, loose, ankle-length gown. She was an honest-to-God voodoo priestess and proud of it. She and Tante Lulu had been gabbing like crazy about love potions and such when they first arrived.

Maybe I need a love potion.

You need something, the voice in his head said.

I was wondering, he said to the St. Jude in his head—hey, he was bored—*when they play the song "When the Saints Come Marching In," do you feel like, well, marching?*

Saints don't march. They float.

Oh. Doesn't have the same ring, does it?

"Who are you talking to?" Grace asked.

His face heated up as he slumped lower in his seat, declining to answer.

The only normal one on the other side of the table was Samantha, the chairman, who had apparently taken an instant loathing to the perpetually frowning Daniel. He had to give the lady credit for chutzpah for her attire, which was beyond hot. She wore a serious black fitted suit over a not-so-serious white silk Victoria's Secret-type thingee that drew male attention like a high-powered magnet. Donald Trump in a bustier, that's what she was. Her skirt was barely knee-high over black silk stockings that went on forever down to black strappy stilettos. Even Daniel gulped a few times on first getting a gander at her getup.

But, really, to Angel, Grace was hotter in her simple blouse and pencil-slim skirt, her red hair tamed into its Meg Ryan flip today, strawberry gloss on her lips.

"First on the agenda," Samantha said, "is a discussion of the Duval family. Ms. Rivard, it is critical that the Duval project be handled privately by your family and not by the foundation. It was started before we were formally incorporated *and* was never voted on by the board."

"If we're gonna hafta vote on every little thing, we'll never get anythin' done," Tante Lulu complained.

"Yes, we will. You'll see." Then, turning to the entire board, Samantha asked, "Is everyone agreed? The Duval project will not be funded by the Hope Foundation. Ayes? Nays? The ayes carry."

"I never expected y'all ta pay fer them chillen," Tante Lulu grumbled.

"Speaking of votes," Daniel LeDeux said.

Which earned him a frown from Samantha. "Can't you wait until new business at the end of the agenda?"

"No, I can't. I expect to be gone by then." Even so, his eyes were glued to her chest and its skimpy, barely-there scrap of silk.

Samantha arched her eyebrows and murmured, "I could only wish!"

"Yer dancin' on my last nerve, boy," said Tante Lulu, who was on Daniel's right, as she turned and swatted his arm with one of the folders that sat in front of each of them. "Shush yerself, boy."

Red-faced, Daniel ignored her and barreled on, "This board is too damn big. I move that we cut its size in half, and I'll be the first one to bow out of the...um, privilege."

"Me, too," said Angel, Grace, John, Remy, and René, one after another.

Which would leave Luc, Charmaine, and Tante Lulu, which was perfect, in Angel's opinion.

"Listen, most of the time, we won't need a full board to meet. And, in fact, schedules usually won't permit everyone to make all the meetings," Samantha explained. "So, I suggest that we keep the board as is, make committee assignments, and see how things go."

The board stayed the same by a 12-6 vote.

Samantha gave Daniel a speaking smirk of triumph, to which he just sank down in his seat, probably to take a nap. But no, he deliberately ogled her breasts, again, which caused Samantha's cheeks to go pink as Maire's suit.

In a whisper that could be heard by everyone in the room, Tante Lulu chastised Daniel. "Sit up straight. How ya ever gonna attract the girl if ya slouch?"

"What girl?" he asked with alarm.

Tante Lulu motioned with her head toward Samantha, which caused her hat to almost fall off and both parties to choke and reach for glasses of water.

Now Daniel's face was pink, too.

"And holy crawfish, when's the las' time ya got a haircut? Charmaine could cut it fer ya. Right, Charmaine? And mousse 'im up good. He's too flat."

Everyone at the table was looking at Daniel, assessing his pink face and flat hair, which looked fine to Angel, but what did he know?

Daniel, wise for a change, said nothing. And he'd stopped goading Samantha with his breast ogling.

Next they adopted a mission statement, approved a bank balance of two million, fifty thousand dollars—a million from Tante Lulu matched by the Starr family, and fifty from the auction held last week—and agreed to the hiring of an office staff.

"Now we need to set up a procedure whereby we decide what projects or individuals or families warrant our help," Samantha explained. "Believe me, this will not be easy. I'll turn this portion of the meeting over to Dorothy Starr, who is a marketing director for Starr Foods. She and her partner did a survey of needs here in N'awleans and southern Loo-zee-anna. Aunt Dot?"

Samantha sat down, and Aunt Dot stood up.

"You're going to be shocked," Aunt Dot said in her raspy no-nonsense voice. "Did you know that there are twenty thousand families still displaced from Hurricane Katrina? Four years and still homeless! It's an outrage. If that's not bad enough, there are ten thousand Katrina orphans who are still in foster care. Of the one thousand children adopted during that period, one hundred were returned or rescued because of shoddy screening proce-dures, everything from abuse to neglect."

He heard Grace gasp at this last statistic but then figured maybe she was reacting to all of it. It *was* sad.

"In addition," Aunt Dot went on, "while salaries have gone up somewhat since Katrina, utilities and rents have shot up almost fifty percent, if units are even available. Records show that there were more than forty thousand affordable apartments in N'awleans before Katrina and Rita, but less than half of them are being rebuilt. So where do people go? Mostly they cram several families into one apartment, or move out of the state or go homeless. All of this exacerbated by Hurricane Ike last year." She paused for everyone to digest what she'd said, then added, "At the present time, we have three hundred and fifty-seven wishes in the hopper, many of which we cannot meet. We have to prioritize. And I'm not just talking about a wish to go to Disneyland or a baseball game. Some of the wishes are downright heartbreaking, like the little girl who lost her mother during Katrina and wants us to find her father, a Marine or navy SEAL—no one knows for sure—who supposedly never knew of his paternity. And illness—I haven't even mentioned the physical problems that aren't being addressed because of our underfunded clinics and uninsured people."

"So, where do we start?" Leave it to Tante Lulu to cut to the chase.

Aunt Dot sat down, and Samantha stood again. "I suggest we set up a number of committees, headed by board members."

Oh, God! If there was anything Angel hated it was committees. They talked everything to death. He would rather be out there doing. Hands-on. Like building a house, which was where he should be today.

"I have office staff that can funnel all the requests for aid or notification of problems to the appropriate committee," Samantha continued. "And I'll serve on each of the committees, as needed. Same for Ms. Rivard."

"Stop callin' me Mzzz. Sounds like a bee. I'm Tante Lulu."

"Okay, Tante Lulu." Samantha smiled.

And for the first time Angel realized what a gorgeous woman Samantha Starr was, with her auburn hair and tall, slim body, despite all the freckles. Probably he hadn't noticed her because of Grace sitting beside him. *Maybe I should make a play for her, just to get Grace jealous. Hmmm.*

"Now, as to the individual committees."

Daniel LeDeux groaned, suspecting what was coming.

"For example, one of the committees could deal with health

issues. Perhaps triaging the most critical cases or pointing out those most easily resolved. Maybe even setting up a Hope clinic in the future."

Everyone, including Samantha, stared at Daniel, who finally shrugged and said, "Okay, dammit."

Tante Lulu swatted him again for swearing.

Samantha shoved toward Daniel a folder that was so thick it caused his eyes to widen. He had to be thinking he'd been had.

"We at Starr have the wish committee pretty much under control, but we'll be coming to you for final approval of the cases and expenditures," Samantha continued. "For example, you'll see at the back of your folder a list that we'll discuss before adjourning today."

"I wanna be on the family one," Tante Lulu said. "Grace and Angel can help me."

So much for volunteering!

And their folder was just as thick as Daniel's.

Holy crap! There must be a hundred applications in there. How is Tante Lulu—how are WE—going to turn any of them away? And hey, I might not even be here much longer.

"I'll serve on yer committee, too, Louise, my dear," Stanley offered.

"Much obliged, Stan," Tante Lulu thanked him with a coy smile. "And Luc can handle legal stuff," she added. "Tee-John kin help him, since he's a cop and knows how ta get around laws and stuff."

"Tante Lulu!" John protested.

"Well, it's true. Remember the time you was a sex cop."

"Tante Lulu!" John protested again, then clicked his tongue and gave up the fight, which was usually the case when dealing with the old lady's outrageousness.

Other committees were established then with Starr and LeDeux family members assigned to serve, including finance, fund-raising, and public relations.

"Speaking of public relations," Samantha said, glancing to her wristwatch, "a *Times-Picayune* photographer should be down in the courtyard about now. He needs us all in a picture to accompany an article about the new foundation."

Most of them groaned but figured there was no use arguing.

Afterward, everyone left, except for Luc, Tante Lulu, Angel, and Grace. Luc said he had something important to discuss.

"I'm hungry," Tante Lulu whined.

"Okay, we can talk over lunch," Luc suggested.

"Since you're all dolled up today, Auntie, how about Antoine's?"

"Yippee! I ain't been there fer a while."

Since it was so close, they began walking through the French Quarter 'til they reached St. Louis Street.

Out of the blue, Tante Lulu remarked, "That Stanley sure is a hottie, ain't he?"

Her remark met with total silence.

"He has a hot cha-cha hiney, ya gotta give him that." More silence.

"Didja know he has a Magic Fingers bed?"

Grace giggled.

Luc chuckled.

And he thought, *Oooh, way too much information. Immediately followed by, I wonder where I can buy one of those.*

"How do you know that, Auntie?" Luc asked.

"How do ya think I know?" She grinned up at her nephew, then said, "Jeesh! You'd believe anything. I was in Montgomery Ward's the day he bought it fer his wife, Sophie. She died ten years ago, bless her heart."

"Oh," Luc said, clearly glad to erase the mind picture they were all enjoying, or not enjoying.

"I'm thinkin' about buyin' one of them beds fer Daniel. That boy needs somethin' ta get his juices goin' again." They all laughed.

"You, too, Grace."

Grace didn't laugh, but he did.

Which prompted Grace to elbow him in the side. "How about me?" he and Luc asked at the same time.

"You two gots enough juice ta fill a punch bowl at Mardi Gras."

He and Luc grinned at each other.

Grace looked disgusted.

Once they arrived at the famous restaurant, Tante Lulu and Grace went in first. Luc hung back and whispered to him, "I hate to say this, but this Duval situation has developed a high Hindenburg factor."

"How so?"

"I talked to a judge yesterday, in confidence. He's a friend. He says we're in deep shit, even if we get the house up ASAP. I have a strong premonition that CPS is going to take those kids away and then let us duke it out in court."

"This is going to kill Tante Lulu."

"Tell me about it."

"Well, let's face facts here. There's no way in the world that Tante Lulu is going to let them separate those kids. She'll go to jail herself first."

"She'd probably consider it a grand adventure."

On that happy note, they went in to have lunch.

CHAPTER 8

Family ties are sometimes cruel...

"That's her. That's the bitch."

Andrea Fletcher cowered in the bedroom closet of her Atlanta, Georgia, home, listening to the railing voice of her stepfather, George Allison. It was always best to hide when he was on a rant...or when he was into the booze. He wasn't an alcoholic, exactly, but he did go on his binges.

As usual, her mother, Ruth Allison, said nothing to stand up to his tyranny, except to insert the occasional, "Oh, George!" Hard as it was to fathom, even after ten years, her mother thought George walked on water. The only saving grace for Andrea was that George was a sales rep for a pharmaceutical company and was often on the road—and the fact that she'd recently graduated from high school and could leave home. Of course, George had spent her college fund, given to her in her adoptive father's will, which George had considered his due. After all, he'd "allowed" her to stay in his house. Now she'd be forced to live at home and attend the local community college, or leave home and get a job with no skills.

"How do you know it's Andrea's mother?"

Andrea straightened, her eyes going wide with shock. "Because I saw those adoption documents you keep hidden, that's how. Grace O'Brien was her mother's name. That's her, all right. The bitch who gave her kid away. Look at the picture in this newspaper, dammit. Same red hair. Same green eyes. They look alike, ferchrissake!"

Andrea's heart was beating so fast she could hardly hear what was being said in the bedroom next door.

"Where did you get this newspaper, honey?"

"New Orleans. When I was passing through last week."

Andrea had known since she was five years old that she was adopted, and until her adoptive father died when she was eight, life had been good. But then her "mother" had remarried, and a day didn't go by without George complaining about all the money her upkeep was costing, how she didn't do enough work around the house, how her grades weren't good enough, how she dressed like a tramp, how she could damn well get a job and start paying rent now that she was out of school or, better yet, move out so they could have some blessed privacy.

Ruth had always told her that her birth mother had no interest whatsoever in her "mistake." That she'd been a slut who couldn't even say for sure who the father was. She would have had an abortion, except she'd waited too long. Otherwise, Andrea would have done a search for her on the Internet. In the past, she'd always thought there was no point, unless she wanted to tell her what she thought of her. Which was sounding better and better by the minute.

In her own sad way, Ruth loved Andrea, but she loved George more. Sometimes—no, all the time—Andrea wondered why she'd ever been adopted in the first place. Weren't adopted kids supposed to be special, the chosen ones? Hah!

"Well, I'll tell you one thing, Ruth. The bitch is gonna pay.

Grace O'Brien is loaded, and believe you me, she's gonna share the wealth."

"What...what do you mean?"

"I asked some folks in the hotel lobby, and they told me the people in this picture just started a foundation. The LeDeux and the Starr families are millionaires, they said."

"But you said Grace *O'Brien.*"

"Don't matter. If she's associating with the jet-setters, she's got cash, too. Guaranteed."

"Oh, George! What are you going to do?"

"Have a little talk with the lady." Andrea could hear the greedy smirk in her stepfather's voice. "If she wants to keep her good name, she'll pay."

"But that's blackmail, honey."

"No. It's payment for all I've done for her girl. Meanwhile, you make sure Andrea sticks close to home. I'll put a hold on her college bank account tomorrow, and—"

You mean the bank account that now has a total of fifty dollars in it?

"—and don't you be givin' her any money. Whatever you do, don't tell her about her bitch mother—not yet. Or she'll be runnin' off to the arms of Mommy dearest."

Not likely! Oh, I'm gonna find her, all right, but not to give her a big hug. No, I'm gonna give her a piece of my mind.

Fat tears slipped out of her welling eyes. Not the first time she'd cried over a mother who hadn't wanted her.

$\sim$

If you're not a lesbian, then what are you?...

GRACE AND LIONEL were sitting at the table in Grace's cottage transcribing Tante Lulu's *traiteur* notes onto a laptop, while Lena was in the bedroom resting.

The computer-savvy boy, whose interest in medicine was

90

stimulated by the herbal remedies, had developed a wonderful program to record the lifelong recipes and observations that clearly had historical value. The software not only indexed the various herbs, but cross-referenced them with their varied uses.

Best of all were Tante Lulu's remarks on the people she'd healed and their life stories, related to each of the remedies. It was a living history, not only of the bayou, its people, its medicinal plants, but of an incredible lady who'd lived an interesting and full life. Grace didn't consider herself competent enough to write a book about Louise Rivard, but someone should.

"Some of this stuff is really weird. Do you think it works?" Lionel looked up from the keyboard and took a sip of sweet tea, a staple here in the South.

"Probably. Every time I scoff, she proves me wrong. Like this 'smoking the baby' business. Really, it sounds awful, but in the end, it's just a primitive way of clearing an infant's lungs. Almost like a vaporizer."

Lionel quirked an eyebrow. "I dunno."

"I read an article in a magazine recently about how alligator blood might be used as a possible human antibiotic. It has something to do with the gators dating back to the stone age, when they had to survive all kinds of mangling and maiming, so their bodies built up these immunities. She may not know all this history, but I'll bet Tante Lulu already knows that alligator blood has its uses."

Lionel's pierced eyebrow was still raised in disbelief.

"I'll take you with us tomorrow when Tante Lulu makes her weekly rounds. She's crazy as a loon sometimes, but believe me when I say she knows what she's doing."

"I like her."

"So do I."

"The only thing she hasn't been able to cure is my thumbnail biting." She laughed and showed him her right thumb with the nail bitten down to the quick. "And believe me, she has tried putting some yucky goop on it. To no avail."

"What's that juju tea she keeps pushing on you?" He pointed to the "Gotta Love a Cajun" mug filled to the brim with a lavender-colored liquid.

Grace laughed. "Juju tea. She claims it's a love potion, but it's just a nice mellow tea, in my opinion. Harmless."

"Are you lookin' for love?" Lionel teased her.

"Hardly. I just humor her."

"Besides you don't need a love potion to get Angel, right?"

"Angel! Why would you say that?"

"Are you kiddin'? When you're not looking, he stares at you like you're eye candy and he needs a sugar fix."

For some reason, a thrill of pleasure rippled through her body. Suddenly, she gave the juju tea a narrow-eyed study, then decided, *No way!* "You're mistaken. Angel doesn't look at me like that. Oh, there was a time when he felt that way about me, or thought he did, but not anymore. Now, we're just...friends."

Lionel grunted his disagreement, then grinned at her. "Maybe I'll get me a jar of that juju tea. There's this girl at school—"

"Forget the tea. You're a good-looking guy." In fact, Lionel was six foot tall and still growing, with a lean, teenage-buff body. Sometimes he resembled a lighter-skinned Samuel L. Jackson. Aside from the numerous piercings and the leather jacket that might just have been glued on, that is. Actually, the piercings were probably a turn-on to teenage girls.

Which made Grace think of the piercing that Angel might or might not still have. *Don't go there, girl!*

"Just ask her for a date," she concluded.

"Hard to go on dates when we're hiding out here."

"It won't be forever."

"Feels like it."

"Angel already has the house framed out. The electricians and plumbers will be there today, and the LeDeuxs will be putting up drywall this weekend. It's taking a bit longer than originally planned, but I predict you'll be in your new house within two weeks."

"Do you really think I'll be able to go to college?"

She nodded. "If that's what you want, Tante Lulu will find a way to make it happen."

"We owe her a lot, don't we?"

"A lot, but she doesn't do it for the kudos. She genuinely likes to help people. The best way you can show your thanks is by doing the best you can to be good people. Adopting St. Jude as your favorite saint helps, too."

Ella ran in then and yelled, "Holy crawfish! Tante Lulu says fer you two ta hurry up. The dilly willy mushrooms are bloomin' t'day, and we gotta go pick 'em lickety-split. They're the bestest thing fer zits and goiters."

Grace and Lionel grinned at each other. The old lady's colorful language was wearing off on all of them.

"And pack a picnic lunch, too," Ella told Grace. "And doan fergit the leftover shrimp hushpuppies and okra salad and a mess of them greens from the garden."

Yep, a definite Tante Lulu influence.

A short time later, Grace was paddling a pirogue down the bayou, heat shimmering off the coffee-colored water, with Tante Lulu in front of her, while Lionel and Miles rowed the second one, with Ella in the middle. A disgruntled Lena was ordered to stay indoors to study for her GED and not to answer if anyone came knocking.

Before they'd taken off, Tante Lulu advised the kids, "Put on long pants and shoes jist in case ya get bit by a snake. That way the fangs won't break the skin."

It was a sign of how accustomed they were all becoming to the old lady's ways that no one had even flinched at the mention of snakes. Actually, Grace wished Miles *would* flinch or say something. He was way too quiet for a ten-year-old boy. If he'd had his way he'd have stayed back at the cottage with Lena, glued to her side.

"And doan be givin' me that Hannah Banana bizness, either," Tante Lulu had advised Ella. "Her clothes is too sexy fer a mite like you."

Ella, who had been wearing a Hannah Montana bandanna, a "Girls Rock" camisole, and too-short shorts, had made a huffing sound of indignation that anyone would criticize Saint Hannah, the idol of adolescent girls and boys. "It's Hannah Montana, not banana."

"Montana, Banana, Fofana, same thing," Tante Lulu had said.

Now, as they skimmed through the tranquil waters in their low-riding pirogue, Tante Lulu, sitting behind Grace, said, "Kin I ask ya somethin', Gracie?"

Oh, boy! Tante Lulu never asked permission to speak. This ought to be good. "Sure."

"You a virgin?"

Grace burst out with a laugh. "Good heavens, no. What made you ask that?"

"Well, I knowed ya a few years now, and I ain't seen ya with any boyfriends."

"There haven't been many lately, but take my word for it, I'm not a virgin." *In fact, I'm a mother.*

"Ya ever been in love?"

"I thought I was once, but it turned out to be puppy love. I was only a teenager."

"Don'tcha think it's time fer love? Ya already lost one good man. Angel. Yer not a young chicken anymore, bless yer heart. Well, yer a young chicken compared ta me, but iffen yer fixin' ta have any chillen, ya best be findin' a man ta marry."

Grace was beginning to learn that in the South you could toss out any kind of insult as long as you attached "bless his or her heart" to it. Like, "Jolie had a baby when she was only seven months pregnant, bless her heart, and the baby weighed twelve pounds." Grace also knew she would never be considered a true southerner, best explained by that famous saying, "I'm a southerner born and a southerner bred, and when I die, I'll be a southerner dead."

But that was neither here nor there. "Tante Lulu, I won't ever marry or have children."

"Fer goodness sake, why not?"

"It's something I don't discuss. Sorry."

"Don'tcha like babies?" Tante Lulu persisted.

"Of course I like babies."

"Is it 'cause you were a nun? I mean, didja take a vow or sumpin'?"

Grace smiled. "No."

"Mebbe ya oughta dye yer hair blonde."

"Why would I do that?"

"Red ain't done much fer ya so far. Besides, they say blondes have more fun."

"I'm having plenty of fun."

"Hah! Hangin' around with an eighty-year-old woman is yer idea of fun?"

Grace smiled. Tante Lulu hadn't seen eighty for a number of years, but who was Grace to correct a woman lying about her age? It was an age-old, God-given right. Eve probably lied about her age to Adam.

"An' ya oughta buy sexier clothes. I'll go clothes shoppin' with ya, iffen ya want. Another thing—ya oughta have Charmaine give ya some of them sculptured nails, too. Ones what are strong as cement and cain't be bitten down."

"Do they make nails that hard?"

"Iffen they don't, we could come up with a concoction." In the middle of her discourse to Grace, she yelled out to the other pirogue, riding beside them, "Miles, stop draggin' yer fingers in the water lessen ya want a gator ta bite 'em off."

The boy immediately shot upright, hands folded over his lap. His little face reddened with embarrassment.

Then Tante Lulu directed her attention back to Grace. "Ya need ta buy yerself one of them push-up, see-through bras and a thong. Me, I cain't see the attraction of having a sling up my crack, but men seems ta like 'em. And a garter belt. Y'know, it's amazing, women in my time hated those seamed stockings and garter belts. We thought panty hose was the best thing since God invented condoms. Who'da thunk they'd come back in style?"

All this was being said to Grace's back, so Tante Lulu didn't even see her gaping mouth, but she did hear Grace sputter, "I do not want or need sexy clothes. When I'm ready for a man in my life, I'll do it the old-fashioned way."

"Oh? What way is that? Sittin' on yer hiney waitin' fer Prince Charming ta come floatin' down the bayou on his white raft?"

"Can we drop this conversation? It's giving me a headache."

"Talkin' 'bout men gives ya a headache? Holey Moly! Ya ain't one of them lesbos, are ya?"

Grace rolled her eyes. "No."

"Well, then, never say never."

"Never."

"Hmmmm."

When silence finally reigned, Grace turned to look over her shoulder at the old lady.

Tante Lulu was deep in thought, but then she said succinctly, "Guess I'll hafta pray on this."

That's all Grace needed.

Gambling on love...

TANTE LULU WAS RESTING on the blanket they'd spread in a clearing along the bayou, which was tranquil today. That was not always the case, but then, that was one of the things she loved about the moody waters of the swamplands. They were never the same. Nor was the ever-changing bayou itself. Often land here today would be gone tomorrow. Like people.

Their picnic was over and most of the herbs gathered, including the rare dilly willy mushrooms, which were poisonous when eaten but great in a paste for roach and ant bites.

The canvas tote at her side held plastic zipper bags of various plants they'd gathered today. Bark from the sassafras tree would be made into a tea good for curing many ailments: poison oak and fever, or into douches to treat bladder infections. Head lice could be killed off with its oils. Then there was ironweed for monthly cramps, spiderwort for stomachaches, trumpet creeper for coughs, bull nettle for mange, stinking arrach for ulcers, and feverfew for migraines.

Cajuns were known for their frugality, using every bit of an animal. No waste. Same was true of plants. There were uses for the leaves, the seeds, the roots and stems. God gave his bounty, and men had an obligation to use it wisely.

"Do you want any more of these cattails?" asked Grace, who was standing with the children at the edge of the water. They already had enough of the tall stems to sink a boat.

"Thass enough," she said. "Be careful. Doan wade in too far. It's not jist snakes and gators ya gotta be careful of."

It was nice to see the three children playing carefree and happy. Their lives had been so worrisome of late. She was gratified to see all of them interested in the things she'd taught them today, especially Lionel, who was going to make a fine doctor someday. She would guarantee it.

But it was Grace that troubled Tante Lulu now. Something was seriously wrong with the girl, and Tante Lulu just couldn't figure it out. Her end goal was to get the girl hitched up with Angel. They were meant for each other. But it wasn't going to be as easy as she'd originally thought. Something deep and important was troubling the girl.

In the meantime, the two of them needed to be together more often for Angel's plan to work. Leastways, she assumed he had a plan. Men were dumb clucks sometimes and thought things could just happen.

"Why so glum?" Grace asked as she walked up and sat down next to her on the blanket.

"Me, I was jist thinkin' 'bout the foundation and all the work that needs ta be done. There's so much ta do."

"You knew that when you started, didn't you?"

Tante Lulu shook her head. Bouncy red curls today that pretty much matched Grace's. "I knew there was a problem, but I never guessed it was so big. I went over that folder of requests with Samantha yesterday, and it jist about broke my heart. So many needy folks!"

"Well, you can't cure the world of all its ills, but you can take one case at a time and make a difference. That's what you always say."

"One thing I'm beginnin' ta learn is that we gotta keep this foundation in the limelight. Allus gettin' publicity. Allus raisin' more money. Otherwise, people fergit and go about their own bizness."

"It's a good thing you joined up with the Starr family, then. It has to make things easier for you."

"Yes, but we LeDeuxs still need ta keep on our toes. Gotta come up with our own new ideas." Suddenly inspired, Tante Lulu said, "Oooh, boy! I jist thought of a way ta raise more money fer our charity."

"Oh?"

"It involves you and Angel."

"Uh-oh!"

"Doan be gettin' yer knickers in a twist. I'm not matchmakin' here." *You believe that 'n ' I've got a gator farm ta sell ya in Chicago.*

"Since you and Angel are experts in playin' poker, mebbe we could set up a poker tournament."

Grace tilted her head to the side. "Hmmm. They do hold them for charities, but you have to be careful of local and federal gambling laws. You know, the RICO Act."

Tante Lulu waved a hand dismissively. "Not ta worry! This is Loo-zee-anna. I know folks."

Arching her eyebrows, Grace continued, "Angel has enough work to do with building the house. I doubt he would have time to—"

"He'll be done with the house in no time. Betcha if ya asked him, he'd stay a bit longer and help plan a poker tournament if you asked him."

"Me? Why me?"

"Well, ya know him better than I do."

"Not anymore."

"Okay, I'll ask him. If he agrees, you'll help, then?"

"Was I just set up here?"

"I doan know what you mean."

～

When clueless men take advice from clueless old ladies...

ANGEL WAS FRUSTRATED BEYOND BELIEF.

And he was damn tired of jacking off in the high-tech sex shower, or waking in the middle of the night with a wet-dream hard-on, or mooning over Grace on the few occasions they were within talking distance of each other, or playing this half-assed pretense game that he was dating other women. Almost two weeks in Louisiana, and his plan for happily-ever-after wasn't working worth jack shit. Something needed to be done.

He was about to pick up his cell phone and call Grace. He'd tell her to get her sweet ass over here so that they could talk...and stuff.

Just then the phone rang.

It wasn't Grace. It was Tante Lulu.

Oh, great!

"I got a great idea."

Oh, great! "I'm glad somebody does."

"Don't be sassy."

"I'm no sissy."

"I said sassy, not sissy. Gol-ly! Best ya get the wax out of yer ears."

"I'm not stepping into that shower again. No way!"

"Huh?"

"What's your latest fool idea?"

"Yer pushin' it, boy."

"Sorry. I'm just frustrated."

"So is Gracie."

"She is?" *Pathetic...I'm damn pathetic.*

"Well, mebbe she is. Or mebbe she's jist not used ta havin' four kids livin' with her. Anyways, you 'n' Gracie are gonna set up a poker tournament fer Jude's Angels. That'll put ya t'gether a lot, I'm leavin' it up ta you ta come up with somethin' really cool at the end so you and that gal will end up in bed. A little hanky-panky would go a long way 'bout now, I'm thinkin'."

"Tante Lulu!"

"Hey, I'm old, but I ain't dead. Yer as bad as Grace. Ain't ya got yearnin's?"

"I've got yearnings, all right." *You don't want to know about my yearnings, you interfering busybody. They are pure, hundred-proof X-rated.*

"Iffen ya need some lessons on how ta get her riled up, I kin send Tee-John over. That boy could charm the undies off a nun. Prob'ly did a time or two."

"Don't you dare."

"Whatever you say," she agreed, way too meekly. "So, will ya do it?"

"Do what? Get Gracie riled up?" *I wish!*

"No—well, yes, but what I meant was, will ya help set up the poker tournament?"

He lifted his free hand in a hopeless gesture. "What do I have to lose?"

Later, he wondered if that hadn't been an ominous question to ask.

CHAPTER 9

Do they make Midol for men?...

*M*en! There was no figuring them out!

Grace sat across from Angel at a folding table in the kitchen of the completed but unfurnished Duval house, watching with amazement as he alternately scowled at her with hostility, then gazed at her with what might be mistaken for longing, then narrowed his eyes with some evil intent, then was so damn polite she itched to smack him over the head, just to get a reaction. She wanted the old Angel back.

"What the hell's wrong with you?" she asked finally.

"Tsk, tsk! Is that any way for an ex-nun to talk?"

She said something so foul that Angel burst out with a hoot of laughter. At least that was like the Angel she'd known and loved. *As a friend,* she quickly amended to herself, *loved as a friend. God! I'm as bad as he is, needing to make that kind of reminder to myself.*

"Why are you being so moody?" she demanded to know.

He looked up from the seating charts they were drawing up for the upcoming St. Jude's Cajun Poker Tournament, which had already met its maximum two hundred entries. And wasn't that ironical? A saint-sanctioned gambling event. The tournament would be held next week in the basement of Our Lady of the Bayou Church hall, right after 11:30 a.m. lunchtime bingo, which was held right after 10:00 a.m. Mass.

"I'm not moody," he grumbled.

"Hah! You've got more moods than Sybil today. If I didn't know better, I'd say you have male PMS."

"Ha, ha, ha. Very funny." He was not smiling.

"Angel, what's troubling you?" She reached across and laid a hand over his.

He flinched...he actually flinched. Then drew his hand away.

That rebuff hurt. Bad. She wasn't going to let him see that, though. The jerk! "So, how's your love life? Still seeing the model?"

"What do you care?"

"Huh?"

"Let's just finish the frickin' tournament charts. We'll start with twenty tables of ten players each. I figure it'll take at least five hours of elimination rounds 'til we get to the final table. We'll take a break then and hold the finals starting at six p.m. What? Why are you looking at me like that?"

"Do you ever miss poker?" she asked, though that wasn't what she really wanted to know.

"Sometimes."

"I can beat you, you know."

He smiled, and the boy did have a knock-'em-dead smile. No wonder women fell like bowling pins before his I-am-so-sexy grins...if not his balls, she joked to herself.

"Honey, you couldn't beat me in a million years."

"Wanna bet?" She'd blurted out the challenge without thinking, and only because he was being such a prick.

He tapped the fingertips of one hand on the table for several seconds while he studied her. It was probably a tactic designed to annoy. "We could have an exhibition game between the two of us the day of the tournament. You know, two ex-poker champs dueling it out."

"Maybe. What would we bet? I mean, what would I get if I win?"

"I'd donate a hundred thousand dollars to Jude's Angels, plus the cost of all the materials I've put into this house. Hell, I'll furnish the damn place."

"You would do all that, just for a bet?" Her brow furrowed with confusion. "And if you win? Not that you would."

The slow, sexy grin emerged again. He tipped his chair back, folded his hands behind his neck, and said, "One night in the sack with you. All night. Anything I want to do."

She gasped and felt her face heat with embarrassment. "Blushes, Gracie? How...sweet!"

Her face heated even more. "You're crazy. Why would you even suggest such a thing? You don't love me."

"What's love got to do with it?"

"I don't know. You tell me."

"I've always been curious about what you'd be like in bed. And the whole friends-with-benefits concept is, I don't know, intriguing."

"No. Absolutely not."

"You're right. It was a bad idea. Even if there wasn't a chance in hell that you could beat me."

She narrowed her eyes at him. "Don't push me."

"Forget I even mentioned it."

"And you won't make all those donations without the bet?"

"Why should I?"

"To be nice?"

"Yeah, right. Bet's off. No big deal."

She inhaled deeply and said, "Bet's on, big boy."

He didn't say anything, just stared at her. His only reaction was a twitch at the side of his mouth. Finally, he said, "Deal."

Almost immediately, she regretted her decision, and she would have recanted, except that she just knew Angel expected her to, and she would be damned if she would do anything to please His Royal Moodiness today.

Angel said the oddest thing then. "I'm done here. I gotta go back to the houseboat and polish up the shower fixtures."

Later, back at her cottage, she asked Tante Lulu, "How about helping me practice my poker skills?"

"Why?"

"I made a little bet with Angel."

"Little?"

"Okay, big."

"Does it involve hanky-panky? No, doan tell me. Let an old lady fantasize."

"So, wanna try a few practice hands?"

Tante Lulu chuckled and said, "Yer on yer own, missy."

∼

A bet is a bet, baby...

ANGEL COULDN'T BELIEVE his good luck. Man, maybe there *was* something to this St. Jude nonsense of Tante Lulu's. He couldn't have wished—*prayed*—for a better opportunity to win Grace's love or, if nothing else, lust.

Grace was trying every which way she could to cancel their bet, but Angel was making sure it held. Like celestial concrete.

Mostly, he avoided her, but when he was unable to do that, he just dodged her verbal bullets.

"You can't seriously think of sleeping with me."

"Why not?"

"Because...because...oh, for heaven's sake, what is this? Some kind of romance novel plot?"

"Could be."

"How can you make love to a woman you don't love?" He

stared at her as if she were missing a few marbles. "Oh, right. I forgot. Men can have sex at will. It's women who need the emotional connection."

"Sex at will? You give me too much credit."

"I hope you haven't discussed this with anyone."

"Nope. It's just between you and me. Should I draw up a contract?"

"For what?"

"The terms of our bet. I'm thinkin' dusk to dawn. The house-boat, unless you'd like to try the honeymoon suite at the Holiday Inn. I hear they have a heart-shaped Jacuzzi. No? Okay. Whatever you say. I need to go shopping. Chocolate body paint—or do you prefer peach? I remember how much you used to like those peach ices. Oysters for an appetizer. Or chocolate. Your choice. Mood music. And, ooh, ooh, ooh, handcuffs. Gotta get handcuffs—and a blindfold. I don't suppose you'd wear a nun outfit for me. Do they make religious thongs?"

"Aaarrgh!"

"Call me crazy, but you sound kinda hot and bothered when you say 'Aaarrgh!' and tug at your hair at the same time with your eyes rolling up into your head. Are you about to have a connip-tion? That's a word Tante Lulu taught me."

"Bite me!"

"I just might do that...if I win. But not to fear. I'll let you bite me back, although I prefer little nibbles."

"You're teasing me. You have no intention of following through on this ridiculous idea."

"Wanna bet?"

"Not that you would win."

"We'll see."

Meanwhile, he was so excited he went back to the houseboat and set the sex shower on permanent ice-cold.

～

You could say it was the Tour de Tante Lulu...

THERE WERE tours of the French Quarter, and then there were whoo-ee hot-damn tours of the French Quarter.

Today Charmaine was driving them through the heart of the Crescent City and its suburbs. Tante Lulu was riding shotgun in her lavender Impala convertible, post-World War II vintage, a gas guzzler to beat all gas guzzlers. Grace and Samantha were in the back seat, mouths agape most of the time at this bizarre adventure.

To say that Charmaine knew things about the Big Easy that weren't on the regular tourist route would be a vast understatement. Add to that Tante Lulu's always surprising input and even Samantha, who'd grown up in the region, was astounded.

And their attire. Both Charmaine and Tante Lulu wore 1940s movie-star-style scarves around their heads with big rhinestone-studded sunglasses. Loo-zee-anna Greta Garbos, for heaven's sake! The only thing missing was cigarettes in fancy holders. Meanwhile, she and Samantha, wearing jeans and tank tops, looked as if they'd gone through a wind tunnel with their hair standing on end, probably collecting every bug within a mile radius. Samantha, for example, with her freckles, resembled a wind-whipped Buckwheat, while Grace's red curls were no doubt now a fire version of Annie.

"That's Madame Claudette's House of Pleasure," Charmaine told them as they passed a seemingly innocent, narrow-fronted, historic Creole house with tall green shutters and intricate grill-work balconies. "Sex with class is the way she bills her fare. I hear that bondage is her specialty. That and ménages."

"Whass a men-odge?" Tante Lulu wanted to know.

"A threesome," Charmaine replied.

"Three of what?"

"Never mind."

"Oh, now I get it. Tee-John was involved in one of those one time, back when he was in college. Talk about!"

"How would you know that, Auntie?"

"Hah! You'd be surprised what I know. Jist 'cause I doan blab it all over kingdom come doan mean I'm ignerant."

Coming from the Queen of Blab, that statement was as outrageous as anything that left her mouth.

"I wouldn't be surprised if you tried it at least once, too," Tante Lulu added to Charmaine.

"I did not! Rusty is more than enough for me."

"You weren't allus married ta Rusty."

"Well, I didn't!"

"Anyways, so this is Claudette's house, hmmm? I knew her grandma, Claudine. The place weren't so classy back then. We called it a cathouse."

She and Samantha looked at each other and choked back laughter.

"'Course, ya coulda got anythin' ya wanted in the old days over in Storyville, which the government closed down when I was a baby. It was sad, really, 'cause those girls dint have no choice in the matter. Some of 'em little more'n chillen, like that old Brooke Shields movie *Pretty Baby.* Tsk, tsk, tsk! It was sell their bodies or starve. Not like t'day where the hookeys gots choices."

"Hookers," Samantha corrected.

"Thass what I said."

"Well, I don't know if prostitution is that different," Samantha inserted, not having yet learned that it was best not to respond to Tante Lulu's remarks. "Many of the prostitutes do it to feed a drug habit. Or to fight poverty."

"It's certainly not about pleasure, from the woman's standpoint," Grace added. "Their bodies are merchandise, pure and simple, for men to use and discard. Like dental floss."

"Mebbe we should start a foundation ta help hookers." Tante Lulu tapped her red-glossed lips thoughtfully.

"Oh, my heavens!" Samantha exclaimed. "Don't you think we should get one foundation under way before starting another?"

"What would you call it? Jude's Fallen Angels?" Charmaine joked.

"Thass a great idea." And Tante Lulu wasn't joking. Grace and Samantha groaned.

"Lookee over there at them midgets comin' out of that place with the sign 'Everything Goes.' Do ya s'pose some women like havin' sex with midgets?"

"Tante Lulu, it's politically incorrect to say midgets. They're 'little people,'" Grace told her in as kindly a manner as possible.

"Pooyie! I'm a little person. They's midgets. Before ya know it, they'll be changin' the name of that chillen's book ta *Snow White and the Seven Little People*. Hah!"

What could you say to that?

Nothing.

"Now, me, I'm for equal rights." Charmaine looked at them in the rearview mirror and grinned. "I think they should have more male prostitutes."

"Like yer husband ain't givin' ya enough lovin'! Praise the Lord, that boy is a reg'lar sex machine, I reckon." Tante Lulu slapped her knee with glee. "How 'bout you, Samantha? You gettin' enough lovin'?"

Samantha jerked up with surprise. She wasn't yet used to Tante Lulu's topics of conversation popping up here and there like fleas. But Samantha was a smart girl who learned quick. She chose not to answer.

That didn't stop Tante Lulu. "Did I tell ya Daniel ain't gay?"

Samantha bared her teeth at Tante Lulu. "Let up on the Daniel LeDeux crap. It's not going to happen. Ever."

"We'll see."

"If I had a bird, Daniel's picture would be lining the bottom of the cage. Is that clear enough for you?"

"That ex-husband of yers musta been a real worm, ta sour ya so on men."

"He was. They considered naming a wing after him at the hospital where he practiced, but not because of all his good works. More like how many of the hospital beds he'd christened by screwing whatever nurse was on duty. He did a couple of patients, too."

"I knew a man like that onct. When he died, they preserved his noodle in brine fer one of those Ripley museums."

"Is she serious?" Samantha asked Grace.

Grace shrugged. You never knew with Tante Lulu.

"Anyways, Samantha, ya know what they say about jumpin' back on a horse once ya been dumped."

"Avoid horses?" Samantha suggested sweetly.

"Nosiree. Ya gotta get yerself a rodeo, girl."

Samantha turned to Grace. "How do you stand her?"

"She's loveable, once you get to know her."

"I allus wanted ta go ta one of them whorehouses." Another change of subject. "Doan ya know anyone who could show us around?" Amazingly, Tante Lulu addressed her question to Samantha. "We could look through a peephole and check it out. Didja know Errol Flynn's wee-wee was so big it stuck up out of the waistband of his trousers? I read that in a book, so it mus' be true."

That was a conversation stopper if there ever was one. "Who's Errol Flynn, Auntie?" Charmaine teased.

Tante Lulu smacked her with her Richard Simmons fan.

"What in heaven's name would make you think I'm acquainted with people in...in houses of ill repute?" Samantha wanted to know.

"Ill repute—thass another name fer it, all right." Tante Lulu hooted with laughter. "I jist figgered, since ya live in N'awleans, ya mus' know everyone."

"Not everyone." Samantha rolled her eyes.

She and Charmaine just grinned, thankful to have dodged one of Tante Lulu's bullets.

But not for long.

"You could learn some stuff in a whorehouse, Gracie. Bein' a nun and all, ya prob'ly doan know many sex tricks."

That remark prompted her usual sputter. "Sex...sex tricks?"

"Like you know that many sex tricks, Auntie!" Charmaine reached over and patted her aunt on the knee.

"You'd be surprised. By the by, ladies"—she was addressing the two of them in the back seat now—"didja know ya could have yer thingamajig sewed back up? Charmaine was fixin' ta do it one time. Coo! Ain't that jist the berries! That was before Rusty came back ta town and put a stop to anything involvin' her private parts."

"She means that I was going to be a born-again virgin and have my hymen surgically reattached," Charmaine explained. And she wasn't even blushing.

Another conversation stopper.

"I had been married a few times by then," Charmaine explained, as if that was any kind of explanation.

"Four, ta be precise," Tante Lulu inserted.

Charmaine stuck out her tongue at her aunt. "Two of them were to Rusty."

"By the by, Gracie, how're the plans comin' fer the poker tournament?"

"Great," Grace replied, thankful for a change of topic. "We had to cut off entries after two days, and businesses have been donating prizes like you wouldn't believe since we can't give cash prizes. Federal and state gaming laws and all that."

"I could talk ta some folks," Tante Lulu offered.

"No, no, that's all right." We've already broken enough laws with the Duvals.

"One thing, Gracie, how come every time I mention the exhibition poker game between you and Angel, he gets a goofy grin on his face? Whass that about?"

Oh, great! That's all she needed, Tante Lulu getting wind of their bet—which wouldn't be a bet if she could ever get him to stand down long enough to cancel that nonsense. "I have no idea."

Liar, liar! that irritating voice in her head said.

"Oooh, ooh, there's the old Pelican Ballroom." Tante Lulu was off on another subject. The place she pointed to was a warehouse; in fact, it appeared to house Starr Foods products. "I usta dance there with my fiancé Phillipe Prudhomme before he went off ta war."

"I didn't know you were engaged," Grace said.

Tante Lulu nodded, for once amazingly lost for words, or lost in memories. "My heart broke when Phillipe died on D-day, and it ain't never been the same."

Grace felt tears well in her eyes, and she knew Charmaine and Samantha were having the same reaction. A love that lasted all those years! How incredible and touching was that?

Of course Tante Lulu broke the mood when she added, "That boy, he could dance, I'll tell ya that, and he dint need no sex tricks, either. Talk about! He could ring my bell, guar-an-teed."

"Way too much information," Samantha whispered to her.

Thankfully, they'd arrived at their destination on the outskirts of New Orleans. Tante Lulu had asked Samantha to show her where some of the people listed in her Jude's Angels folder were living.

It was a rundown, dilapidated low-income housing project. Apparently, it had survived Hurricanes Katrina and Rita, but not by much. Hurricane Ike's rain and winds had done a job on it, too. The brick was covered with mold. Some of the windows were broken. The window trims hadn't been painted in at least twenty years. In fact, not surprisingly, there was a sign out front that said this was the site of a future condo community called Magnolia

Gardens. Clearly, not for poverty-level folks. Which meant the displacement of an estimated one hundred families.

As they walked around the grounds outside the buildings, where almost no grass grew, and children played on hard-baked dirt and rusty slides and swings, Tante Lulu's mood got stormier and stormier. Once inside, it was even worse. Doors with broken locks. Smells in the hallways that defied description, and not just food.

"Believe it or not," Samantha told them, "people would stand in line to get one of these units. That's how scarce housing is in New Orleans these days. *Affordable* housing, that is. Those families who can afford it have sent their children to live with relatives else-where—and are glad to be given that opportunity, despite sepa-rating parent and child, or siblings from each other."

"I've seen enough," Tante Lulu said with a fierceness that Grace knew would be translated into her new foundation. She stamped out of the building on her wedgie sandals, her little butt swinging in a pair of tight red capri pants. Forget Greta Garbo— Tante Lulu, in her own inimitable style, was the cat's meow, and then some.

Next they went to a ranch-style house that had withstood the rigors of the hurricanes, better than the projects, anyway. There was a neat lawn here, and a deck out back with a barbecue grill and children's toys. The problem was that three families, related by blood, lived in the three-bedroom residence. The Arnauds included seven adults, four teenagers, six children aged three to thirteen, and two babies. An impossible situation!

They were sitting on the back deck sipping at glasses of cold iced lemonade and eating beignets that Tante Lulu had purchased at the French Quarter Market on the way there. With them were several members of the mocha-skinned Creole families, all with the surname of Arnaud. Cecile, a divorced single parent, nursing a darling baby boy, was a hairstylist for an upscale New Orleans beauty salon. Her mother, Eulalie Arnaud, a waitress at one of

Emeril's restaurants, laughed when Tante Lulu proclaimed Emeril
a hottie, second only to Richard Simmons. Also joining them was
Eulalie's glowering husband, Martin, a plumber, who was suspicious of these four visitors to his home.

"I know a Josephine Arnaud up Houma way," Tante Lulu
announced out of the blue.

"That's my sister," Martin said.

"They dint get hurt none by the hurrycanes, did they?"

Martin shook his head. "No, but after Katrina, she had to take
in our mother and father and two cousins."

"How do you manage with so many people in one house?"
Grace wanted to know.

"We do everything in shifts," Eulalie said with a booming
laugh. "Even the bathroom. Honest to God, I cain't remember the
las' time I took a bubble bath."

"You don't need no bubble baths anyhow, Lallie. Uses too
much water," Martin complained.

"Oh, you!"

Samantha explained the Hope Foundation in general, and then
Tante Lulu gave her spiel on Jude's Angels and how they were
working to keep families together.

Martin went all stiff. "We don't need no charity. All you do-
gooders are the same. Wanta come into our homes and neighbor-
hoods, lookin' down yer fancy noses at us poor folks."

Eulalie was about to chew her husband out for his rudeness,
but Tante Lulu raised a halting hand at her and instead addressed
the man. "Doan be a horse's ass, Martin. We all need a helpin'
hand sometimes. I ain't allus been in high cotton, y'know. I been
poor a time or two myself—mostly poor. So doan be takin' that
attitude with me."

Martin ducked his head, but still he grumbled, "There are folks
worse off than we are."

"Yer prob'ly right." Tante Lulu squeezed his forearm in forgiveness, even though he hadn't apologized. "But all we kin do is take

one step at a time. And frankly, we'd appreciate all the advice we kin get from folks like you."

Just then a teenage girl stuck her head out of the sliding glass doors. "Gram, can you gimme five dollars for some ice cream? I aim ta take Billy for a walk." Behind her was one of those reclining-type wheelchairs holding a boy, no more than seven, with severe disabilities, probably cerebral palsy.

Grace was shocked, and so were Tante Lulu, Charmaine, and Samantha. Not by the disability itself, but by the realization that this family had suffered and continued to suffer more than they let on. But the raised chins on the three Arnauds out here on the deck precluded any mention of their hardships regarding the boy.

Good heavens! How did they all manage in a house this size, with a wheelchair-bound boy, as well?

On the way to the car, Tante Lulu muttered, "This family is gonna get help, fer darn sure."

The four of them had lots to talk about on the way back to Houma. Samantha, who had a home in the Garden District of New Orleans, was coming back to Houma with them to look over the progress on the Duval house and to have a meeting with Grace and Angel over final plans for the poker tournament.

"Well, that settles one thing, fer sure," Tante Lulu said finally, with a long sigh.

"What's that?" Charmaine asked her aunt.

"I'm gonna hafta live ta be a hundred ta take care of all the work ta be done."

Grace could swear that infernal voice in her head said, *Amen!*

CHAPTER 10

Did the angel have horns, or was he just a horny angel...?

*A*ngel said hello to Tante Lulu, Charmaine, and Samantha, who went inside the Duval house, then turned to Grace, and winked.

Grace was wearing white jeans and sandals and a low-cut lime green tank top. Her breasts weren't big, but they weren't small, either. Her butt was tight for a thirty-five-year-old woman. Her red hair was piled on top of her head with one of those claw thingees, wisps of it straggling about her face, which was flushed with pink—probably from riding in the sun with the top down, not because she was excited to see him. Darn it!

She looked so good to him. In the best of all possible worlds, he would pick her up, lay her down over there in the shade, and fuck her brains out for about three hours. Then she would do the same to him. *Whoa! Better think about something else before a part of my body starts to greet her in a way she might not appreciate.*

"Hey, baby!" he reached out and picked a bug from her hair.

She swatted his hand aside. "Don't you 'baby' me, you...you lech. Was that your girlfriend we passed on the lane coming in?"

"What girlfriend?"

"You have so many? The one in the green Volvo."

"The woman you passed was Sherry Romines, a student at Tulane. She's waitressing over the summer at the diner where I eat most nights. She volunteered to help with the interior painting here."

"I'll bet she volunteered for a whole lot more than that."

"Jealous, Grace?"

"Absolutely not! Just an observation."

"I asked you for one night of sex, cupcake. I didn't ask you to go steady."

"Don't be an ass. Just for the record, if you don't put a shirt on, I'm not sitting in on this meeting."

Huh? "Why?"

"It's narcissistic of you."

He laughed. "I can't even say that word."

"And it's, well, indecent. I've told you that before."

"Ah. The belly button. You know, Grace, despite your protests to the contrary, it just shows that even you can be turned on without being wildly in love."

"Who says I'm turned on?"

He gazed pointedly at her nipples, which were now definitely, well, pointy.

"Jerk," she said, folding her arms over her chest.

"By the way, *have* you ever been wildly in love?"

"No, unless you consider being an out-of-control teenager who had sex with every reasonably attractive boy with a hard-on being wildly in love."

"What? You? I don't believe it."

"Believe it."

"And then you took a vow of chastity to repent?"

"Something like that."

"How come I couldn't have been around then? Pre-repentance, I mean." He pulled a fake pout.

"You wouldn't have liked me then."

He smiled widely, just to irritate her, but then he defended himself. "I've been working, Grace, installing the kitchen cabinets. Hot work. The air-conditioning isn't set up yet."

"I know that," she conceded. With the other three women inside the house, Grace got the opportunity he'd been forestalling for days. "About that bet of ours—"

"Don't even think of reneging. A bet is a bet."

"It's a silly bet."

"Not to me. What do you say to a little dress rehearsal—or undress rehearsal?"

He stepped toward her.

She stepped back, hitting the wall. "Why me, Angel? I'm not a young chick. I'm not hot. You could have any woman you want."

"Not true," he said, even as he leaned closer and inhaled her scent. *Lemons again. Must be her perfume, but I'm coming to consider lemons an aphrodisiac. Get a grip! Next I'll be like Pavlov's dog, drooling every time I drink a glass of lemonade.*

She arched her brows in question.

"It's not true that you're not hot, or that I could have any woman I wanted." *I really, really want to lick your skin and see if you taste like lemons.*

"Puh-leeze!"

"I can't have you." *Do I sound pitiful or what? Curb your enthusiasm, boy.*

"You said you didn't want me anymore."

He shook his head. "I said I wasn't in love with you anymore. I said I no longer had marriage in mind. I never said I didn't *want* you."

"Sex," she concluded.

"Damn skippy!"

"This is all about you being horny."

"More like sexually focused."

"I'm disappointed in you, Angel."

"Nice try, kiddo, but that tactic won't work. The bet is still on."

"Well then, I guess I'll just have to beat you." Her chin rose about two inches.

"Take your best shot, sweetheart." For the coup de grace, he added, just before sauntering by her into the house, "One more thing, Gracie. Wear that halter dress the night of the tournament. You know, the white one with the big-ass red flowers that you wore to Ronnie and Jake's wedding. And, oh, did I mention...don't wear any underwear. You just might be able to distract me." *Or blow my mind—and other body parts.*

She was still sputtering behind him after he entered the house.

He could only hope that she was as turned on as he was.

~

C'mon, baby, light my fire...or else put the damn thing out...

As ANGEL WALKED the three women through the house, using a punch list to check off work done and work yet to be done, Grace seethed.

The question was whether her seething resulted from anger over the stupid bet and his suggestive teasing, or from the sexual heat raised at the prospect of losing the bet.

It was beyond Grace's understanding how she could suddenly find the man so attractive. Well, that wasn't quite true. She'd always known he was attractive; she'd have to have been blind not to see that. But he'd never been attractive to her in a sexual way before. He was now.

She fanned her face with a sheet of sandpaper.

Angel glanced her way, then arched his brows in question.

Hah! Like she'd tell him *that*.

Even though he'd pulled on a long-sleeved denim shirt, he'd left it open. And her eyes kept straying down to that darn belly button. And lower. In addition to a buff body, he had a killer smile and dark chocolate eyes with incredibly long lashes. When he turned, his butt got her attention. From front or back, his long, muscled legs drew images that caused Grace's face to heat up. Heck, she even thought his knees were sexy.

"Gracie, yer mind is wanderin' again. Ya dint answer Angel's question," Tante Lulu said, a knowing smirk on her wrinkled face.

"Huh?" She deliberately avoided looking then at Angel, who chuckled, surely suspecting where her thoughts had been.

"We were discussing whether to bring the kids to see their new house yet," Samantha recounted. "Charmaine and I think we should let them get involved in the painting project on Friday."

"I wanna wait and have a big surprise *fais do do*, a party ta beat all parties, where they get to see the place when everything is done. Charmaine and me is goin' furniture shoppin' t'morrow. Charmaine has great taste."

She and Samantha exchanged doubtful looks about the taste thing but said nothing. There would probably be zebra-print sofas and white furry rugs, not to mention lava lamps and velvet paintings.

"We've waited this long. Another week or two shouldn't matter," Grace said.

"We oughta call that TV show what gives people new houses jist ta show 'em what other folks can do," Tante Lulu added.

"No, no, no!" Angel inserted. "We're avoiding publicity, remember?"

"Oh, yeah," Tante Lulu agreed.

"All right, then, Tante Lulu, we'll wait to give the kids their first walk-through on"—he consulted a calendar on the kitchen wall—"June twenty-fifth, a week from Saturday's poker tournament." Angel winked at Grace after mentioning the tournament.

"Will you be done by then?" Charmaine wanted to know.

He nodded. "As long as everyone helps with the painting. Starr Foods is sending over some ceiling lights and electricians to install them. Some of the ladies auxiliary at Tante Lulu's church are making curtains. The wives of the LeDeux men are donating bed linens, towels, and kitchen supplies, like pots and pans. I'm going to finish the deck. That's about it. There's always something that comes up in the end, though."

"I thought we'd be done by now," Tante Lulu told Angel, "not that I'm complaining about you, bless yer heart."

Not offended, Angel said, "We could have been if we'd launched a full-blown building project with everyone here every day to help out, but you wanted to keep it low-key."

"Yer right." Tante Lulu patted his hand, which was resting on the countertop, a cheerful red marbled granite someone had found at a builders' surplus outlet. The curtains were going to be red and white checked, while the cabinets were a light oak with brass handles.

As an indication of the sad state Grace was in, she found herself staring at that hand. Long fingers with nails cut short. Calloused palm. What would it be like if those fingers—

"Whatsa matter, honey?"

Grace stared blankly at Tante Lulu.

"You groaned," the old woman explained.

Everyone looked at Grace with concern, except Angel, who smiled.

"That wasn't a groan—it was my stomach growling," Grace lied. "I'm hungry."

"I'm hungry, too," Angel said, and by the way he ran the tip of his tongue over his lips, there wasn't a person in the room who thought he was talking about food.

~

Dumb, dumb, dee dumb...

IT WAS FRIDAY NIGHT. Tomorrow was the most important day of his life—the poker game with Grace. And he was in the Swamp

Tavern with four of the LeDeux men, sucking up suds and other good stuff, or bad stuff, depending on your definition. How dumb was that?

"I still say the answer is oyster shooters," René told him, waving for the bartender to set up another round in front of them.

Forget about martinis and cosmos and other sophisticated cocktails, oyster shooters were a real man's, or real woman's, drink. A concoction of one raw oyster with its natural juices was put in a shot glass, covered with Tabasco Sauce, tossed back without chewing, and followed by a shot of hundred-proof bourbon. It was one of those stomp-your-foot, yell-"Yee-haw" kind of drinks that was popular here in Dixie land.

"What the hell does booze have to do with getting Grace to fall in love with me?" Angel wasn't tickled pink that everyone in the world, or at least Houma, Louisiana, knew that he was mooning over Grace. He had Tante Lulu, the bigmouth of the South, to thank for spreading that news hither and yon. *Hither and yon? Crap! I'm even beginning to sound like the old biddy. Next I'll be developing one of those hokey southern drawls and saying "y'all."*

"You'd be surprised what liquor can do for a woman's inhibitions. The ultimate thigh opener." This from Luc LeDeux, who should be the last person to give advice, since rumor was he'd gone practically kicking and screaming to the altar after imbibing some kind of crazy love potion jelly beans. Okay, Luc had been crazy in love by the time they got him to the church, but he was definitely not the one to give advice.

"Once Grace sobered up, she would feel the same way as she does now," Angel pointed out. He hated the pitiful tone of his own voice, so he downed another oyster shooter. He wasn't sure if this was his fourth or fifth, but he was pretty sure his eyes were starting to bulge. His tongue was for damn sure numb.

"See, here's the thing."

Oh, no! John LeDeux, the wildest thing to hit womankind

before his recent marriage, was about to impart his own brand of wisdom.

"I think Grace is already halfway in love with you, *cher*, but she just doesn't realize it yet. It's up to you to jump-start her love engine."

"I can't believe you just said that," Remy LeDeux said. Remy was a really good-looking guy—or so women said—but on only one side of his face. The other side had been deeply scarred from burns suffered in an explosion of his plane in the first Gulf War. *"Love engine*, ferchrissake! Where do you get this bullshit?"

"From Tante Lulu," the rest of them answered as one.

Which called for another round of oyster shooters.

"What makes you think she's, uh, halfway in love?" *Pathetic. I am beyond pathetic.*

"The way she avoids you," John replied.

"Oh, that's a clue. Not!"

"Seriously, if she wasn't falling, she would have no trouble being around you. In fact, she'd be cozying up to you, trying to persuade you to be buddy-buddy again."

"Well, all I know is that if I don't win tomorrow, it's over. No more fallback positions. I'm not going to continue beating my head against her brick wall."

"And if you do win?" René inquired with raised eyebrows.

Angel tried to raise his eyebrows back at René, but for some reason he couldn't make them move.

"I mean, do you have a plan?" René elaborated.

"Sort of."

"What the hell does 'sort of' mean? You can't seduce a woman without a plan."

"You can't?" Luc and Remy asked.

John just nodded.

"My only plan is to win the poker game and get Grace into my bed. I'll play it by ear after that."

"Or by cock." This from Remy, who usually wasn't that crude.

He must be as blitzed as the rest of them.

"Sex doesn't necessarily lead to love," John declared, "but take it from the love doctor"—

Four sets of eyes rolled at that one.

—"good sex can lay the road to love, and I mean that pun intentionally."

More rolled eyes.

"Listen up, Sabato, you're gonna lose your key to hunkdom if you don't develop some Rhett 'Frankly, Scarlett, blah, blah, blah' talents. Southern men, like good ol' Rhett, might not subscribe to *GQ*, but we know how to be cool, believe you me."

"Hunkdom?" the rest of them exclaimed.

"Yeah. We're all hunks, right? Therefore, hunkdom."

"You are full of shit," Angel told John.

"I was reading this article in *Cosmo*—" John started to say.

"You read *Cosmo?*" With a hoot of laughter, Remy slapped his knee and almost fell off his barstool.

John's face didn't even get red, that's how confident the bozo was of his masculinity. "I was in Charmaine's beauty shop to get a haircut, and I read this article. Did you know you can make a woman have multiple orgasms, one after another, bam bam bam, just by doing this one little thing?" And he proceeded to tell them what that one little thing was.

Angel, Luc, Remy, and René's mouths were hanging open with shock when John finished. Angel hadn't thought he could be shocked by sex stuff anymore. He'd been wrong.

"I would never do that." Luc raised his chin self-righteously.

"I would," the rest of them said.

"Okay, maybe I would, too." Luc grinned at them.

"I'm going to start reading *Cosmo*," Remy decided.

They all laughed then, just as Charmaine and her husband, Rusty, walked in the door. Apparently the bartender, a friend of the family, had called her to come pick them up, not wanting any of them to drive.

Charmaine took one look at them and made *tsk*-ing sounds of disgust.

"Do you ever read *Cosmo?*" Angel asked Rusty.

Rusty winked at his wife before saying, "All the time."

"Then you know about..." Luc proceeded to mention the *thing* John had told them about.

"Sure." Rusty put on his poker face.

"Well, how come you never told us?" Luc was genuinely disgusted.

"You never asked," Rusty replied.

"You just lost your membership in the LeDeux dude club if you need to be asked. Talk about!" This from René, who also appeared genuinely offended.

Hunkdom and dude club! These LeDeuxs are nuttier than squirrel poop.

I can't believe I just said, uh, thought that. Tante Lulu really is wearing off on me.

"Tee-John LeDeux!" Charmaine put her hands on her hips— very nice hips, by the way, as displayed in shrink-wrapped black jeans leading down to red cowboy boots. If that wasn't bimbo message enough, she wore a stretchy red T-shirt that said, "I Do Men...and Women." On the back it said, "Charmaine's Beauty Salon, Houma, Louisiana." Glaring at her half brother, she accused John, "You've been reading my *Cosmos* again, haven't you?"

John smirked.

A while later, as Rusty drove them all home, Charmaine leaned back over the front seat of the SUV and handed a business card to Angel. "I made an appointment for you. Tomorrow morning. Nine a.m."

"Huh?" He switched on the interior light in the back seat where he was sitting. They'd already dropped off Luc and John. Remy was half asleep beside him. The card read: "Eveline's Magik Shop, Eveline Anjou, Voodoo Priestess, St. Charles Avenue, New Orleans, Love Potions Our Speciality."

"Voodoo? Tante Lulu would have a fit. Somehow I don't think the black arts go very well with St. Jude and the Church."

Charmaine chuckled. "What she doesn't know won't hurt her."

An hour or so after that, when Angel entered the houseboat, he noticed a blinking red light on the answering machine. It was Tante Lulu, who apparently did know everything, contrary to what Charmaine had said.

"If you go ta that voodoo schmoodoo, St. Jude's gonna drop ya like a hot brick. Y'hear?"

~

You're never too old to have mojo...

LATE SATURDAY AFTERNOON, Tante Lulu preened as she walked around Our Lady of the Bayou Church hall on the arm of Stanley Starr. Everything was going well with the poker tournament, so far. In fact, they'd made twenty-five-thousand dollars, just from the cover charge and buy-in fees.

"What's that perfume, darlin'?" he asked, leaning closer as he linked the fingers of one hand with hers. "You smell like spring-time on the bayou, I do declare."

Glancing down at their combined pale skin mottled with age spots—flowers of death, they were called, of all things—she smiled and swatted him playfully on the chest with the fan in her free hand. "Ya allus were a charmer, Stan, even when ya was courtin' Sophie."

"Once a charmer, always a charmer, m'dear. It's in the blood." He waggled his white eyebrows at her.

"An' I mus' say, yer Old Spice is mighty nice, too."

"You told me one time that it was your favorite," he reminded her. "That's why I wore it t'day."

She couldn't imagine when that mighta been. If it was pre-Sophie, it had to be more than fifty years ago. Still, she felt an uncommon thrill ripple through her old body that he'd paid attention to her wants.

Yep, all these years, and I can still get a date with a smooth talker. How cool is that?

As they passed the refreshment stand, where jambalaya, gumbo, lazy bread, oyster po' boys, and beignets were the big sellers, that busybody Stella Guenot gave her a dirty look and muttered to Lily Beth Morgan, loud enough for her to overhear, "Some people doan know when ta act their age."

So, of course, Tante Lulu muttered to Stan, loud enough for Stella to overhear, "Jealousy turns some folks green as grasshoppers, don'tcha agree?"

"Absolutely," he said, chuckling as he raised their linked hands so he could kiss her knuckles.

Tante Lulu about peed her padded panties with surprise and, yeah, felt her sagging, almost nonexistent breasts perk up with interest. *Imagine that!*

To avoid embarrassing herself, she studied her surroundings. Lively Cajun music blared from the loudspeakers, now that silence, or at least muted music, was no longer required during the tournament. Banners inside and out announced the event— the first annual St. Jude's Angels No Limit Texas Hold 'Em Poker Tournament.

She was wearing her favorite red chiffon cocktail dress; her Marilyn Monroe wig; professional makeup, thanks to Charmaine, which meant subtle liquid makeup, the kind that didn't clog in the wrinkles; a bit of transparent red lip gloss, which also didn't clog in the wrinkles; and a quick brush of mascara. And she wore red patent leather pumps, which were killing her feet. After the tournament, she and Stan were going out to dinner, if her arches didn't collapse before then.

"You know what they said in the old days, Louise?" Stan said, close to her ear. "A woman wears red shoes as a surefire signal that she wears no underpants."

"Oh, you!" She swatted him again with her fan.

"I didn't mean no insult," he immediately apologized, not that she'd taken offense. "You look terrific, honey." Stan looked good, too, in his white planter's suit with a sky-blue shirt to match his eyes, blue suede shoes, and Elvis tie. She hadn't noticed before, but he had Elvis sideburns, too. White ones, but sideburns nonetheless. As far as she was concerned, the fact that he had any hair at his age was a plus. All this, on top of his Old Spice cologne, just about made her swoon. She did like a man in Old Spice. Although her swooning might be due to her pinched toes, she had to admit.

In the midst of a two-hour dinner break, the two of them watched the tables being dismantled and reassembled for the final round, to be held in the center of the room, which was fenced off from spectators by velvet ropes they'd borrowed from a local movie theater. Before that final round to determine the grand-prize winners, Angel and Grace would be displaying their championship talents by playing the best out of three games of poker for some bet they refused to discuss with anyone. Like her.

The tournament had started at 1:00 p.m. and proceeded quickly until 5:00, when the field had been narrowed to ten, out of the original two hundred. Even the losers appeared happy with their donated prizes, which included restaurant meals, spa treatments, airplane tickets, weekend getaways, pizzas, autographed sports memorabilia, a set of golf clubs, skis, and Roller Blades. The final ten would each get a DVD player, and the grand-prize winner would get a laptop and an all-expense-paid trip to Las Vegas, where some hoity-toity national poker championship was to be held.

As they made their way to a table reserved for the LeDeux and Starr families on the sidelines, a middle-aged, scowling man bumped into Tante Lulu, almost knocking her over.

"Hey, watch where you're going," Stan said, helping her to regain her balance.

"Butt out, you old geezer," the man snarled. "Why don'tcha go back to the nursing home where you belong?"

What a slimebucket! The guy was wearing glasses with thick lenses and old-fashioned black frames, instead of them new-fangled wire-rimmed ones. Maybe he had trouble seeing and wasn't really a slimebucket.

Instead of apologizing, the slimebucket swore and demanded of Tante Lulu, "Where's Grace O'Brien?"

"Huh?" She scowled, not liking his slimy attitude at all. "Why would a jerk like you be lookin' fer Grace?"

"Never mind!" He stormed past them and into the crowd.

She and Stan exchanged glances.

"Some folks is jist born ornery, I reckon," she concluded.

With a deep sigh, she sank down into a chair and toed off her shoes. *Lordy, Lordy, I doan think I'll be able to put them toe-pinchers back on.*

When Stan went off to get them both an iced sweet tea, she scanned the room, looking for the Duval children. There they were, helping to fold tables, except for Lena, who was at the cash register by the drink table, where lemonade and sweet tea were being served. Nothing alcoholic. Tante Lulu had wanted the kids to be involved today. Even so, she'd asked Tee-John to keep an eye on them, just in case those snoopy government folks were about. On Friday they would be holding the *fais do do* housewarming party right after the kids moved into their new house. Then this whole mess would be over. She hoped.

When Stan came back, she sighed loudly and said, "Ya know what the best thing is about today's doin's?"

"What?"

"It's all fer a good cause, but everyone's havin' such a good time. Even the volunteers who're helpin' out. Didja know there are twenty of us LeDeuxs here t'day, countin' the grandkids?"

"That's nothing, darlin'. There are thirty-some of us Starrs floatin' around, too. You could say we're straight-shootin' stars, if you get my meaning."

SANDRA HILL

She laughed at his racy humor. "Look, it's pert near time fer Angel and Grace ta start their playin'. Doan she look pretty in that white sundress with the red peonies? And Angel, whoo-boy, that is one good-lookin' feller!"

As if he'd heard her comment, Angel turned and sauntered over to their table, then hunkered down, with his jeans straining his outspread thighs, to be on eye level with her. The boy was hotter than a two-dollar pistol. If she was younger, she would be checking certain things out.

"Whass a matter, sweetie?" she asked.

"I'm so nervous. I'm gonna blow this, I know I am."

"It's jist a game. Take it easy. Yer as jittery as a fart in a fryin' pan."

"Oh, there's an image I'm going for!"

She smiled and patted his shoulder.

"This game, well, it's my last shot. If I don't win, it's over."

"You and Grace, y'mean?"

He nodded.

"Ah, sweetie! Ya should know better than ta put all yer eggs in one basket."

"All my eggs are about to go rotten."

"Grace is a hard nut ta crack, I'll give ya that. But I think she's been softenin' up toward ya lately."

"Really?" His brown bedroom eyes widened with hope, and, yes, she still knew how to recognize a man with slumberous I-can-make-a-woman-scream-in-bed eyes. "What makes you say that?"

"Jist a feelin'. Y'know, Angel—never mind."

"What?"

"There's some reason Grace is holdin' back. I doan know what it is, but ever'time I ask certain questions, she almos' looks scared."

"I know what you mean, and dammit, I can't believe I never saw it all these years. The little bit I've learned lately, and it's not much, about her lousy home life is more than I gleaned over a ten-year period." Had he just been insensitive? Or had she done such a good job hiding things? "What could be so awful, or hurtful, that she would need to keep it secret?"

"Doan know, but here's somethin' else ta chew on. Didja know she gave away most of her poker and treasure-huntin' money?"

"*What?* That's impossible." Angel knew practically to the dollar how much Grace had won and earned. Not as much as him, but a huge amount, nonetheless. At least two mil.

Tante Lulu shrugged, then patted him on the arm. "What kin I do ta help?"

"Say a rosary. Or a novena. Put a voodoo spell on her. Now, don't go ballistic. I know you said no voodoo. I was just kidding. But really, can't you do something? Like pray? You're closer to God than anyone I know."

"Oh, my! Askin' God ta help ya gamble...I doan know 'bout that."

"Is it any worse than praying for me to be able to seduce Grace into my bed? That's what you said you were doing last week."

"Ya got a point there, 'ceptin' ya cain't get the bacon ta sizzle if ya don't add some flame. I take it my prayers dint work in that area."

His pretty face bloomed with color. "No, but like you, I think she's, um, softening."

Tante Lulu nodded. "Okay, guess we gotta call in the big guns."

Angel's eyebrows rose a notch. "St. Jude?"

"That goes without sayin'. Nope, I'm talkin' 'bout the LeDeux family love committee, better known as the Cajun Village People."

"Forget it!" he said with a grunt of disgust, rising to his feet without his knees even creaking, which was an amazing feat to Tante Lulu. "I'll trust in my God-given poker-playing talents. And luck."

"Good luck," she called after him but added under her breath, "Dumb cluck!"

CHAPTER 11

How much does a slimebucket hold...?

*G*eorge Allison tapped his foot with impatience as he watched from behind the rope fence. Grace O'Brien, the object of his pursuit, was about to sit down at a table across from Angel Sabato.

Tournament workers were quickly putting up signs beside each of them. "Angel Sabato: 1st place, World Series of Poker, 2001, 2002; 2nd place, 1997, 1999." Then, "Grace O'Brien: 1st place, World Poker Tour, 2000; 2nd place, 1997, 1998; World Series of Poker, 12th place, 2001."

George had arrived at the New Orleans airport this morning, hired a car, and pulled in to Houma by noon. With a little Internet Googling, he'd had no trouble getting Grace O'Brien's address. Thanks to some discreet questioning at a podunk general store along the way, he'd learned that Grace lived next door to Louise Rivard, the matriarch of the LeDeux clan. He'd also gleaned good information about Grace's affiliation with these rich Cajuns, only to find that the two cottages were nothing special as a reflection of wealth. But then, lots of the high and mighty liked to live down, displaying a humble lifestyle at home, while they gallivanted around the world with the jet set. He figured that must be the case with the LeDeuxs and Grace. Once he'd hit Bayou Black, he found out from a neighbor that Grace and all the LeDeuxs were back in Houma at some charity event, where he was now.

Oh, well, he had plenty of time.

And look at her over there now in her slut dress. Probably wasn't even wearing any underwear on top with her whole back exposed, practically down to her butt. Her poker partner certainly had his eyes glued to her exposed body parts. The bitch sure didn't have any problem making a spectacle of herself, either, prancing around the center of the room to play a game of poker, like she was the queen of some damn ball.

Two women stepped in front of him. He was about to protest, or shove them aside, but stopped himself when they began to gossip.

"I hear she was a nun at one time."

"No way! I hear she entered a bunch of poker tournaments and won a couple million dollars."

"A nun who played poker?"

The two of them giggled.

"And now she's livin' out there on Bayou Black, next door to that crazy old woman Louise Rivard."

"She might be crazy, but I hear she's loaded. All them LeDeuxs are. Apparently, they got a big part of the pirate treasure that was discovered down the bayou last year. Grace O'Brien was part of that treasure hunt, too, if I recall. I heard the treasure was worth about ten million dollars."

"That must be true, because Tante Lulu put up a million of her own dollars to start this Jude's Angels charity. How come I never get so lucky?"

"You? Hah! I can't even win the lottery."

So, George thought, Grace not only associated with millionaires, but she was a millionaire herself, from poker winnings, but also from her share of that pirate loot. No reason for guilt, then, in taking some of it from her, to cover all his pain and suffering in raising her bastard. Not that he was feeling guilty, anyway. Nope, he was entitled.

A voice came over the loudspeaker then, drawling in one of those slow, hokey southern accents. "Ladies and gentlemen, René LeDeux here. Y'all are about to witness top-notch poker playing by two of the best, Grace O'Brien and Angel Sabato. I'll be givin' ya a runnin' account of the games, but you can also watch what's happenin' on the big-screen TVs at each end of the hall. Are you reee-aaaa-dy? Let the play begin!"

George had intended to confront Grace here right after the poker tournament, but he was rethinking his plan now. Maybe it would be better if he waited for her to return to her cottage. Make it a private meeting. Only later would he go public, and then only if she didn't hand over the cash he deserved.

Yep, that's what he would do. Tell her nice and polite, at first, how much he had done for her bastard—uh, kid—over the past ten years and how much payment—uh, thanks—he thought he deserved. He wouldn't be greedy, and this would be a onetime deal. After all, he wasn't a blackmailer. Just a regular guy wanting his just desserts.

So, what would be fair? Maybe ten thousand per year for the past ten years, or a hundred thousand payoff. No, he would start by asking for thirty thousand per year and negotiate down to two hundred thousand.

He already had some big plans. Lasik surgery for the vision problems he'd had since he was a kid. A widescreen TV. A new car. Maybe a vacation in Vegas for him and the wife. So many things he needed. He better insist on at least three hundred thousand, after all.

But what if she refused?

Well, then, the bitch would find out what a big star she was when the tabloid headlines read: "Rich Nun Gave Her Baby Away."

~

Baby, will you play with me...?

GRACE TOOK a deep breath and tried to calm her nerves. She always felt a fierce adrenaline rush just before a competition, but this was different. More like an adrenaline gush, from every pore in her body.

What is wrong with me?

Tuning out René LeDeux's play-by-play on the loudspeakers and the murmuring of the crowd behind the rope fence, she tried not to chew on her thumbnail but instead concentrated on the cards in front of her in this "Heads Up," two-handed round of cards. Or tried to.

Ever since Angel had mentioned this stupid bet, it had been all she could think about. And not whether she would win. More like what she would gain if she lost. Like wild sex with a guy who was too hot to handle by any woman's standards. And the most tantalizing thing—and wasn't it every woman's fantasy?—was that she could indulge all her secret wicked yearnings, guilt-free, since she was "forced" to do it.

Studying him for a quick second, she noticed he was clean-shaven and must have had a haircut that day. He wore a pure white T-shirt under an open denim shirt. The shirt and his faded denim jeans looked as if they'd been ironed. Whether it was his Italian or Hispanic genes, he was one good-looking man, and he knew it. Well, why wouldn't he? Women buzzed around him like horny flies.

Except her.

She'd sat beside him in dozens of poker tournaments. She'd gone on motorcycle trips with him. They'd even slept in the same motel room a number of times, albeit in separate beds. She'd seen him naked, and not just in that magazine. Nope, she'd accidentally walked in on him in the shower. Twice! And none of it had prompted her to jump his bones or even drool a little. A year ago, when she'd told him that she thought of him only as a friend, it had been true. And it still was. Pretty much.

She was so confused.

When she'd tried to discuss it with Tante Lulu, the old lady had just patted her on the shoulder and said, "Sometimes our true feelin's are buried so deep, we doan even know they's there. An' they kin only come out when they's ready."

Whatever that meant!

Then Tante Lulu had added, "If I was you, I would kiss that boy like he just came home from the wars, and see what happens."

Grace knew exactly what would happen, but she hadn't made a smart remark about it to Tante Lulu because the old woman had probably been thinking about her own soldier boy who'd never returned to her.

Angel examined the cards fanned out in his one hand and remarked in a voice thick and sultry as a midnight bayou breeze, "So, you wore the dress. Just like I told you."

He was probably trying to distract her from playing well.

"That's all I did."

He glanced up from his cards, tossed two down, and motioned for the dealer, Luc LeDeux, to hit him again. "Meaning? You're wearing underwear?"

Luc pretended not to have overheard, but a grin tugged at his lips.

She ignored Angel's question, even as his eyes skimmed the upper part of her dress with the exposed back, knowing she couldn't possibly be wearing a bra, unless it was paste-ons. And darn it, his scrutiny caused her breasts to pearl and tighten with a deep ache. Good thing he couldn't see through the fabric.

"Panties," he concluded.

Well, two could play this distraction game. "Bikini panties, if you must know."

"Oh, well, I can handle panties, even bikini ones."

"Lace bikini panties."

He grinned, slow and lazy. "Score one for the lady. Gracie, Gracie, Gracie! I am so going to enjoy...you."

"In your dreams!"

"In case you're wondering, I fulfilled my part."

She frowned, having no idea what he meant.

"I'm going commando. Don't want to waste any time, after the games are over and the real games begin."

Enough was enough! "You overconfident oaf! You're assuming you're going to win." They had both been given an equal number of chips for their bankrolls, presumably worth a million each. Pushing a short stack to the center, she spread out her flush and gloated, "I call." He had two pairs, so an easy win for her.

The whole time, René had been discussing strategy and odds of each turn of the cards over the loudspeakers.

"That's just one hand, baby," Angel said. "Let's see what you can do this time."

"Bring it on, big boy," she replied as they both put their antes front and center.

She thought he muttered something about being big, all right.

This time, while René was expounding once more on the art of poker playing and all the permutations of how this particular hand could be played, Angel did indeed win with bullets, a pair of aces, to her queens. The teasing smile that spread across his mouth was pure deviltry. And temptation on the hoof.

"That's one-one, cupcake. Care to sweeten the pot?"

"No."

"Afraid?"

"No."

This was the third and final hand. They each put out their blind bets before being dealt two cards, facedown; these were their hole or pocket cards. She peeked at hers, a queen and a jack. Angel did the same to his. Of course, nothing showed on his face, expert that he was.

She checked, and he did likewise.

The dealer, Luc, turned the flop, the three cards face up in the; center of the table. A queen, queen, and jack.

Wow! Talk about luck! At the very least, she was going to end up with a queen-high full house, almost unbeatable; the only thing that could beat her would be king-or ace-high full house.

She doubled her bet, and Angel matched her.

Luc turned over one more card...a three of hearts.

Well, that didn't help her, and she couldn't see any way it would help Angel, either.

She checked again, and once again he checked, too.

Was he bluffing? Hmmm.

Luc turned over the river card. A ten of diamonds.

She placed her bet.

He matched hers and raised.

Grace knew she had him beat, she just knew it, but still she looked across the table at him. For just a second, the king of no tells had the most vulnerable, hopeless look in his eyes.

And her heart literally ached.

Without hesitation, Grace surprised even herself when she made a life-changing decision. "I fold."

He flipped over his Big Slick, one of the best starting hands in Texas Hold 'Em, an ace and king, giving him an ace-high straight, a good hand but not good enough to beat hers. Angel cocked his head to the side in question.

"Win some, lose some," Grace said, trying her best to maintain an expressionless face.

Sliding her two cards into the muck, face-side down, she said, "You win."

Angel seemed shocked. "Come on, show us your hand," Angel prodded, clearly suspicious. She must have given off some tells that he was now having trouble interpreting. Reaching across the table, he went to turn over her pocket cards. But she slapped a hand over them, not about to let him see what a fool she was.

But then the implications of what she had done hit her. *Oh, my God! Oh, my God!*

She lifted her gaze to look into his eyes, expecting him to gloat or say, "I win! I win! You are mine...for tonight!"

He did neither. He just stood, did a little bow at the applause, then began to walk away from the table. When he was only a table-length away from her, he turned and said, "See you." Then left the room.

That was all.

But oooh, boy, it was enough!

~

And so the game began...the REAL game...

IT WAS DARK, and she hadn't arrived.

Angel wasn't sure if she would show up, but still he was all amped up...and prepared.

Lights off, candles lit. White wine, Grace's favorite sauvignon blanc, on ice. Soft music on the built-in sound system—Grace's favorite, Alicia Keys. That la-de-da gourmet cheese that Grace liked; it cost about the same per ounce as gold these days. Fruit was chilling in the fridge, but no strawberries. Grace was allergic to strawberries. And French bread on the counter, the ridiculous kind that if not used today would be hard as a rock tomorrow.

If he was a nice guy, he would have called off the bet, or at least told Grace she didn't have to fulfill her part after he'd won. Apparently, he was not as nice as everyone thought he was because he was for damn sure going to demand everything he could get from Grace and let the chips fall where they may.

He grimaced at his own corny play on words but then stiff-

SANDRA HILL

ened. He heard the faint sound of high heels on the wood deck surrounding the houseboat, getting progressively louder.

With heart racing, he waited, not turning even when he heard the screech of the screen door. When he did turn, finally, she just stood in the middle of the room.

"I'm here," she said, her voice a combination of belligerence and nervousness.

Hell, he was nervous, too.

In the muted candlelight, she was a picture of pure femininity. Creamy white skin, with long legs leading down to white high-heeled slingbacks. Her shiny red hair was straightened tonight but already reverting back to curls in the swamp humidity. Dangly pearl earrings. A cupid's-bow mouth outlined in sexy red lip gloss. White clingy halter dress with red flowers. Think Marilyn Monroe standing over the air vent in *The Seven Year Itch*, except Grace's dress wasn't totally white. *Where's an air vent when you need one?*

It seemed like forever that he just stared at her before replying, "I'm glad."

"Huh?"

"I'm glad you're here." He leaned back against the wall, arms folded over his chest, to keep from leaping on her like a teenager in testosterone overload. He should take things slow and easy. Have a drink. Chitchat. Maybe steal a kiss or two or twenty. But no, he was too far gone for that. "Will you take your dress off for me, Grace?" *Nothing like putting all my cards on the table, with no warning.*

More card puns! I am definitely losing it.

She blinked at him.

"Real slow."

"You probably think I won't."

"I'm hoping you will."

As she began to undo the braided belt at her waist, she held his gaze. "I know that you think I'm shy, practically a virgin, but I'm

140

not. I was wild years ago. I still am, underneath, even if I don't always act on it."

He smiled. He couldn't help himself. "Be wild for me, Gracie."

"You're going to hate yourself tomorrow, Angel."

"I seriously doubt that."

"I'm not your usual sweet young thing. I'm thirty-five years old, and it shows."

"What makes you think I'm attracted to sweet young things?"

She shot him a look of utter disbelief.

"Anymore."

She dropped the belt to the floor, which caused the gathered fabric to balloon out, making it a loose, shapeless dress, held on only by the ties at the back of her neck. "You'll regret having forced me to do this," she said, at the same time she was raising her hands to her nape.

"If you want to think you're being forced, go right ahead."

"I always pay my debts."

"Is that what this is about?"

Instead of answering strongly in the affirmative, she hesitated. "I don't know."

Hope soared—that's how pathetic he'd become. Vaguely, he wondered exactly what she meant. Maybe it wasn't what he hoped. Whatever. He would puzzle it out later. For now, he waved a hand for her to continue undressing.

Even from here, he could smell her Jessica McClintock perfume. Lilies of the valley. He knew because he'd asked her one time when they'd been seated next to each other in a poker game, and her scent had distracted him...in a nice way.

"Take it off," he repeated.

Her eyes blazed green fire at him. Anger, yeah, but it could also be signs of arousal. Maybe he was building dreams on the tenuous framework of hopes, but he could not care less.

Grace undid the ties, held them out from each side of her neck, then let them drop, causing the dress to slide down and pool at her feet.

For a long minute, he couldn't look below her haughtily raised chin. But then he did.

"Oh, sweet Jesus!"

She was everything he had dreamed of and more, wearing nothing but sexy high heels, which caused her body to arch, belly forward and ass back...pure centerfold posture...and a pair of white, high-riding-on-the-sides bikini briefs, which were lacy, like she'd said, but she'd failed to mention that they were embroidered all over with tiny roses. Standing long and tall, she was one frickin' flame-haired goddess. Her breasts, topped by tiny pink nipples, were perfect half globes, bigger than he'd imagined, but that was possibly just the contrast with her slim frame. Her waist was narrow and her hips just wide enough. He was even rather fond of her stubby, bitten-down right thumbnail. She wasn't the most beautiful woman he'd ever seen, and her body wasn't that of a perfectly toned twenty-year-old, but, oh, baby, he loved the way she looked.

"Why are you standing all the way over there?" she sniped.

"Because I need the wall to prop me up. Otherwise, I might faint."

She tilted her head in question, a little Mona Lisa smile tugging at her ruby lips.

"You make me breathless just looking at you, Grace. My heart is racing, the blood is draining from my fool head, and I feel humbled just being here with you, like this."

"Wow! Such flowery words! Be still, my heart."

"I've also got a hard-on that could lift a locomotive, just from looking at you."

She laughed. "That's the Angel I know and"—she hesitated—"recognize."

Ouch!

"Listen, let's just do it. Get this stupid bet over with. Okay?"

"*It?* As in singular? You've got another think coming, babe. I'm calling the shots here. You promised all night, and I for one don't intend to waste one minute of it. I can sleep next week. Tonight I fuck."

"Oh, that was nice."

He shrugged. "And by the way, this was not a stupid bet. In fact, it's the smartest bet I've ever made. Should have done it years ago."

"You didn't want me—*that way*—years ago."

"Oh, sweetie? I was ready to jump you like a dead battery, from the get-go." He shoved away from the wall and started to walk toward her. "No, don't move. In fact, turn around. Slowly."

Now he got a view of the small of her back, always a tantalizing part of the female anatomy to him, and rounded buttocks that, yeah, had a bit of cellulite, but not a deterrent to him. Nope, he chose to be more fascinated by the dimple in each cheek, each of which he was going to enjoy kissing. The dimples, not the cheeks. Well, both.

"Raise your arms and lift your hair," he said in a raw voice, little more than a whisper, once she was facing him again. He was still several feet away. "That's it. Now hold that pose."

"If I'm going to stand her like a bleepin' nude statue, you should get naked, too."

"I thought you'd never ask." He smiled and toed off his shoes and yanked off his denim shirt and the T-shirt underneath. He popped the snap of his Levi's but didn't unzip.

Her lips parted as she stared at his chest and his belly button.

God bless belly buttons.

There you go again, Angel, my son, asking God to bless the oddest things.

Maybe I oughta get a belly button ring.

Was the penile piercing not enough of a mistake for you?

Okay, maybe not!

Then he began to circle her. Not touching. Just memorizing

everything he could about her body. All his big plans for all the wicked things he'd systematically do to seduce Grace flew out the window. Angel had been a player for a long time, like forever. He knew fifty, no, a hundred ways to melt a lover. But right now he was like a pilot with a destination in mind and not a clue how he was going to get there. All he knew was that he wanted to take the slow route. Real slow. But his system was on automatic pilot, and his glider plane was fast turning into a supersonic jet heading for home.

Grace glanced down and stared meaningfully at the jeans he still wore, unsnapped, riding low on his hips.

"Not yet."

She shot him a glare of irritation. "If you're going to keep looking at me like that, I'm going to come, and that would cut your party short."

Wha-what? "Gracie, Gracie, Gracie, you can't say things like that to me."

"Why not?"

"Because you'll make *me* come."

She smiled, as if that had been her intention.

He was having a hard time understanding this Grace standing before him. She was throwing off opposing signals like an out-of-whack neon sign.

So, he decided to test the neon waters by reaching out and strumming the back of his knuckles over her nipples.

She gasped as the tips hardened even more, into pink pearls.

He did it again and husked out, "Do you like that?"

"No, my nipples are hard because of the Arctic wind blowing through here. Pfff!"

He thought about reacting to her sarcasm with an equal dose of his own, but he had more important things on his mind. "You are everything I've ever dreamed you would be," he murmured, instead, moving around to her back again.

"Been dreaming about me a lot, have you, Angel?" she inquired over her shoulder.

"Oh, yeah."

"Eeeek! What are you doing?" she yelped with surprise as he knelt on the floor behind her and licked the back of first one knee, and then the other.

"Smelling the roses."

"Jerk!"

He licked again.

"Are you trying to give me a heart attack?"

"Nope, just a lust attack." He put his hands on her waist to prevent her from turning around. "Ticklish, are you?"

"I never thought I was before."

"Don't move." He took his hands off her waist and began at the side of her foot, skimming his fingertips over the outside of her calves, thighs, hips, waist, rib cage, and underarms.

A full body shiver rippled over her.

He pulled on the elastic waistband of her bikini briefs, tugging them down to her ankles. After she stepped out of them, along with her shoes, he urged, "Spread your legs a little bit, honey."

She hesitated, then did as he asked.

Now he skimmed his fingertips over her high arches, grazing the soft skin of her inner ankle, then her inner calves, her knees, and the tops of her thighs. But then he stopped and traced a fingertip over the crease of her buttocks, the small of her back, and her spine all the way to her nape.

"Aaaaaahhhh!" she moaned, and her legs started to buckle.

Quickly he stood and held her back against him, one arm around her waist, the other free to do...other things. Looking down over her shoulder, he stared at her begging-to-be-sucked breasts and the thatch of red curls below.

"You remind me of one of those Vargas pinup paintings that used to be in old *Playboy* magazines."

"You're crazy. Those paintings depicted women with almost too-perfect bodies."

"Precisely," he said and kissed the curve of her neck. She still had her hands raised to her head. "Like these," he murmured, cupping her breasts from underneath, using the rough pads of his thumbs to strum the nipples into even greater hardness.

"Oh. My. God!" She dropped her hands and rested her head back on his shoulder, pressing her breasts into his hands. He could feel the nipples against his palms. "Don't you dare stop," she gasped out.

While he played with her breasts, he made love to her ear, whispering erotic promises of everything he wanted to do to her, making the whorls and center of her ear moist before stabbing them rhythmically with the point of his tongue.

He could tell that she was approaching her first climax by the way her body went rigid. She tried to shove his hands off her breasts and move out of his embrace. "Stop...wait...I need to...I can't concentrate, dammit...too many things at once."

Instead of stopping, he drew her earlobe into his mouth and plucked at her nipples, over and over.

She began to keen. "Oh...oh...oh." He placed the fingertips of one hand at the pulse in her neck and the other hand over her flat stomach. The hard ridge under his fly was nestled against the crease of her buttocks. Despite the fabric, when he thrust once, then again, he felt heaven, and she must have felt it, too, because her lower body jerked.

"Let it come, sweetheart," he whispered.

And she did, head thrown back, breasts thrust forward, with a long shudder that went on and on and on.

When she started to collapse, he picked her up and carried her into the bedroom. Placing her carefully on the bed, he noted her glazed eyes and parted lips.

She stared back at him, at first unfocused, but then her gaze went downward to his still-unshucked jeans. He hadn't even kissed her yet, and he was as turned on as he'd ever been.

When she arched her brows at the prominent bulge at his crotch, he shrugged and grinned.

"Well, sweetheart, that was nice for an appetizer."

CHAPTER 12

Oops, she did it again...

Grace lay splayed out on the bed staring up at Angel. She should have been embarrassed by her nudity, but her body was still humming in post-orgasm mode, where modesty was the last thing on her mind.

"That's for sure it was only an appetizer," she said. "I haven't had sex in two years, and if I'm going to ruin a good friendship, I want the real deal for my main meal."

"Meaning?"

"Puh-leeze! You know exactly what I mean." She glanced pointedly at the stack of foil packets on the bedside table. "And, by the way, a bit of an optimist, aren't you?" She pretended to be mentally counting the number of condoms. There were ten.

He smiled.

"Stop smirking."

"That's not a smirk. I'm just happy. I finally have you where I want you after all these years." He kept surveying her body like she was the present under his personal Christmas tree.

"Finally? That is such a crock. This I-want-you-Grace-baby

business is a new idea of yours. Probably midlife crisis or a testosterone-overflow situation."

"I'm not that old, and my testosterone levels are fine, thank you very much."

"Take off your pants."

"I like a woman who knows her mind."

"Take them off real slow," she said, repeating his earlier order to her. Propping herself up on her elbows, she prepared to watch.

The top snap was already undone. He unzipped his fly, just an inch or two, then walked over to a wall switch that turned on dim lights. Then he fiddled with the dials on the bedroom speaker for the houseboat music system. Barry White began to wail out a hokey love song.

"Angel," she said in a sudden panic.

"Don't worry, Grace. It's not my CD. It was here when I moved in. No hidden messages. I'll change it." His back was still to her, and she couldn't help but notice how stiff it had gone, the muscles bunching with tension.

She had hurt him, Grace realized, and was embarrassed by her overreaction. "That's all right. I like Barry White." But her demur came too late.

Another song by another artist came on. More mournful love lyrics. They both burst out with laughter; this was even worse than the first one.

But then her attention was diverted as she noticed that Angel's jeans had slipped down almost to his butt. He'd been telling the truth back at the church hall. He wore no underwear.

He changed the CD anyway to Coldplay, then turned.

No longer smiling, he walked toward the side of the bed. Holding her gaze, his eyes a smoldering dark chocolate, almost black velvet, his wide lips parted, he told her, "Watch."

Slowly, he unzipped his jeans the rest of the way, then shimmied them down over lean hips, a flat, ropey-muscled belly, a blue vein-popping erection, and long, long legs, 'til they pooled on the

SANDRA HILL

carpeted floor. Without glancing down, he kicked them aside, then stood, legs slightly apart, waiting. For what? Her approval?

"Well, well, well, aren't you the big boy? I don't see any piercings, though. What happened to the bolt you had in that *Playgirl* picture?"

"It was hell going through metal detectors at airports."

She rolled over on her side, to the edge of the mattress, and reached out with one hand to touch him.

He flinched, but then he let her cup his balls, which were lightly furred and heavy. When she traced a fingertip down his penis from base to head with its drip of pre-come, he took her hand in his and showed her the grasp and motion he liked. He allowed that for only a moment before he groaned and moved onto the bed, lifting her to the middle and coming up over her. Taking care to position himself, he nestled his erection between her thighs, and his belly pressed her down.

"There are so many things I want to do to you," he murmured against her lips. "But first..."

He kissed her.

And kissed her.

And kissed her some more 'til she was a moaning, melted mass of yearning.

He licked her lips. He nipped her bottom lip, then sucked it into his mouth. He shaped her lips with his 'til he got the perfect fit, then alternately pressed and drew on her. The kisses started gentle and seeking, then turned wet and voracious. His tongue entered her mouth, deep, and coaxed hers into his. He opened his mouth wide over hers, as if so hungry he could eat her whole.

Meanwhile, her arms were wrapped around his shoulders. Sometimes her hands caressed his back, sometimes tunneled into his short hair, holding his head in place. At one point, fighting the waves of passion riding over her, she tried for a bit of sanity. "Just because I'm behaving like this doesn't mean I'm going to marry you."

"Who asked?" Angel replied, biting her on the shoulder.

"Ouch! Well, just so you know. It's merely sex, and—"

"Shut up, Grace."

Sliding downward, he gave his full attention to her breasts. "You're really sensitive here, aren't you, honey? There aren't many women who can climax just from having their breasts fondled."

"That and the ear sex," she gasped out, because he was already massaging them with big sweeping circles of his rough palms. While he flicked both nipples with his middle fingers, he asked thickly. "Do you taste as good as you look?" Before she could answer, he was sucking deeply on her, drawing the full areola into his mouth, then pulling out slowly on a suctioning clasp 'til just her nipple was between his teeth and he was vibrating it with the tip of his tongue. Over and over. So intense was the pleasure she would have fainted if she weren't already lying down. When she thought she could bear no more and was begging him to stop, he moved to the other breast, but not before eying with satisfaction the wet, rosy distension he had created.

He was right about her nipples being sensitive, though, because every tug of rhythmic suckling created an answering tug between her legs.

"Tell me what you like, Gracie," he husked out. His eyes were slumberous with desire and his mouth swollen from his kisses and deep sucking.

"Everything...everything you're doing."

"This?" He pinched her nipples lightly.

"Oh, yes!"

"This?" He slid farther down her body, kissing a line from her breast bone to her navel, where he proceeded to repeatedly stab his tongue inside.

She moaned in answer and spread her legs wider, wanting him there, inside her. Taking hold of his arms, she tried to pull him up. "No more...no more foreplay. I want *you*."

"Not yet, baby."

"Please. Oh, God! I can't stand any more."

"Sweetheart, you are not taking control of my game." She arched her hips up off the bed as he put his mouth to her pubic hairs, rubbing his face back and forth 'til her slick folds opened and welcomed the most intimate, delicious torment of all. "Melted honey," he murmured. "My own personal honey pot."

She wanted to tell him that he was no Winnie the Pooh, and she was no bee comb, but all she could say was, "Aaaaahhhh!" The blood drained from her head, her eyes probably rolled back in their sockets, and she bucked up against his open mouth.

Putting his hands under her buttocks, he lifted her and used his shoulders to further spread her thighs. She was totally exposed to his sensual exploration then. And explore he did. He used his tongue like an erotic torture instrument. Licking and further opening her folds. Poking inside her. Stroking and stroking and stroking. Everywhere but where she really wanted him.

"You are so pretty here, Grace, did you know that?"

She made a gurgling noise in response.

"All pink folds with this rose here in the middle. Why do you suppose it's swelling up like that?" he teased. "It almost seems to be pulsing. Can you feel it?"

She nodded, hardly able to see him through the erotic haze covering her eyes.

"Do you want me to touch you there?" He blew on her to show just where he meant.

And her clitoris did in fact pulse and swell some more.

He kissed it, just a mere brush of his moist lips, and she stiffened at her approaching climax. This was not the way she wanted to come again. Not alone.

"No, no, no! I want... stop...dammit... inside. Nooooo!"

He watched her reaction even as he sucked on the distended bud, slowly, and she was lost. She screamed as the most intense pleasure pounded at her there and throughout her body in wave after wave after wave.

She must have lost consciousness for a moment, because when Angel said thickly, "Open your eyes, Grace," his face was above hers. He had her knees up to her chest and spread wide. Only then, when he had her full attention, did he enter her with one long, hard thrust.

And her traitorous body began a new round of convulsions, her long-unused inner muscles clenching and unclenching his shaft. He filled her, and all of his penis wasn't even inside her.

"Take all of me," he urged in a hoarse whisper.

How? she wondered, but then she half sat up, put her hands on his shoulders, and bucked up against him, once, twice, three times 'til she could swear her womb moved and made room for him to slide in even farther.

They were both stunned for a moment.

Sensing that he was pinching her, he waited, soothing her with soft crooning sounds and gentle kisses. Once she relaxed and her inner muscles shifted to accommodate his size, he began long, agonizingly slow strokes in and out of her tight channel.

"You feel like a hot velvet glove with fingers grasping and ungrasping me. How do I feel to you, Gracie?"

"Warm marble. With a pulse," she replied with a choked laugh.

After that, one unending orgasm roared through her, especially when he moved to short, hard, pounding thrusts that hit her clitoris with his pubic bone each time.

He reared back, the cords in his neck sticking out with tension, and let out a guttural masculine groan. She was shaking all over, unable to stop yet another violent full-body orgasm. Then all was quiet except for their heavy breathing, the music in the background, and her wildly racing heartbeat, which could surely be heard in the silence.

She had never experienced anything like it before. She would have liked to attribute it to the culmination of a celibate lifestyle, but deep down she knew it wasn't true.

When Angel raised his head and looked down at her, brushing

some damp curls off her face, his expression was not hard for her to read. He didn't need to say the words. He loved her, and what the two of them had just experienced was Angel expressing that love.

The question was: Did Grace love him in return? Was everything she had done a subconscious manifestation of that love?

If she did, this was an even more tragic situation than it had been a year ago when Angel had professed his love. Because there was still no future for them. And now two of them would be hurt. They were digging a hole with no easy exit.

Thankfully, no answers—or digging—were required at this time. Angel rolled over onto his back, taking her with him to lie on her side. He tucked her face into the crook of his neck and placed her arm across his chest.

"That was amazing, Grace," he said, running a light caress up and down her back.

"Well, it certainly rocked my world," she replied, going for a lighter note. "Probably happens to you all the time, but not to me."

"Maybe it was your dormant sex drive kicking in."

"Maybe."

"Or something more?"

"Maybe."

"Did I hurt you?"

"A little. At first. But it was worth it."

"Good." He kissed the top of her head.

"How long before we can do it again?" she asked, even as a wide yawn escaped her lips.

He smacked her on the butt.

She nipped his shoulder.

And, amazing sex kitten that she was, she snuggled closer...and fell asleep.

$\sim$

It was going to be a love fest...uh, feast...

GRIMLY, Angel stood leaning on the rail of the houseboat's deck as he sipped at a Dixie longneck. It was midnight. Grace had been asleep for an hour. And there were only six or seven hours left of this interlude to go before Grace, sure as sunshine, went back into her stinking friend mode.

After that, Angel was going to let her go. Wasn't that what all the psychobabble-ists said you had to do if you really loved someone? The only difference was, in letting Grace go, Angel had no delusions that she would boomerang back to him.

He had to stick around until after the housewarming, and he had lots of loose ends to tie up before then, but after that...well, he wasn't sure. But whatever he decided, it wouldn't be taking place in redneck heaven Louisiana.

For now, though, he thought on a long sigh, he had a whole lot of lovin' to pack in a few short hours. Memories that would have to last him a lifetime.

The sex had been great, and he planned on more, but he knew deep down that the intensity of the pleasure had been due to love guiding his every touch. He couldn't imagine how spectacular it could be if that love were reciprocated.

But that was pathetic, futile, dumbass mental whining on his part. He refused to take the sheen off the golden lovemaking to come.

So, he went back into the houseboat. Put cheese and crackers on a tray, along with two peeled peaches, one cut in slivers and the other in circles minus the pit; small rindless wedges of watermelon, cut in strips; some peeled navel orange sections; and pitted maraschino cherries. Then he poured two plastic stemmed glasses of wine and headed for the bedroom, where he arranged everything on the bedside table.

Grace was still sleeping soundly, flat on her back in the center of the mattress, arms thrown over her head, legs parted. Sated, and very sexy. He recalled reading a magazine article one time by a sexologist—*that is what they call those goofy psychologists, isn't it?*—that said you could predict the type of sexual partner a person would be by the way they slept. Front, back, fetal, side, whatever. He was pretty sure Grace's sleep posture would be deemed hot, hot, hot. He liked to think she was his very own amazing Grace.

He sat down on the edge of the mattress and for a long time studied Grace, trying to figure out just what he loved about her. Oh, she was attractive enough, despite her age and body issues. And he and Grace certainly had the sexual-compatibility thing down pat. Over the years, though, as they'd traveled and played poker together, and later joined the treasure-hunting crew, together, he'd come to respect her caring personality and sense of humor. There wasn't another woman who could put him in his place with a mere look. *Let's face it*, he decided, *it's not any one thing. And I'm a fool to even try to understand.*

Time to get down to business. Fun business. Not funny business. Although it could be funny, as well as fun, he supposed. Yep, he was going to prepare a feast for Grace she wouldn't soon forget, to titillate taste buds she'd never realized she had.

He started by placing cherries on her nipples and in her belly button. Watermelon slivers ran a straight line from her collarbone down to the red curls of her pubic hair, which he framed in peach slices. The coup de grace was the honey he was drizzling over her lips from the nozzle of a little plastic bear.

Only then did he start to croon, "Oh, Graaa-cie! Time for dinnnn-ner!"

~

Her soda fountain was hot...

GRACE WAS in the middle of the sweetest dream.

She was lying in the grass in a citrus grove where the tart scent of the ripe fruit teased her nostrils. But, no, it was a peach orchard. Luscious with the juicy fruit. *Can they have peaches and oranges in the same grove?*

It was a warm day. She was so relaxed. But there was a drip on her mouth. Then another. Was it starting to rain? She ran her tongue over her top lip.

Honey.

Her eyes shot open.

Angel was on his side, leaning over her. When she opened her mouth to ask what he was doing, he squirted some honey into her mouth from a Winnie the Pooh dispenser.

She swallowed the honey, then glanced downward.

"Oh, my God! What have you done?"

"I figured this was a BYOF party, as in Bring Your Own Food." He swooped in and gave her a quick kiss, which involved lapping at the sweet substance in and out of her mouth.

Then he handed her a glass of wine to sip. "Be careful," he said while he helped her recline against the pillows. "Don't want you to jerk and upset my masterpiece." He grinned down at her. "Now, listen up, sweetheart, there is a good way and a bad way to eat fruit."

"And you're going to show me the bad way?"

"Exactly!"

Aside from her moans and occasional gasps, he was the only one talking during his demonstration.

"The thing about cherries is you need to suck the juice out first before chewing.

"And watermelon! All that sweet liquid. Once you eat it, you almost always have to lick up the excess. Like so.

"And peaches—oh, baby, I do love peaches." He squeezed the peach slices into her hair *down there,* made her spread her thighs, and squeezed more juice and then the pulp into her slick folds. And then he ate her.

After that climax, which had her lifting her hips, then

stomping her feet on the mattress, she shoved him over onto his back and informed him huskily, "Have I told you I make yummy cherry jam and watermelon wine slushes?"

"Knock yourself out, baby," he encouraged her.

He, too, was soon groaning at the delicious torture she inflicted on him. And even though he hadn't wanted to, she'd brought him to orgasm with her honey-coated, peach ring "banana" split.

Afterward, they were both breathing hard and laughing, at the same time.

"Is there anything sexier than a man who can make a woman laugh in bed?" she wondered idly, tracing a finger through the sticky hair on his chest.

"Maybe a woman who can make a man smile in bed?" He gave her a quick kiss and a slap on the butt and in a hokey southern drawl said, "Come on, sweet thang, these sheets are a mess. What we need, darlin', is a shower."

She looked at him and grinned. "I swan, Rhett, ah thought you'd nevah ask."

CHAPTER 13

Water sports can be so invigorating...

ow, that's what I'm talkin' about."

Angel adjusted the many knobs and faucets in Remy's high-tech Hugh Hefner shower and positioned a stunned Grace right where he wanted her. *If only it were so easy to place her where I want her in my life!*

"Good heavens! This is like *Star Wars.*"

"If *Star Wars* were a porno movie."

"We're going to make a porno movie?"

"A virtual one."

"Sounds good to me."

First, using the soft soap that was there—a minty scent—he made her stand still while he soaped every inch of her body, from her toes to head, giving extra attention to some places in between. Then he shampooed her hair.

By now they were both primed for more. And he didn't mean soap.

"You have to do everything I tell you to." He backed her up against the far wall.

SANDRA HILL

"Oh, I do, do I?"

"Yep. It's for your own good."

"Pfff!"

He adjusted the ten or so faucets so that some were hard streams, others misty showers. Then he aimed them at some strategic spots on Grace's body, which was already flushed from the steam, and hopefully aroused. "Spread your legs, honey." He knelt down to show her how he wanted her. "That's good."

Then he handed her the soft soap and propped himself against the opposite wall of the huge shower stall.

At first she seemed confused.

"I think you're still a little sticky," he explained.

When she understood, she let out a little choked laugh. "You do get your money's worth when you gamble, don't you?"

"Damn straight."

Grace squirted a huge dollop of soap into her palm and put the plastic bottle on a shelf. Then, at first closing her eyes, she began to lather her neck and shoulders and arms, then her breasts. At first she just massaged her breasts in a circular fashion with her palms, but then she was strumming the erect nipples with the fingers of both hands in a washboard fashion, finally flicking them with both middle fingers. There was a jet stream hitting both nipples straight on.

Her eyes, open now, took on the glassy glaze of green crystal. Her lips parted. And she glanced his way, unfocused.

He reached over and handed her the bottle.

She put another dollop in her hands, braced her shoulders back against the tile wall, and soaped her belly and the red curls below. When she began to apply the rest of the soft soap to her inner folds, which were also being hit by a strategically aimed stream of water, he knew she was approaching climax. Spreading her thighs wider and arching her belly out so the water hit her clitoris, she began to moan.

That was his cue. Quickly slipping on a condom, he stepped

forward, lifted her up by the buttocks, and entered her already convulsing inner muscles.

Surprised, she stared at him in confusion...at first. But then she wrapped her arms around his shoulders, burying her wet face in his neck, and lifted her legs higher to straddle his hips. He was already too far gone, and so was she. It took only a half-dozen thrusts before they came together. Short but sweet.

"Are you trying to kill me?" Grace gasped when he finally pulled out of her.

"Oh, yeah. I don't want you to ever forget this night."

"Oh, Angel," was all she said, but it sounded like a death knell to him.

∼

Hello, heartbreak...

GRACE WAS the one to initiate sex the next time, when she awakened in a sleeping Angel's arms. Several hours had passed, and it was almost dawn. Their night of loving was almost over, after which all bets were off. Literally.

This was the best and worst experience of her life. Best because making love with Angel was more than sex; it had been almost magical in its intensity. Worst because there was still no happily-ever-after for them, and now that she knew what she'd be missing, her future looked bleak.

Still, how could something that felt so right be so wrong?

Not wrong, exactly. Just hopeless.

Nothing in this world is hopeless, she could swear that blasted head-voice said. Really, she was hanging around Tante Lulu too much if she was now channeling St. Jude.

But honestly, Grace had more baggage than a Samsonite factory. Her personal issues were so overwhelming, there was no way she could be in a committed relationship. And no matter what Angel said, that was precisely what he wanted from her.

A man like Angel would want children. He'd said as much in the past. How could she contemplate having children of her own, or even adopting, when she'd already killed one and given away the other? Impossible!

If only...

No, no, no, I am not going to start that game.

Grace eased out of Angel's embrace and knelt down on the floor beside him on the bed, just studying him. He was so damn beautiful. In repose, he really did resemble an angel. Maybe a fallen angel, considering the bad-boy past he sometimes referred to, but an angel just the same.

His dark, almost black, hair was short, and although there had been a certain attraction to him in his long ponytail, she had to admit she liked this style better. Sort of devil-in-a-conservative-suit kind of thing.

His facial features were pure Hispanic. Or Italian. Probably a mix of both. As attractive as the sculpted cheekbones and full sensual lips were, they were nothing without the spark of mischief evident when his eyes were open.

His body...well, what could you say about a body like his, except "Wow!" He had six-pack abs, long muscular legs, and the to-die-for belly button. And then, of course, there was the main event. And was it ever! Even in "at ease" position, it was very nice, indeed. She wondered idly if he still had piercing marks under the base. Tilting her head to the side, she tried to see better.

And noticed that his soldier was no longer at ease but starting to salute.

Her eyes shot to her left to see Angel watching her. "Don't stop now, baby."

"Oh, you! You were awake the whole time, weren't you?"

He grinned.

"I was just checking to see if you still have the piercing where that bolt was in the *Playgirl* picture..." Her words trailed off as she realized she was rambling. And blushing.

"Go ahead. Check."

"No, I'd rather do this." And that was when Grace began to make love with Angel. Really make love. Like she meant it.

And he reciprocated. Kiss for kiss. Caress for caress.

It was a long, gentle loving.

At one point, while she was straddling him, and he was deep inside her, she said in a sex-hoarse voice, "Look at us." Her red hairs were mixed with his black ones. Like woven fleece. "Aren't we pretty?"

His response was to roll his hips from side to side.

Which caused her to climax. Again.

Afterward, he held her tight as if he didn't want to ever let her go. He didn't say those three precious words, but she imagined he was thinking them.

A short time later, when Angel was asleep once again, she slipped away and dressed. She thought about leaving a note, but what could she say that hadn't been said before?

How about, "I love you?"

Grace shook her head. Expressing that sentiment would just open a can of worms she wasn't prepared to discuss with him now. Or ever.

Not surprisingly, Grace cried the whole way home.

And so it ends...

ANGEL STARED AT THE CEILING, dry-eyed, but crying inside, as Grace's car drove off.

He'd sensed when she got up and went out to the other room to dress. He really hadn't expected her to stay, or to say good-bye. What was the sense in that?

Still, his heart—no, his whole body—ached with the yearning for something more. How could he love a woman capable of cutting him off like this, especially after the most incredible night of lovemaking?

With a deep sigh, he went out into the empty great room and sat down at his laptop. After logging in, he sent an e-mail to Ronnie at Jinx, Inc.

<<HEY, Ronnie!
What's the next project on the company agenda?
I'm free to go wherever as of next week.
Angel>>

~

It was a good news/bad news kind of thing...

GRACE WAS COMING out of the shower when she heard a knock on the door.

It was too early for Tante Lulu to be sending the Duval brood back here. They usually slept in until at least nine on the weekends.

Could it be Angel? Grace had mixed emotions about that possibility. It would be better if they ended things without hashing it out. On the other hand, she missed him already. Parts of her body bore bruises and aches that would be a reminder of him for days to come. She would have to put makeup on her face to cover the whisker burns.

Tying a robe about her waist and tunneling her fingers through her wet hair, she went to the door. Belatedly, she recalled that none of them were supposed to be opening their doors these days without checking who was on the other side.

It was a strange man. Middle-aged. No, probably mid-fifties.

Bit of a paunch. He wore a plaid shirt, khaki pants, and thick-lensed glasses with black frames. His nose was kind of swollen and reddish with what Tante Lulu called gin blossoms, sure sign of an alcohol-loving man.

"Are you with CPS?"

"Huh? I'm from Atlanta."

"You're not with Child Protective Services?"

"Hell, no...I mean, no. My name is George Smith." She could tell he was lying by his hesitation over the last name. "Can I come in?"

"I don't think that would be a good idea. My, uh, husband is in the shower."

"I know you don't have a husband. But looks like you've got yourself a man." He gave her whisker burns and kiss-swollen lips a smirk, then shoved the door wide and strolled into her small living room, big as you please.

The man looked harmless. Maybe he was just an aggressive salesman. There had been that insurance guy last week. But, no, she was getting a bad feeling. "How do you know I don't have a husband?"

"I know everything about you."

"Whaaat?"

Surveying his surroundings, he remarked, "Not much for a rich gal."

"Maybe because I'm not a 'rich gal.' "

"I noticed a Beemer outside."

"That BMW is eight years old."

"Looks fairly new to me."

"I take good care of it."

"Make us some coffee. We need to talk."

The nerve! "No on the coffee. And no, we are not going to talk." She was inching toward the umbrella stand by the door. "Get the hell out of my house before I call the police."

"Oh, I don't think you'll want to do that."

"Why is that?"

"Because then the world will know about you and Andrea."

She had an umbrella in a double-handed clutch, holding it in front of her like a sword. "Okay, I'll bite. Who's Andrea?"

He flashed her a smile that could only be described as evil. "Your daughter."

"I beg your pardon? I don't have a daughter." Suddenly, there was a buzzing noise in Grace's ears.

"December 10, 1991, ring any bells?"

The blood drained from her head, and she plopped down onto an overstuffed chair. He sat down on the sofa across the room, grinning at her shock.

Oh, God, oh, God, oh, God! "Tell me."

"My wife and her first husband adopted Andrea when she was only a few days old. Harald died ten years ago."

"And?"

"I figure you owe me bigtime for taking care of your girl all these years."

"Owe you?" Her brain was still muddling through the fact that she was finally going to learn something about the baby she'd given away, but never in a million years had she imagined it would happen like this. *Andrea.* What a pretty name! She would have to stop calling her Sarah in her thoughts.

"Yeah, three hundred thousand oughta do it. Thirty thousand a year expenses ain't too excessive."

"And if I don't come up with the money?"

"Well, I seen your picture in the newspaper with that Louisiana charity foundation. I wonder what everyone would think if they knew Ms. Goody Two-Shoes O'Brien was helping every southern redneck in the world when she tossed away her own child."

She gasped. "I did not toss—"

He waved a hand with rude dismissal. "Whatever."

"You're blackmailing me."

"No, no, no. I'm just giving you a bill for legitimate expenses."

"I only have a hundred thousand in CDs, and another hundred in a retirement fund. It would take a couple days to access the money."

"Well, see, I'm a sensible fellow. We compromise on two hundred thou. How 'bout we meet at the Lafayette Hotel in Houma on Thursday at noon. Bring the cash, and I mean cash."

"Wait a minute. I'm not giving you anything without information about my...daughter."

"Whataya wanna know?"

"Everything."

"She looks just like you." He said that as if it was not a compliment.

But a daughter who looked like her? Tears welled in Grace's eyes, and she put a hand to her heart.

With seeming reluctance, he pulled out his wallet, then handed her a photograph. Grace could barely see through the haze of tears. Wiping her eyes with a tissue, she stared hungrily at the picture. A girl with bright red hair was standing under a flowering magnolia tree. She had green eyes and a stubborn chin like Grace, but apparently she was tall, like her father—her real father, with whom she also shared a wide mouth and straight nose. "Tell me more."

"She's real smart. Was gonna go to university next fall, but the college fund Harald set up for her ran out."

Grace would just bet it had.

"Now she'll probably get a waitress job 'til she earns enough for tuition, or maybe go to the local community college."

Not if I can help it.

"Does she...does she ever ask about me?"

"No. Until recently I didn't even know about you. She thinks you didn't want her."

Grace stifled a moan.

Just then Ella came rushing in the back door, followed by

Lena, Lionel, and Miles. They were up earlier than she'd expected, after all, probably due to Tante Lulu's prodding. The old lady didn't sleep much.

"Grace, Grace! Guess what?" Ella yelled. "We're going to the mall. Tante Lulu and Lena are gonna shop for furniture, and Tante Lulu said I can buy a Hannah Montana CD and Miles a game. Where's my 'Girls Rock' T-shirt?"

"On the dryer."

Just then, they all seemed to notice the strange man in the room, and Lionel particularly stared with suspicion at the umbrella in her hand.

"Grace," Lionel moved closer to her, "do you need some help?"

"No, no that's all right. Go in to your bedrooms and change. Maybe I'll go to the mall with you." *Or not. I'm too stunned to move.*

Reluctantly, they left her alone again.

George sneered at her. "You adopted a bunch of colored kids, but you had no time for your own brat?"

"I haven't adopted them. They're only here temporarily. And I do not appreciate your use of that word."

"Brat?"

"No. The other one."

"Colored?" He laughed. "I coulda used a worse word."

"How can you refer to your daughter—your adopted daughter —as a brat?"

"Hah! I never adopted Andrea. Why would I?"

Grace cringed to think that her daughter had been raised under the roof of this insensitive bigot. "Does Andrea know you're doing this?"

"Hell, no! What business would it be of hers, anyway?"

Well, since he was using the young girl to extort money, Grace would guess a lot, but she couldn't antagonize him...yet.

She had no idea what she was going to do about giving him money, or somehow connecting with her daughter...or not. She had to get him out of here so that she could clear her head.

"You got any whiskey? I sure could use a drink to wet my whistle."

"No, I don't, and I think you should leave. I'll be there on Thursday. Do you have a card or something?"

"You must think I'm dumb."

As a rock. "How can I contact you if there's a problem?"

He shook his head. "There better not be a problem."

Once he left and she cautioned the Duval kids to stay put for a little bit, she rushed over to Tante Lulu's cottage. The old lady, who was washing dishes, looked up at her with surprise.

"Gracie? Whass the matter, honey?" She was already wiping the soap suds off her hands with a dish towel.

Grace plopped down into a kitchen chair, cradled her face in her trembling hands, and began to bawl, loud and long. Finally, when her crying bout was over, she looked up at Tante Lulu, whose wrinkled face was even more wrinkled with concern.

"It's about my daughter."

~

The cure for everything is tea...and St. Jude...

TANTE LULU PUT a cup of tea and its saucer on the table in front of Grace and sat down beside her. The poor girl had just told her the most amazing story between sobs and hiccoughs and sighs of regret. Bad parents. A lost child. A slimy blackmailer.

Where to start unraveling this mess? Tante Lulu smiled to herself. Unraveling was what she did best.

"Drink up, honey. It's my special blend fer soothin' the nerves. Then we'll talk."

Grace took a long drink, then placed the cup carefully on the table, tracing the rim with a forefinger, deep in thought.

The cup and saucer, one of a set of six, had been hand painted many, many years ago by her almost mother-in-law Betty Prud-

---

homme. Betty had been color-blind and not much of an artist, bless her heart, so the roses looked more like tulips and the leaves were more purplish than green, but Tante Lulu loved them just the same.

"What should I do?" Grace asked.

"What do ya wanna do?"

"See my daughter. Reconnect in some way, if I can. I don't really know."

"That goes without sayin', sweetie, but first ya gotta decide what ta do 'bout this George fella."

Grace nodded. "Maybe I should just give him the money, on the condition he sets up a meeting with my daughter...if she's willing."

"No, no, no! Givin' in ta bad people is lak pouring water in a leaky bucket. Doan think fer one second that this worm won't keep comin' back fer more."

"I won't have any more to give him."

"That won't matter none." She scrutinized Grace for a few seconds. Wasn't hard to miss the whisker burns and kiss-swollen lips, and neither of them was caused by crying, either. "I notice ya hooked up with Angel las' night."

Grace blushed. You had to love a spinster gal who could still blush, and in Tante Lulu's book a thirty-five-year-old gal who'd never gotten married was a spinster. Not that that couldn't be corrected—the unmarried bizness—and it for darn sure was on Tante Lulu's agenda.

"Why not tell Angel about this shyster's threats and let him help you?"

Grace was horrified. "No! I wouldn't want him to know—no! It's better that he doesn't know about my...past."

"Sweetie, let's get one thing straight. People make mistakes, we all do, but there's a shelf life on penance. Ya cain't let yer mistakes rule yer whole life, and thass what ya been doin'. Fer goodness' sake, ya were only sixteen when ya had a baby. Do I think ya shoulda kept the little one and raised it yerself? Well, yes, I do, but it 'pears as if ya had no one ta turn to fer help back then. Now ya do."

"But I should have known better. I had an abortion the year before. Wouldn't you think I'd have the sense to at least use birth control after that?"

"Sweetie, why are ya beatin' yerself up over things that cain't be erased? The question is what ta do now?"

"Not Angel!"

Tante Lulu narrowed her eyes at her. "Thass why ya broke the boy's heart, ain't it? Ya got this fool notion that ya gotta be punished fer yer sins. Let me tell ya, girlie. God doan like humans goin' inta the punishin' bizness. If there's any punishin' ta do, it's up ta him and no one else. And—no, doan interrupt me—there's another thing. God forgave ya a long time ago. Doan ya think it's 'bout time ya forgave yerself?"

Grace burst out into a whole new set of bawling. Lordy, Lordy, who knew one body could hold so much water? When she was finished, and had gone through three more tissues, Tante Lulu suggested, "How 'bout talkin' with Tee-John? He's a cop. He could handle this lowlife, guaranteed."

"No! There's too much I need to know yet before I can contact Andrea. Him being in jail, at least at this point, would only be setting up walls. Not that I want to pay him any money. I'd rather use it to pay for her college education."

"Luc, then. He's a lawyer. He would know what ya should do."

Grace nodded.

Tante Lulu took her hand and bowed her head. "Dear St. Jude, please help Grace. She ain't hopeless, but ya allus was the best saint fer those in despair. And dear God, please be with Grace in her time of need. Amen."

"Thank you," Grace choked out, squeezing her hand.

"About this Andrea gal," Tante Lulu said then. "I wonder if she has a hope chest."

CHAPTER 14

As the world turns in Loo-zee-anna...and turns...and turns...

Everyone was behaving really weird.

As Angel worked to finish all the little projects on the Duval house that week, he got help from many of the LeDeux men, each of whom gave him funny looks—and more unwanted advice than Dr. Phil. Was it because he had nailed Grace? Nah! They had all done enough nailing in their time to be licensed sex carpenters. They could hardly be judging him. Besides, it had been a willing event.

Event? I'm losing my mind here.

Finally, the last straw came with John LeDeux, who kept giving him odd glances while they were putting up crown molding in the kitchen.

He growled, "What?"

"Nothin'."

"Don't tell me frickin' nothin'. It sure as hell is somethin'."

"Not for me to say."

"Who, then?"

John refused to meet his gaze.

"Grace?"

John shrugged.

"Is something wrong with Grace?" Holy crap! She couldn't be pregnant, could she? Noooo! Even if he hadn't used protection, it would be too soon to know. "Is she sick?"

"Nope."

"In some kind of danger?"

"Ooops, I just remembered I'm on duty tonight."

"When it comes to artful dodges, that one stinks."

"I have to be in Baton Rouge for a stakeout."

"How'd you like to have a stake up your sorry ass?"

"Tsk, tsk, tsk! Tante Lulu doesn't like potty mouths, *cher.*"

"Tante Lulu isn't here. And I'm not your dumbass *cher.*"

"Chill out, Sabato."

"You are pissin' me off."

"Listen up, birdbrain, Grace only told Tante Lulu and Luc. She doesn't want anyone else to know about...well, stuff. I only know because I overheard them talking. And Remy only knows because Tante Lulu wanted to buy a gun. And René...well, René could always worm anything out of Tante Lulu. So, really, it's only Tante Lulu and Luc who know."

"What a crock! Whoa! Did you say something about a gun? That's it. I'm outta here." He laid down his hammer and headed toward the door.

"Where you goin', *cher?*"

"To Grace's cottage. She'll tell me what's goin' on, or...or else."

"She's not at home."

Angel turned slowly, inch by inch, to glare at the dickhead who was grinning at him. "Oh?"

"She's at the Lafayette Hotel in Houma."

"Alone?"

He shook his head.

"She has a lover?"

"Oh, puhleeze! After boinking away with you for seven

straight hours, I hardly think she's gonna be lookin' for more action."

Does everyone know my business? I need to get out of Louisiana before I go totally nuts. "Tell me exactly...no, forget it. I'll find out myself."

He was already halfway to his pickup truck when John appeared in the doorway and yelled, "Good luck!"

Angel was really, really afraid, not just because of the grim expression on John's face, but because he sensed that once again, his life was about to take a major turn. And he hated like hell to have it all depend on luck.

You could try prayer, St. Jude said in his head.

~

Trust me, baby...

GRACE KNOCKED on door number 217 at the Lafayette Hotel.

Luc was hiding at the far end of the corridor, keeping out of sight. Tante Lulu was waiting down in the lobby, fuming because they refused to let her come up with them.

The plan was for Grace, who carried a huge purse—one of Tante Lulu's—that contained mostly cut-up newspapers with some bills on top, to enter the hotel room and leave the door unlocked so that Luc could later come in and scare the spit out of this slimeball. The police would not be involved, because Luc planned to get some critical information out of George Smith before kicking his butt out of Louisiana. Like where was Grace's daughter, and how could they arrange a meeting? As it was now, they had only his probably fake surname, and a home in Atlanta, which might also be a lie, and even if both of those were true, how many George Smiths might there be in a city that size? Hopefully, all would be handled in a calm, nonviolent way.

"You're late," George snarled as he opened the door and shoved her inside.

Luckily, she was able to kick one leg back to keep the door from slamming shut. It appeared closed but was not totally.

George wore a "Got Hurricane!" T-shirt, which celebrated the famous French Quarter drink, not the natural disaster, tucked into a pair of pleated navy blue polyester pants. On the dresser was a bottle of Jim Beam and a half-filled glass of amber liquid. *At noon?* A suitcase lay open and packed on the bed; George must have been planning an immediate flight after their meeting.

"Actually, I'm right on time," she said.

"You got the money?"

She nodded and dropped a heavy bag on the floor at her feet. "But first I want some answers."

He immediately went on red alert. "Like what?"

"Like an address and phone number where I can make contact with my daughter." She put up a halting hand as he began to protest. "I'm not looking to retaliate for the money I'm giving you, but I want to meet with Sar—I mean, Andrea, if she's willing."

"And if she's not willing? I know for a fact she never went on one of them Internet sites where adopted kids search for their parents. How interested could she be?"

"I don't care. I want to communicate with her, either by phone or mail. At the very least, I want her to know that I tried."

"A bit late for that."

She remained adamant.

"How 'bout I tell her that her birth mother wants a meeting, and then I'll contact you."

She shook her head. Once the sleazeball left, she might never locate her daughter.

Just then the door swung open, striking the wall, and Luc strolled in like John Wayne in a business suit, all guns blazing. Except that he carried no weapons. They were depending on

Luc's slick tongue, which some courtroom adversaries claimed was a formidable weapon in itself.

"You bitch! You called the cops."

"No, Luc is my lawyer."

"We just want to talk," Luc said. "I've brought some documents for you to sign."

"I'm not signin' nothin'."

"Calm down, man. We'll negotiate a fair deal. Cash for information." Luc walked slowly over to the bureau. "Let me pour myself a drink, and we'll all behave like reasonable people. Grace, do you want a drink, too?"

Me? Whiskey, straight up? No, not at any time of the day, thank you very much. "Sure."

But they both underestimated George. During that second when Luc and Grace were distracted, George rushed for the open doorway, shoving Grace to the floor and grabbing the purse with his other hand.

Luc was out of the room before she was, but George had already got into the elevator, and Luc was running down the stairway, with Grace in hot pursuit. When they emerged in the lobby, George was at the other end, heading for the revolving door.

Just then, Tante Lulu stood with a—*oh, my God!*—pistol in her hand, and yelled, "George?"

Surprised, George hesitated, and Tante Lulu fired the weapon, missing George and wiping out a wooden Native American that stood in front of a Houma Indian craft store among other lobby shops. In the melee that followed, George tripped, dropped the loot bag, and took off running down the street. They were unable to catch him.

Grace would have laughed if she wasn't so sad over this lost opportunity. In fact, while the police were talking to Luc and Tante Lulu, she began to bawl, something she did way too much lately. The words *blackmail* and *assault* were being bandied about, even though Luc kept saying they didn't want to press charges. As for Tante Lulu firing a pistol in a public place, the old lady was already on Luc's cell phone to one of her cronies in high places.

Grace tried to pull herself together and was wiping her eyes with a tissue. They might be able to salvage this whole fiasco if there was some information in the suitcase George had left behind in his hotel room. She turned, about to do just that before the police swept the room.

And there stood Angel, staring at her with confusion...and hurt. "Grace?"

"What are you doing here, Angel?" She couldn't keep the panic from her voice.

"What's going on?" He looked at her, then at Luc, Tante Lulu, the police, the strident hotel staff, and curious onlookers.

"Nothing. Please go away."

"Who was that guy running away?"

"Nobody. I mean it, Angel, go away."

"I heard the police say something about blackmail. Surely...Grace! Is someone blackmailing *you?*"

"Don't be silly."

"What's silly to me is everyone up and down the bayou knows what this big fuckin' secret of yours is, but not me. Why is that, Grace?"

"That's not true. The only ones who know are Tante Lulu and Luc." Immediately, she realized her mistake. "I mean...there is no *big* secret."

"Bullshit!" He narrowed his eyes at her. "This has something to do with why you can't get married and have kids, doesn't it?"

She would have tried to deny his claim, but a blush betrayed her.

"Damn!" he said and punched his fist into a column beside him, which caused the police to look their way. "Why can't you trust me, Grace?"

She wanted to examine his grazed knuckles but knew he wouldn't let her. "It's not a question of trust."

"Yeah, it is. And I'll tell you this, babe, if anything convinced me that I don't stand a shot in hell with you, this is it. Forget about love. You don't even respect me."

"Not true! But this is not the time for this discussion."

"When *is* the time?"

She had no answer.

He shook his head with hopelessness. "I've never been bullet-proof where you're concerned, Grace, but I'll be damned if I continue to be your bullet-riddled target anymore."

With a grunt of disgust, he turned and walked away.

～

The Hitchhiker's Guide to the Galaxy...*uh, bayou...*

LENA WAS SITTING in the yard behind Grace's cottage helping Ella tie long strings on the balloons that Lionel and Miles were inflating with a helium tank on the back porch. They would be part of the decorations for the big housewarming party at their new home tomorrow night.

Hard to believe how much had happened to them in the past month or so. Tante Lulu and her family and friends had been like angels sent by God to help them while she was ill and recovering. Not only were she and her family to have a new home, but a trust fund had been set up to support them until they all, even she, had completed college. In addition, papers were being filed to give her full guardianship over her siblings, which should get CPS off their backs for good. She was still stunned by it all.

Grace came out with a tray and placed it on a picnic table. "I've set out lunch for you guys. If you need me, you have my cell number. I need to take Tante Lulu to the grocery store. We should be back in an hour." She turned to Lionel then. "We're going to visit some of Tante Lulu's *traiteur* clients this afternoon if you're interested in coming along."

"Yeah. Sure. Hope she smokes a baby again."

To show how accustomed they were becoming to the old lady's weird ways, none of them even questioned Lionel's outrageous statement.

After Grace was gone and she heard her car drive away, Lena put a CD on the portable player, and they all listened in an almost prayerlike fashion to their mother and father singing "Devil Blues," followed by "Stormy Monday," "Baby, Please Don't Go," and "Hard Luck Blues." A series of Bessie Smith hits came next, including those old standbys " 'Taint Nobody's Bizness if I Do" and "Nobody Knows You When You're Down and Out." They all knew these homemade CDs by heart, and, although Lena had no great musical talents, she was thinking about studying music history in college. So maybe her parents had passed something on to her.

Lena glanced up from her balloon stringing, then did a double take. A young girl, about her age, was standing on the road in front of the cottage. With long red hair pulled back into a ponytail, she wore a black Atlanta Braves T-shirt and shorts leading down long legs to athletic shoes with no socks. She carried a worn purple backpack.

Although they'd been warned not to talk to strangers, this girl looked harmless. Lost, actually. The odd thing was, there was no car or bike. How had she gotten here?

Standing, Lena cautioned with a motion of her hand for the others to stay put. Walking around the house, she asked, "Can I help you?"

"Is this where Grace O'Brien lives?"

Lena nodded. "But she's not here right now."

The girl nodded back, studying the place. "It's pretty here."

It was pretty, Lena had to admit, with all the pink roses climbing up the sides of the cottage, but it had been a tight squeeze these many weeks with all of them inside and only one bathroom.

"Do you wanna come back and have some lunch with us...while you wait?"

The girl licked her dry lips. She looked hot and sweaty, but then, everyone got hot and sweaty in this humidity. Still, she must be thirsty.

Without waiting for an answer, Lena turned to walk back around the house.

The girl followed.

"I'm Lena Duval. This is my sister, Ella, and my brothers, Lionel and Miles." She arched her brows at the girl, who was shifting her weight from hip to hip.

"I'm Andrea Fletcher."

"C'mon. We were just about to eat."

"Where you from?" Lionel asked as they each loaded up with homemade po' boy sandwiches and potato salad, accompanied by frosty glasses of the sweet tea.

Andrea, who had been eating ravenously, wiped her mouth with a St. Jude paper napkin and replied, "Atlanta."

"How'd you get here?" Miles wanted to know.

"Flew in to New Orleans, took a bus to Houma, and then hitched a ride out here."

"Hitchhiking is dangerous, isn't it?" Lena would never hitchhike herself. That was just asking for trouble.

Andrea shrugged. "Seems everyone in Houma knows who Tante Lulu is."

"You'll understand that when you meet her." Lena refilled all their glasses from the big St. Jude pitcher.

"She's crazy," Ella said.

"Ella!" Lena told Andrea, "Tante Lulu is a little eccentric, but she's been very kind to us. So has Grace."

"They built us a house. That's more than kind," Lionel pointed out. "We're moving in there tomorrow."

"And they're payin' fer all of us ta go to college someday," Miles added.

Andrea's jaw dropped open, before tears welled in her eyes. "Grace O'Brien is paying for a house and *college* for four people."

"Well, not just Grace. Mostly the LeDeux family," Lena explained, "but I guess Grace is like an honorary member of that family."

"Are they rich?" Dubious, Andrea gazed at Grace's cottage and Tante Lulu's next door.

"Oh, yeah," Lionel said. "Don't judge them by the way they live. They're loaded, all right."

Lena smacked Lionel on the arm. "It's not nice to say that."

"Well, it's true," Ella backed up her brother. "Grace used to be a nun, she tol' me so, but then she became some kind of world poker champion, then a treasure hunter. So she must be rich."

"A nun and a...a poker player?" Andrea was clearly stunned. Who wouldn't be?

Still Lena couldn't let Ella get away with that kind of gossip. "I swear, Ella, your tongue must have a motor on it. Some things are meant to be private."

Ella ducked her head sheepishly.

Andrea swiped at the tears that continued to brim her green eyes and lifted her chin pridefully.

The tears puzzled Lena, but she wasn't sure how to ask what they meant.

"So, are you all Grace's children? Adopted children, I mean."

"Nope. Not even foster children," Lena informed her.

"Grace has just been letting us stay with her while our trailer was torn down and a new house built. Our parents are dead. It's a long story."

"What are all these statues around the yard?"

"St. Jude. Tante Lulu's favorite saint." Lena laughed, surveying the St. Jude shrine, surrounded by a circle of flowers, the St. Jude birdbath, and the St. Jude wind chimes. "He's the patron saint of hopeless cases."

"Hmpfh! I could use a pigload of those. What's with all the balloons and crepe paper?"

"We're making decorations for the big housewarming party tomorrow night," Lionel said. "Wanna come? Our house is at the other end of Bayou Black, about ten miles away, on Live Oak Lane."

"I don't know. Maybe." Andrea's expression was really sad, Lena realized, and she wasn't sure what to do about it. She wished Grace or Tante Lulu would hurry home.

"Can I use your bathroom?" Andrea asked suddenly.

"Sure. You can't miss it. The left door off the living room. You'll probably find Ella's Hannah Montana pj's on the floor."

"Are not!" Ella protested. "I put them in the hamper."

"For once," Lena commented.

After Andrea entered the house, taking her backpack with her, they all turned to Lena with questioning eyes. "Who *is* she?" Lionel wanted to know.

"She asked a lot of questions about Grace," Miles said.

"She kinda looks like Grace," Ella remarked.

They all went silent at that last observation, then turned as one to stare at the house where Andrea had gone. Could it be?

CHAPTER 15

The long-lost daughter wasn't lost anymore...

$\mathcal{A}$ ndrea could barely restrain herself from sitting on the edge of the bathtub and bawling her eyes out, but she knew that once she started she wouldn't be able to stop.

When she'd arrived in New Orleans yesterday, she'd worried that she might run into her stepfather. Luckily, she hadn't. He was probably already here knee-deep in his blackmail attempt. What a scuzzball! Why couldn't her mother see what a creep he really was? Well, she would be out of their home soon, for good, although she had no idea where she would be living or what she would be doing.

After washing the tears from her face, she left the bathroom and glanced through the window to see the Duvals still out in the back yard, which gave her the opportunity to snoop a bit. There were only three tiny bedrooms. She was interested in the one that must be Grace's.

She immediately homed in on the bureau, where a number of framed photographs were displayed. One of those showed Grace with a handsome, dark-haired man, their arms looped around each other's waists. Was it her boyfriend? *Oh, God! Could it be my father?* Another photo showed Grace with a trophy, smiling at the camera, with a banner behind her reading "World Texas Hold 'Em Poker Championship." In yet another photo, Grace wore a nun's habit. Everything the kids outside had told her must be true. Then there was a picture with a gang of people, including Grace and the dark-haired man, standing in front of a pile of gold. Beside the photo was a framed newspaper article about a Jinx, Inc., treasure-hunting team finding pirate coins right here in Bayou Black last year.

So, that was probably the reason why her mother had given her away. A baby had been disposable in this woman's full life. Still, how could she?

My own mother gave me away, and yet she's helping to give four strangers not just a new home, but college educations. And here I don't even have enough money to go to community college.

It hurt. No doubt about it, Andrea was hurt. Deeply. She wanted to confront the woman who had given her life and tell her what she thought of her. She wanted to hurt her in return...almost eighteen years of hurt.

How best to do that?

Maybe she should show up at that party tomorrow night and humiliate her in front of all her friends? Yeah, that would be good. Let her feel what it was like to ache so bad you just wanted to curl up in a ball and die.

Then she could get on with her own life.

Alone.

But not hopeless. She wouldn't let her life be hopeless. Somehow she would work her way through college and prove she didn't need a mother who had never wanted her.

Just then, the sound of adult voices came from the back yard. Oh, no! Andrea wasn't ready to confront Grace yet, not in light of all she'd just learned. She had to get out of here. There was a campground about a mile back that she should be able to afford for one night. Yeah, that's what she would do. Wait 'til the party tomorrow night. Make a big splash, then head out of Dodge for parts unknown.

She grabbed her backpack and was sneaking through the front door when she heard Lena call from the back porch, "Andrea, Tante Lulu and Grace are back. Come out and meet them."

A surprised and confused Lena entered the house and searched each room, soon realizing that Andrea was gone.

∾

She loves him, she loves him not, she loves him, she...

"Do you think it was my daughter?"

Grace was sitting out on her back porch later that night after everyone else had gone to bed. Apparently, the old lady had trouble sleeping, too; so, seeing her light on, she'd come over to chat, bringing a bottle of her dandelion wine with her.

"Prob'ly. Didja check the bus station in Houma?"

"Yes. And every other place I could think of." After they'd got home this afternoon, and Lena had relayed the story about the red-haired stranger arriving unexpectedly, Grace had suspected it might be Andrea. And it broke her heart to think the girl had needed to come searching for her, and not vice versa. And it scared her to death to think of where she might be wandering on her own out there tonight.

Ever since the disastrous meeting with George two days ago, Grace had hired a PI friend of John LeDeux to investigate a George Smith from Atlanta. And now she also had him looking for Andrea.

"What a mess!" Grace said on a sigh. "I've dug myself into such a hole, I don't think I'll ever get out."

"Well, now, honey, there's a rule of thumb about holes."

"Oh?"

"When yer in one, stop diggin'."

"What does that mean?"

"It means that all this started with lies and secrets. Ya gotta undo that mess first."

"You mean tell Angel."

"Thass a start. Even if ya have no desire ta wed up with him, he deserves ta know the truth."

"If you could have seen his face that day at the hotel—he was so hurt. I've tried to call him at least a dozen times since then, but all I get is voice mail."

"What do ya really want, Grace? It ain't fair ta go cozyin' up ta Angel again iffen ya doan plan on marryin' him."

"I haven't thought that far ahead."

"Do ya love the boy?"

"I don't know. All I know is I ache over the hurt I've caused him, and...and I do miss him."

"How's the sex?"

"Tante Lulu!"

"What? Ya think I doan know nothin' 'bout hanky-panky?"

"I'd rather not talk about it."

"That good, huh?"

She had to smile at the old lady's persistence.

"Ain't it 'bout time ya stopped bein' such a scaredy-cat?"

It was true. Her whole life had been based on guilt and the fear of discovery. She still felt guilty, especially since she might have to explain herself to the child she'd left so cavalierly. And she was embarrassed, if not fearful, of what people—especially Angel— would think of her now. "Will Angel be at the party tomorrow night?"

"Prob'ly, but that sure is waitin' 'til the horse has left the barn, sweetie. His plane is leavin' from N'awleans at nine a.m. on Saturday."

"It's hopeless, isn't it?"

Tante Lulu chuckled. "Ya came ta the right place with that question." She pointed to the yard.

Thanks to a full moon, one particular star seemed to radiate in a straight line down to the St. Jude mini-shrine.

As a sign of her disintegrating mind, she could swear the statue winked at her. Accompanied by freakin' celestial music.

It was probably just a blink of the starlight and some frogs ribetting.

I beg your pardon!

~

Thunder on the bayou...uh-oh!...

ANGEL WASN'T GOING to the party. There was only so much battering of the heart that one guy could stand.

In fact, he had this image of himself as the donkey at this affair —more exactly, the donkey's ass—and all these tails being pinned on him. Each of those were the many slings and arrows tossed his way by Grace.

Feeling sorry for thyself, my son?

Oh, shut up!

Is that any way to talk to God?

I thought you were St. Jude.

Is that any way to talk to St. Jude?

I give up!

Are you perchance...hopeless?

"I'm out of here, and just in time," he muttered aloud, "before I go totally bonkers. I wonder if anyone has ever been committed for St. Jude Syndrome."

Tsk, tsk, tsk!

"Or Tante Lulu-itis?"

She's a saint, you know.

Oh, good Lord! Angel would have put his hands over his ears—

187

as if that would do any good!—if they weren't needed on the steering wheel.

His bags were packed and in the back seat of the pickup, his flight booked for tomorrow morning, all loose ends tied up with the Duval house project, and he had an appointment with Ronnie at the Jinx offices on Monday. As for the LeDeux gang, good-byes weren't his style, and he sure wasn't looking for thanks.

He probably could have uncovered Grace's big honkin' secret by pumping one of the LeDeuxs, but he'd be damned if he'd pursue her anymore. What was the point? Still, he'd been stunned that she could confide in others and not him. Even if she didn't love him, he'd thought she trusted him.

It was still daylight, and nothing of interest was on the TV, so he'd decided to clear out of the houseboat early.

Maybe he'd go over to the Swamp Tavern and have a beer before getting a room near the airport in New Orleans.

Cruising down the rural two-lane road, he noticed a back-pack-carrying young girl hitchhiking. Was that stupid, or what? Girls today should know better. Didn't she watch any of the crime shows on the tube?

He glanced her way as he approached, her red ponytail catching the late-day sun. Then he did a double take as he passed.

"Oh. My. God!" He slammed on the brakes and pulled over to the side of the road. Turning in his seat to look through the rear window, he saw the girl approaching. She must think he had stopped to pick her up.

The girl was Grace, except younger, probably still a teenager. The red hair was longer, the green eyes a little darker, about three inches taller, but he would bet his left nut that this doppelganger was Grace's sister.

No, no, no! That's not it.

It's Grace's daughter.

Holy shit!

So this is the big secret.

But how could it be? At closer range, he could see that she was over sixteen, and Grace was almost thirty-five. When she gave birth, she would have had to be only fifteen or sixteen, at most, he swiftly calculated in his head. "Oh. My. God!" he muttered again.

As the girl opened the passenger door, she inquired, "Hi! You goin' anywhere near Live Oak Lane? It's at the other end of Bayou Black, I think."

The Duval house. He inhaled and exhaled several times before he said, "Sure. Hop in. You goin' to the party?"

"Um, sorta."

Sorta? Okaaay! Once she closed her door and snuggled as far away from him as she could, he put the truck in gear and drove on.

"How'd you know about the party?" Even her voice was Grace-husky.

"Honey, down the bayou everyone knows everyone's business."

"You're not from around here, are you?"

"Nope. Mostly New Jersey, but I move around a lot. You?"

"Atlanta. But I sorta expect to move around a lot now, too."

He didn't bother to probe further about that enigmatic response; she probably wouldn't tell him, anyway. In the ensuing silence, he kept glancing her way, repeatedly. The resemblance to Grace was uncanny.

Was this how Grace looked in pre-nun days?

Was this why she became a nun?

Was this why she was so screwed up emotionally?

No, no, no, I am not belly-smacking into that pool again. Ill drop the girl off at the end of the lane and get the hell out of stinkin' Louisiana as soon as possible. Maybe I can even get a standby flight tonight.

"I'm Angel Sabato. What's your name?"

She hesitated, then said, "Andrea Fletcher."

"How old are you?"

"Why?"

Good Lord, she probably thought he was fishing to know whether she was jailbait or not. "Just making conversation."

"Almost eighteen."

He smiled at that. As if almost eighteen was tons better than seventeen! "You been in Louisiana long?"

She shook her head. "Just two days."

"Staying long?"

She shook her head again.

He pulled into the parking lot of a Kluck-Kluck Chicken Palace, turned off the motor, and stared at her.

"What?" The girl had one hand on the door handle, ready to bolt.

"Let's cut to the chase here, sweetheart. You're Grace's daughter, aren't you?"

Instead of acknowledging his observation, she did the damnedest thing. She burst out crying, and he found himself with a teenage version of Grace in his arms, comforting her with pats on the back and stupid-ass promises of, "Now, now, everything will be all right," while she blubbered out incoherent stuff about George, blackmail, adoption, a bitch mother, betrayal, an unwanted baby, stepfather, Daddy dying, trust fund, and college for the Duvals.

An hour later, he was at a mom-and-pop motel in Houma, registering for two rooms with a connecting door. When the owners gave him a disgusted look, probably figuring he was getting it on with a child, he gave them a black look right back, one that put them in the category of dirty old geezers.

He told Andrea to stay put, gave her a couple of twenties to order pizza, and assured her that everything would be resolved in the morning, when he would bring her birth mother to meet her. Andrea would either vent her spleen or be reunited with her mother.

Andrea had a ton of questions to ask about Grace, most of them negative. He didn't have a lot of answers because, sadly, he was finding he didn't know Grace as well as he'd thought. In fact, not at all.

Personally, he had a spleen to vent with Grace, too.

Someone should have paddled her ass a long time ago. And he didn't mean that in a sexual way. Or not hardly.

But whoo-boy, Grace was going to be pissed that he was involved. Good! He lived to piss her off.

Andrea suddenly gave his face intense scrutiny. "Are you Grace's boyfriend?"

"Why would you ask that?"

"I saw your picture in her bedroom, and you two were looking at each other like...well, you know."

At one time, Angel would have been pathetically happy to know Grace kept his picture in her bedroom. Not anymore. His hopes had been shot down, stamped on, and buried.

Surprisingly, the sun hadn't set yet when he was again back on the highway. A road he hadn't ever expected to travel again. And he wondered how he'd managed, once again, to get himself involved in what they used to call in the navy a SNAFU. Situation Normal, All Fucked Up.

Royally, he added.

He heard thunder in the distance and a bolt of summer lightning crossed the sky. He was pretty sure it was an omen.

~

Even Angels have bad moods...

EMOTIONS WERE BANGING off the wall this evening, Grace's, most of all. In fact, her fragile nerves were close to breaking.

There was no word yet on the location of George Smith.

Her daughter hadn't shown her face again. Anywhere.

Police Lieutenant Clifford "Tank" Woodrow, a friend of John LeDeux, was hitting on her. Bigtime.

SANDRA HILL

Angel hadn't come to the party. MIA.

She was seriously considering a return to the convent. Well, not seriously, but life had definitely been more calm and uncomplicated back there.

On a happy note, the scene when Grace, Tante Lulu, and Samantha Starr had arrived earlier to show the Duval children for the first time their new house had been touching beyond belief. They kept weeping and screaming for joy at every little thing they discovered. The sunny yellow paint in Lena's small bedroom, the Hannah Montana curtains in Ella's equally small bedroom, the two desks complete with new PCs in the large bedroom shared by Lionel and Miles, the shower stall *and* tub in one of the two bathrooms, along with a supply of bubble-bath products. Then there was the furniture. And St. Jude canisters. And a satellite dish.

Dusk was coming quickly over the bayou. The sumptuous Cajun dinner was over, though snacks were still out, and drinks flowed, both alcoholic and nonalcoholic. Few people had left, all basking in the joy of a job well done. Some were dancing to the rowdy Cajun music in the living room and out on the deck that wrapped around three sides of the house. Occasionally, Ella, dressed to the hilt in Hannah Montana attire, would manage to sneak in a Miley Cyrus song. And Lionel, with all his piercings, was especially attractive to the young ladies present. Even Miles was coming out of his shell, as he smiled and was more talkative than usual. Especially heartening was to see Lena engaged as a girl her age should be in a little flirtation with Andy LeDeux, the young New Orleans Saints football player. Right now a fast rhythmic song about a Cajun guy being in the doghouse was playing, and every time the music came to the stanza, "Knock, knock, knock, let me come in," everyone sang along.

A crowd was forming around John LeDeux, who was dirty dancing around his seemingly uptight wife Celine, trying to get her to dance with him. "C'mon, *chère*," he coaxed in an exaggerated Dennis Quaid *Big Easy* fashion, "show me your moves. You know which ones, darlin'. Oh, yeah!" The funny thing was that their son, Etienne, was dancing around both of them, and he wasn't half bad.

"That little one, he is gonna be wild when he grows up, jist like his daddy," Tante Lulu predicted. She had come over to stand next to Grace, wearing her *fais do do* outfit, which, in her case, was a square-dancing dress, with big crinolines. On her feet were flat ballet slippers. On her head, which came up only to Grace's shoulder, was a mass of blonde Shirley Temple curls, tied with a band of pink ribbon and a bow on top. A Lawrence Welk dancing hobbit.

"Angel should be here," Tante Lulu said.

"Are you blaming me?"

"If the thong fits."

"I can't believe you said that."

"Word's gonna come out soon 'bout Andrea, sure as God made little St. Jude statues. I jist doan see why ya couldn't tell the boy yerself."

"Maybe because he would judge me and deem me an unfit female and mother."

"You doan know that."

"I certainly judge myself by those criteria. But, really, I have too much going on right now...too many crises looming to even think about a relationship."

"Since when does love wait fer the right time? When the thunderbolt—"

"Who said anything about love?"

Tante Lulu gave her one of her looks, the one that said you couldn't fool her. "Sweetie, yer like Job with all the problems of the world weighin' ya down. That wall 'round you gots ta come down. Too late fer Angel, I 'spect, but mebbe there's other apples in yer orchard."

All those misplaced metaphors were enough to make Grace

dizzy. And even though Grace knew it was too late for Angel, she didn't like anyone else saying so.

Tante Lulu was looking over Grace's shoulder and smiling.

Half turning, Grace saw the six-foot-plus Tank looming.

"I'm juicy," he said. "You could just call me Delicious...or McIntosh."

"Oh, good grief!" He was referring to Tante Lulu's orchard remark. "Do you ever give up?" she laughed.

"And thick-skinned. You can climb my *tree* any time you want, sweetheart. Wanna dance?"

"No," she said.

"Yes," Tante Lulu answered for her at the same time. "Show her how ta booger, Tank, Cajun-style." Then she walked off—to harass someone else, no doubt.

"She means boogie," Grace said.

"I figured." He smiled down at her.

"Are you Cajun?"

"Honorary. C'mon, they've slowed the music down. We won't have to make fools of ourselves."

So, Grace found herself dancing with the handsome cop. Not as handsome as Angel, of course. Still, maybe he could take her mind off the mess that had become her life.

"Is it true that you used to be a nun?"

That again! Grace rolled her eyes. "Yes. A long time ago."

"I used to be a priest."

At first she just stared at him, slack-jawed. Then she laughed. "Nice try!"

"Hey, can't blame a guy for throwing a pitch."

"Some game! What is it with men and this sex-with-a-nun fixation?"

"Good girl on the outside, bad girl on the inside. Ultimate male fantasy!"

"Not mine!"

He put both arms around her waist and tugged her closer,

forcing her to link her hands behind his neck. "So what are your fantasies?" he purred into her ear, at the same time lowering his hands to her butt and pressing her even closer. She felt every button on his shirt, his belt buckle, and something down lower.

"Not *that* fantasy," she told him, grabbing his arms and pulling upward to remove his hands from forbidden territory.

"You still hung up on that Angel dude?"

"I'm not hung up on anyone," she lied. "How about you? You hung up on anybody?"

"Nah, I'm just hung. Oh, that was bad. Sorry."

She shook her head at his crudity, then had to move his hands off her butt again.

"Uh-oh!"

"What?"

"I smell a halo burning."

"I'm no angel," Grace protested.

"Yeah, but he is."

Grace turned in Tank's arms, and, yep, there stood Angel in the doorway, staring at her behind, then raising his eyes, glaring like she was a world-class slut—Bathsheba tempting David in the temple.

Without preamble, he walked up and told Tank, "Get your frickin' hands off her ass."

Then he pointed an angry finger at Grace. "Get your flirty ass in the kitchen. I have something to tell you."

Flirty ass? Grace was too shocked to speak.

"That is one badass angel," Tank said.

"Tell me about it."

CHAPTER 16

When Grace takes a dive, beware the big splash...

Grace didn't immediately follow Angel into the kitchen, which was a good thing. In his present mood, he might very well have throttled her.

Everyone kept coming up to him, handing him a beer, shaking his hand, expressing thanks for his stopping by, congratulating him on a job well done with the house. No one mentioned his leaving the state, avoiding it like the big white elephant in the middle of the room. Except Tante Lulu.

"Still runnin' away t'morrow?"

He had a hard time not gaping at her attire. Beverly Hillbillies meets the Little People. "I'm not running. I'm just—" He stopped himself. There was no point in arguing with the old fossil.

"She loves you, y'know."

"She has a strange way of showin' it. Anyhow, I'm way beyond that."

"Pfff!"

"Sometimes a guy just needs to fish or cut bait. My fishing days with Grace are over."

"Here comes yer trout now." Tante Lulu chuckled as Grace approached. "Doan she look pretty in that yellow sundress with the white polka dots? Sorta like a red-haired speckled pup."

Not exactly the way he would describe her, since her outfit was strapless, with built-in cups on top and a wide belt cinching the waist, leading to a full, swishy above-knee-length skirt.

"I don't appreciate you giving me freakin' orders," Grace said right off.

"I don't appreciate the frickin' way you've messed up my life," Angel said right off.

"And I don't appreciate yer language, either one of y'all," Tante Lulu said.

"Me? What *I've* done?" Grace squawked as his words sank in.

He grabbed her by the forearm and hauled her into the laundry room, just off the kitchen, slamming the door behind him, leaving behind a disgruntled Tante Lulu, who would have loved to be a third party to their argument.

"Are you insane?" Grace yanked her arm out of his grasp and smacked him on the shoulder to emphasize her irritation.

Propping her against the opposite wall in the small room, he tried to tamp down his temper. "I must be insane to be wasting my time on you."

"Who asked you to? I thought you'd be off to wider horizons by now, marrying another stewardess."

He couldn't help but grin. "They don't call them stewardesses anymore. That's considered sexist. They're flight attendants. Besides, I'm aiming for a model this time. Or an actress."

"Oh? And is the only criterion an empty head?"

"As long as she's not a redhead."

She inhaled and exhaled several times. "What's your problem, anyway? Why did you come back?"

"For you."

She gasped and went into her stiff-as-a-poker, I-told-you-I-don't-love-you demeanor.

SANDRA HILL

"Not for *that*, Grace. If you really want to know, I came here baited for bear, *red-haired bear*; truth be told, after spending half the day with your daughter, only to find you sucking tonsils with some Cajun boy toy."

"More like man toy," she goaded him.

"Believe me, babe, you do not want to goad me today."

"And I was not sucking—" Her eyes went wide and she put a hand over her cups...uh, heart, as understanding seeped in. Then she moaned. "You know about my daughter?"

The tears welling in her eyes made them look like deep green pools seen through a hazy fog. And her lips were quivering.

He refused to be swayed from his fury. "Yeah, imagine that! Now I'm not the only one this side of the Mason-Dixon Line left in the dark. Your big fat hairy secret is out, sweetheart."

"I never meant to exclude you. I just—"

"Save it, Grace. I'm not interested in your lame excuses. The only reason I'm here is to arrange for you to meet your daughter. Then I'm out of here, for good."

"Andrea wants to meet me?"

"Yeah, but don't go getting all warm and fuzzy. She probably wants to tell you what a lousy excuse for a mother you are."

Grace winced. "Did she say that?"

"Pretty much. As far as she's concerned, you gave her away because you couldn't be bothered and haven't had a second thought since. In fact, you would have had an abortion, except you waited too long. Furthermore, she was told that you were a slut who had slept with so many boys you didn't know who the father was. Does wild teenager ring a bell with you?"

Grace inhaled sharply. "Oh, my God!" Then she inhaled sharply again. "Do you believe that?"

"I don't know what to believe anymore."

She held herself tightly with arms folded over her chest and rocked back and forth in distress.

There was a knock on the door. If it was Tante Lulu, he might very well pop her into the dryer and turn on the spin cycle. Knock a little sense into the interfering lady.

But it wasn't Tante Lulu. John popped his head in. "Angel?"

"Not now, LeDeux."

"Sorry to interrupt," John said, clearly not sorry at all if the grin on his face was any indication.

"I mean it, LeDeux. Get lost."

"I've gotta leave, but Luc asked me to give you something before he went home. I probably won't see you again before you head back to Jersey tomorrow." Digging in his pocket, he pulled out some playing cards, five of them, which he fanned out. A queen-high full house, three queens and two tens.

"What the hell? Why would Luc give me these? And why now?"

John shrugged. "He said you would understand."

Grace made a small sound of distress behind him. He turned to look at her and saw her staring, red-faced, at the cards he held. Where a few minutes ago her expressive face had reflected the pain of her daughter's opinion of her, now she was mortally embarrassed.

Why? He turned to LeDeux again for answers.

"Yankee men are so thick, I swear y'all could take lessons from southern men. Especially us Cajuns. Do you need a thunderbolt to open yer closed mind, *cher?*" On those words, he had the good sense to leave before Angel belted him a good one.

And suddenly Angel saw the light. Slowly, he turned his attention back to Grace, who would have bolted if he wasn't closest to the door.

"Grace?"

She refused to look at him.

He walked over and tipped her chin up so that he could see her reaction to the question humming in his brain. "Call me crazy, but was this your final hand in the poker tournament?"

"Don't be silly."

She was lying. The blush on her face and the nervous fluttering of her fingers gave her away.

Okay, these were the facts occurring to him like dominoes flipping over:

—Grace claimed not to be in love with him.

—Grace had kept the news about her daughter a secret from him.

—Even if they were only friends, lack of trust was a relationship killer.

—Grace, who had always been the soul of honesty when it came to card playing, had deliberately taken a dive in the poker game with him.

—Grace had a daughter.

On the other hand:

—Grace had deliberately *chosen* to make love with him. How amazing was that?

—Grace had not wanted him to find out.

—Grace must have strong feelings for him, maybe even...

—Grace had a daughter.

What does it mean?

His emotions had reached critical mass. Hurt, anger, disappointment, wounded pride, but also hope, and, maybe, still love. Or maybe not.

But all he could say was, "Grace, you are going to be the death of me yet."

Bless me, Father...uh, Angel...for I have sinned...

Warily, Grace walked around Angel's motel room.

Warily because Angel now knew her secret—well, most of it—and already he seemed to be judging her and finding her wanting. Wary because there was only one double bed, which posed some interesting possibilities. And wary because on the other side of the wall was her daughter, sound asleep now but capable of awakening at any moment.

Grace was not prepared for any of those events.

"The bathroom's all yours," Angel said. He had one towel wrapped around his waist and was using another to towel-dry his hair. The scent of fragrant soap, or shampoo, filled the air. And his belly button drew her eye like an erotic magnet.

"I don't have anything to sleep in," she croaked, not about to bring up the sleeping accommodations. Let him be the one to decide.

He rooted in a rolling duffel bag and pulled out a light blue Jinx, Inc. T-shirt. Despite its extra-large size, it would probably only hit the top of her thighs. Oh, well.

"First, can I...can I see her?" Angel had already informed her that Andrea was expecting to meet her for the first time in the morning.

"She might wake up. Are you prepared to talk tonight?"

She shook her head, but then she persisted, "I'll be real quiet, and I won't turn on a light, other than the one in this room."

He hesitated, then opened the door, stepping back so that she could go through.

Grace's heart was beating so fast she could scarcely breathe. Andrea's hair was red, like hers, but long, probably down to her shoulders, and no frizzy curls, thank you, God! Wearing an Atlanta Falcons football jersey with nylon boxers, Andrea was lying on her back with her arms thrown over her head. The covers had been tossed off.

"She's beautiful," Grace whispered.

Angel walked up on silent bare feet to stand beside her and nodded. "She looks like you, only a little taller."

"And thinner," she observed.

He chuckled under his breath. "She even snores like you."

"I do not snore," she protested as he prodded her back to the other room with a hand at the small of her back. "Yeah, you do, but it's more a snuffle than a snore."

"We know each other too well."

"Ain't that the sorry truth?"

She hadn't meant it as an insult.

Grace took a shower then. A long, contemplative shower until the hot water began to run tepid. Still no answer about what to do, but she felt more calm and resigned to accept what fate would throw her way. She did have the good sense to say a quick prayer to St. Jude to help her.

When she returned to the bedroom, the lights had been turned low. Angel lay on his stomach, facing away. The cover and sheet had been turned back on the other side. He was fast asleep.

She turned the lights out. Except for the stream of light coming from the almost closed bathroom door, the room was in darkness. For a long time, she lay on her back, trying to digest all that had happened to her that day, and what was coming up. No way could she sleep.

"Angel?" she whispered.

There was no answer. At first. Then she heard him sigh, turn his head to her side, and say, "What?"

"Are you asleep?"

"Not now." Angel had hoped to avoid any conversation tonight. His emotions were still too raw.

"Can I tell you something?"

"Do I have a choice?"

"Yes."

"Go ahead, dammit."

"My parents were not nice people."

"Big whoop! Do you think I lived with Mother Teresa?"

"At home, anyway," she continued, ignoring his comment. "At church, at Dad's office—he was an accountant—at Mom's prayer groups, they appeared like normal, caring parents. But I was an embarrassment to them because of their age and I guess because people would know they'd actually had sex at least once. Because they considered me a punishment of sorts from God, they were especially harsh. I can remember being three years old, maybe four, and having to kneel and pray for hours because I didn't eat all my oatmeal. In the end, my father forced the cold glob down my throat 'til I puked. Then he started all over again."

She waited for him to say something, but he didn't. Yeah, her parents were idiots, maybe even cruel idiots, but what did that have to do with now?

"Are you awake?"

"I'm awake." *But I wish I weren't.*

"I wasn't allowed to participate in any after-school activities. Friends never came over, but then, who wanted to associate with a girl who dressed like one of those LDS kids? You know, long plain dress, hair in long braids. I looked like I belonged on *Little House on the Prairie*."

I would have liked to see that. A sexy Laura Ingalls. Hubba hubba! He barely stifled a chuckle. I'm going off the deep end here.

"By the time I was a preteen, I began to rebel. You know the adage—you might as well be hanged for a saint as a sinner. At thirteen and fourteen, I became wild. The harsher the punishment, the more I pushed the bounds of promiscuity. Anything with two legs and a penis was fair game for me."

Okay, I am officially a dog. Because I wish I'd known her then.

"Of course, there were consequences." She couldn't go on, now that she'd come to the real confession.

Angel turned over on his side to stare at her. She was trying her best not to cry. To enforce that self-imposed edict, she bit her bottom lip, painfully.

He reached out and tugged her hand away. When he did, he continued to hold it loosely, reluctantly. "Go on," he urged.

"When I was fifteen, I got pregnant and had an abortion. Anne Marie."

Oh, shit! "You named your fetus?"

"I named my baby."

Oh, that's better. Naming a fetus in the womb.

"The baby I killed."

You were fifteen years old, ferchrissake!

"Anyhow, my parents found out and went ballistic. It was the first time my dad hit me, and he hit me good. Black eyes, cracked lip, welts, contusions. Good thing my mother locked me in my bedroom for two weeks, because school authorities would have been on them like gangbusters for child abuse. They gave me only bread and water during that 'incarceration.' I was allowed to use the toilet but not shower or brush my teeth."

Death-row inmates get treated better than that. Angel reeled with shock and fury at parents who could so mistreat a child, and that's what she'd been, even if she had been fifteen. If they were here now, he didn't think he could restrain himself from giving both of them equal batterings and a few years in jail.

Too choked up to speak, Angel twined his fingers with hers, and his thumb caressed her wrist in a comforting way.

"You'd think I would have learned my lesson, but, no, I got pregnant again. To a different guy, and, contrary to what Andrea's adoptive parents told her, I know who her father was. This time, out of fear, I didn't tell anyone. But, of course, I started to show eventually."

For some reason, Angel's heart ached at the image of a pregnant Grace.

"My parents went ballistic again, but they restrained their violence, barely, and instead sent me away to a Catholic home for unwed teenagers. So, a few days after my sixteenth birthday, I gave birth to a baby girl. Andrea, although to my mind she was Sarah. That's how I've always thought of her, and no matter what anyone believes, I have thought about her often. I never saw her when she was born, and she was adopted out with my parents' consent within hours. I can't say that I protested at the time.

Maybe I just wanted it all to be over." She paused. "So, there you have it."

Grace might be able to control her tears, but he couldn't. Thank God for the near-darkness of the room. He didn't want her to see how deeply he was touched. Anger and hurt warred within him against pity and admiration for her survival skills. "And that's why you entered a convent?"

"Better that than return to my home. God only knows what they would have done to me."

"Okay, so I'm beginning to understand your history, but you have to know, I am very angry with you, Grace."

"I know."

"But my anger has to do with your lack of trust, not with your teenage pregnancy or giving your child up for adoption. Hell, you were little more than a child yourself."

"That's no excuse."

"Self-flagellation accomplishes nothing. Why didn't you ever try to find your child?"

"I didn't deserve that second chance. Plus, I would have had to talk with my parents to initiate the search."

"You haven't talked to them since then?"

"Since I left the convent," she corrected. "That was the death blow for them. I won't tell you what they said to me. It was so vicious. The kind of thing that can never be forgotten."

He could imagine.

But all this was neither here nor there, with regard to him.

Sitting up suddenly, he swung his legs over the side and reached for his jeans. Slipping them and a pair of flip-flops on, he stood and tugged a T-shirt over his head.

Grace jackknifed up in bed and stared at him with incredulity. "What are you doing?"

"Going out."

"Why?"

"I need to walk."

"Why?"

"Did you think telling me all this, at this late date, would make everything all better?"

Her silence told the story.

"I sympathize, Grace. I really do. But I know damn well I'll make love to you if I stay in that bed."

"And making love would be such a bad thing?"

"Yeah, it would. Sexual gratification, sure, but it would only muddy the already muddy waters of you and me—if there ever was or ever will be a you and me."

She winced.

"There are still too many unanswered questions. Like, do you love me? Why did you fake being a loser in the card game? Was your lovemaking the real deal, or more fake crap? Why did you say you would never marry and have kids? Most important, do I even care at this late date?"

"What do you want from me, Angel?"

"I don't know. I honestly don't know anymore. Maybe nothing. I just know that I've been on this roller coaster with you far too long. I jumped the tracks a year ago, I jumped the same tracks yesterday, and I'm not sure I want to get back on."

She looked crushed. And she looked cute, too, with her red hair all mussed up and curly from having climbed into bed with it wet. He refused to be tempted by either. A clear head was in order, and walking was the only thing he could think of that would provide that. Although a barrel of booze held a certain appeal.

"I'm sorry," she whispered as he opened the door and was about to walk out.

Without turning, he told her, "So am I."

And he left.

But a minute later he was back. Stomping over to the bed, he yanked her up 'til she was kneeling on the bed. Then he kissed her, brutally. A harsh, ravaging movement of mouth and teeth and tongue. Demanding and erotically raw. Fortunately, or unfortunately, she returned the kiss with equal fervor.

Then, just as suddenly as he'd begun the kiss, he ended it, shoving her back to a half-reclining position against the pillow. Staring up at him in confusion, she asked, "What was that about?"

"Hell if I know!" His heart was racing so hard he could barely breathe. "Consider it thanks for your dive in the poker game, or punishment for your dive in the poker game. Maybe both."

Then he left again.

CHAPTER 17

When redheads collide...

ﬡ ndrea stood in the park across the road from the motel, watching Grace O'Brien walk toward her.

She was wearing a strapless yellow sundress with white polka dots and high-heeled sandals, probably the same clothes she'd had on at the party last night. Had she slept with Angel last night? Probably. From what her mother had told her about her mother, or hinted, anyway, she was so loose she gave sluts a bad name.

Her red hair, the same color as hers, was a messy mop of lopsided bedhead curls—or did they call it sex head? She wore no makeup, except for lip gloss. Kissed off?

But Andrea had to admit she looked pretty good for being so old. Not at all the way she'd expected her mother would look.

Angel sat on a bench behind her, whispering encouragement, "Go for it, kiddo. She's your mother. You'll like her."

Yeah, right.

Andrea wanted to hate this woman. She'd certainly written her enough unmailed letters over the years telling her just that, but she was finding it hard to hold on to that hatred as Grace got closer. Tears were running down Grace's face, and her lower lip trembled. Thankfully, she stopped several feet in front of her. Andrea didn't think she could handle it if the woman tried to hug her.

"Hello, Andrea."

Andrea just nodded. She tried for a mature, unaffected expression, but it probably came off as just surly.

"I've been wanting to meet you for a long, long time."

"That is so bogus!" Andrea snapped out.

Grace flinched.

"Andrea," Angel chastised behind her.

"Sorry," she said, "but, c'mon, you gave me away, like a doll, or something. An unwanted doll."

"Let's sit down over here," Grace said, motioning to a nearby picnic table.

When they were sitting opposite each other, and Angel had moved to lean against a tree a few yards away, she asked, "Do you even know who my father is?" She was having trouble keeping the contempt out of her voice, despite all of Angel's pep talks last night and this morning about not making assumptions about her mother.

"As a matter of fact, I do. His name is Alexander Pappas. His friends called him Alex. Last I heard he was running his own restaurant in Philly. A Greek restaurant. Your father is Greek. You have his height. He was six-two."

Wow! She'd never thought her father would be Greek. She'd imagined all kinds of scenarios, but never Greek.

Not that there was anything wrong with being Greek. "Were you in love with him?"

"I wish I could say yes, but no. I was only fifteen, and he was a hotshot football player a few years older. Very good-looking."

A football player? A good-looking football player? Wow!

"Does he know about me?"

She shook her head. "But I'll contact him if you want me to."

"No. At least not yet. Do I have, like, half brothers or sisters?"

"I don't know."

She scowled at Grace. She should know that kind of thing, shouldn't she?

"Honey, I haven't seen him in eighteen years."

She didn't like Grace calling her honey; she had no right. "My stepfather is a scumbag."

"I know."

"Oh, God! Did he come here and try to blackmail you?" She was so embarrassed.

"Yes, but he didn't succeed."

"Good. Is he going to jail?"

"No. Unless he does something more."

Andrea let out a breath she hadn't realized she was holding. "It would kill my mother." And just make him more angry.

Grace winced, probably at her calling someone else mother, but what did she expect? As if she had any rights!

"Your mother...did she...does she treat you well?"

Andrea shrugged. "She's so in love with the scumbag that nothing else matters, but she's not mean. Most of the time. And she was lots different when Harald, her first husband, was alive."

"Why did you come to Louisiana, Andrea?"

"I overheard my stepfather talking to Mom about you, and I decided to come and tell you that I hate you, and I don't think much of a mother who gives her kid away, and you must have been a real skank and maybe you still are, and how can you have as much money as my stepfather says you have and I can't even go to college, and—"

Grace reached a hand across the table to take hold of one of hers, but she jerked it away. But not before noticing her neatly trimmed nails, covered with light pink polish...except for the thumb, which was cut to the quick. "You bite your nails," she blurted out.

"But only the thumb," Grace said, with a small smile, noticing Andrea's stubby thumbnail, too.

"It doesn't mean anything," she snarled.

"Of course it doesn't." Grace withdrew her extended hand. "Okay, I respect your right to hate me, but what do you want to do in more general terms? I mean, will you come back to my cottage and stay with me for a while so we can get to know each other?"

"Will Angel be there?"

Grace and Angel exchanged a look that she couldn't interpret.

Grace answered for them both. "Angel has other plans." Her voice sounded kind of choked, but then she cleared it and went on. "He has to leave today for New Jersey, where he has a job."

Angel made a rude sound at her explanation but offered nothing different.

"If not staying here with me, for a visit, is there a college you're interested in...where you've been accepted? Because I'm certainly willing to help you achieve that goal."

"I wouldn't take your money if you...if you paid me."

Grace released a long exhale. "Or would you just rather flay me with insults and go back to your home in Atlanta?"

"I'm *not* going back to Atlanta."

"Where, then?"

Actually, she hadn't planned anything beyond contacting her birth mother.

"Are you two shacking up together?" she asked both of them.

"No, we are not shacking up," Angel answered, "and Grace is right, I'll be catching a flight to Jersey this afternoon, once we've finished here." Just then, his cell phone rang.

She and Grace stared at him, thankful for the break.

"What?" Angel growled into the phone. "Grace? I don't know. Let me ask." He put his hand over the phone. "Grace, where's your cell phone? Apparently, Luc and Tante Lulu have been trying to contact you."

She pulled it out of her purse, then grimaced. "I forgot to recharge it last night. Yikes! Ten missed calls."

Angel was talking on his phone again. "Son of a...gun! How did that happen? Slow down, Lena. What? Oh, crap! Where did they take them? Is Luc on the case? And Tante Lulu? What jail?"

Andrea and Grace were both standing now, sensing Angel's alarm, waiting to hear what he had to say.

Finally, he ended the call and looked at them. "CPS showed up at the Duval house early this morning with a police escort. They took the three younger kids into foster care. Tante Lulu tried to fight them off. When she pulled out a pistol, they arrested her. Didn't matter that the thing wasn't loaded. That incident on top of the one at the Lafayette Hotel cooked her goose. She's in custody."

"What can we do?" Grace asked.

"Let me call Luc first."

While he punched in the number, Grace told Andrea, "Luc LeDeux is a lawyer."

LeDeux, LeDeux, LeDeux, that's all I've heard since I came to Louisiana.

After Angel ended his call, he told them, "Luc is on his way to the courthouse. Apparently, he had already filed guardianship papers for Lena this morning, now that the house is complete, and that's what prompted this SWAT-type swoop down on them. Luc says Lena is a basket case and is alone at the house. Can you go over there, Grace? I need to contact the other family members. He hasn't been able to reach anyone. Apparently, everyone is either hung over or sleeping in from the party."

"Of course, but you'll have to drop me off, since my car is still there."

He nodded. "After you settle Lena down, maybe you can come with me to the courthouse."

"Tante Lulu must be distraught," Grace said, then laughed. "On the other hand, she's probably enjoying the experience."

"You got that right." Angel smiled back at her.

And Andrea realized that, just like that, her grand reunion had turned into a great big bust. Her mother, if you could call her that, cared more about these LeDeux people, who must be nutcases by the sound of it, than she did about her. They didn't even realize at first that she'd stood and walked away.

She was halfway to the road when Grace yelled, "Andrea? Where are you going?"

When she declined to answer, Grace ran after her. Pretty quick, too, considering the grass and her high heels. Grabbing hold of her arm, she stopped Andrea and demanded, "Where are you going?"

"What does it matter to you? You've got your family here."

"Of course you matter to me."

"Angel can't hear you from back there, so you don't have to put on any fake show of motherly love."

"I do love you, Andrea. And furthermore, you're not going anywhere 'til we've settled things between us. You're coming with me."

"Who are you to tell me what to do?"

"Ah, sweetie! I'm your mother."

They were both crying when they got to Angel's truck. And, honest to God, she could swear there were tears in Angel's eyes, too.

~

How many boulders could life put in her path?...

GRACE WAS BEING PULLED in fifty different directions, and she wasn't sure how much emotional drama her nerves could take. At least Angel was sticking around—for a while.

While he was in the kitchen, calling the numerous LeDeux family members, and Samantha and Stanley Starr, too, she sat in the living room with Lena and Andrea. Putting an arm over Lena's shaking shoulders, she tried to comfort her. "Honey, you have to trust that Luc will take care of this. He's a wonderful lawyer."

"But they must be so scared. Especially Miles."

Grace was sure they were. "No harm will come to them, and Luc is working as fast as he can to get a temporary restraining order against CPS. They'll be back with you in no time, pending a court date."

"It's a weekend. The courts aren't open on the weekend, are they?"

Grace had no idea. "I'm sure they convene for emergency situations." The only question was, would some golf-playing or sports-fishing judge be willing to give up an afternoon for what could be postponed until Monday? If Tante Lulu weren't in jail, she'd be calling in dibs from her high-placed friends. Barring that, they might have to work within the system, like regular folks.

"I knew this would happen. I just knew it would. I told everyone that it was better if we laid low in our trailer and didn't call attention to ourselves."

"That couldn't have gone on forever. Besides, you were sick, Lena, and the children are getting older, needing more than you would ever be able to offer. Like college at some point."

She nodded.

"And don't be worrying about Tante Lulu. Believe me, she's probably having the time of her life."

Lena tried to smile. "I appreciate everything you've done for us, Grace. And Tante Lulu, too. She's one crazy old lady, but she's been like a mother to us. You both have."

She could tell that remark didn't go over well with Andrea. "Tante Lulu has been good to us all, honey."

"*Honey,*" she heard Andrea repeat, in a mutter, from across the room.

She raised her eyebrows in question at Andrea, but she just

scowled at her. Apparently any sentiment left from that little weeping session at the park had worn off. She suspected that Andrea resented the attention she was giving to a "stranger" while she had just met up with her daughter for the first time a few hours ago. Grace felt obligated to help Lena, but at the same time perhaps her first concern should be for Andrea. *What to do? What to do?*

"Andrea, *honey*, would you mind sitting here with Lena while I go talk with Angel? You and I have lots to talk about, and I hope you won't begrudge me the time to settle things here first."

Obviously, she did begrudge the time, because she sat, unmoving, in her chair, pouting. "Don't worry about me. You never have before."

"You don't have to stay with me," Lena told Andrea.

Which at least caused Andrea's face to bloom pink with embarrassment as she realized how small-minded she must appear. Getting up, Andrea went over to sit next to Lena and directed Grace, "Go. We don't need you here."

~

The LeDeux Principle: If trouble brews, a LeDeux is probably stirring the pot...

"THIS IS A WORLD-CLASS FUBAR SITUATION," Angel, leaning against the kitchen counter, told Grace as she sat down at the small dinette table. He'd just finished his last call.

"FUBAR?"

"Fucked Up Beyond All Recognition."

"How so? I mean, how so more than usual?"

"Tante Lulu is refusing Luc's efforts to get her out on bail. On some Cajun principle or other. Stanley Starr is at the jail demanding to be incarcerated with Tante Lulu, if they won't drop the charges, which are numerous, by the way. CPS is pissed about

SANDRA HILL

being duped and kept out of the loop where these Duval kids are concerned. The kids' whereabouts at the moment are unknown. There are about two dozen LeDeuxs converging on the courthouse, as I speak. That's just for a start."

"Add to the mix my daughter Andrea coming on to the scene."

"You said it, babe."

"Thank you for sticking around, Angel."

"How could you even think I would skip town at a time like this?" When he'd seen Grace at the Lafayette Hotel, he'd determined to put up this glass wall around himself—a Grace-repellant glass wall—where he would be shielded forevermore from anything to do with their lost cause. The glass wall was still there, but that didn't mean he would abandon her in her time of trouble. As a friend. There was no longer any hope of a future for the two of them.

The voice in his head said, *Oh, you of little faith!*

"I've given you more than enough reason."

"Yeah, you have."

"What should we do?"

"About what? Tante Lulu, the kids, or us?"

"Is there an us?"

"No. I don't know. Hell, no! I'm so damn mad at you." He stared at her for a long moment. She looked crushed. In any other circumstances he would take her in his arms, to offer comfort, as a friend, and she knew it, too. He couldn't do that now. He just couldn't. And, clearly, his lack of action was hurting her. Big deal! He'd been hurt by her a lot, and over a long period of time.

"Is there anything we can do, other than stay here with Lena? I feel so...ineffective."

"Me, too. How 'bout we go visit Tante Lulu, if they'll let us, and see if there's anything she wants us to do? To close up her cottage or whatever."

"Good idea."

"Will Andrea be okay staying here with Lena?"

"Probably. They're both so miserable. They can cry on each other's shoulders. Teenage angst and then some."

"Andrea's strong, just like her mother."

Grace's face brightened. "That's a scary thought. Two Graces." She laughed.

"That's my girl," he said.

"I wish," he thought he heard her say before she went back into the living room to inform the girls of their plans.

If he was smart, he would drop Grace off at the jail and head for the hills. But when had he ever been smart when it came to Grace?

~

She's in the jailhouse now...

"ADD THIS TA THE LIST, Gracie. I need 'bout two dozen of them little plastic St. Jude statues fer us jailbirds here. See if ya kin find one of them orange prison jumpsuits fer me; they dint have any my size here a-tall, can ya beat that? Make sure ya water my vegetable patch, pick a mess of that okra, and give it ta Mr. Boudreaux down at the general store, and set out some Cheez Doodles fer Useless. An' take over more of that salve fer Lester Sonnier's noodle."

Grace was taking notes as fast as she could in the visitor's room at the parish inmate detention center, where Tante Lulu was sitting on the opposite side of one of those bulletproof Plexiglas partitions that separated visitors from the bad guys—or gals. As if Tante Lulu was dangerous to anyone but herself! And, really, how long did she expect to be here?

"Noodle?" Angel mouthed to her. He was standing at the beverage machine, which was eating up his quarters like a coin-eating piranha. At the rate he was going, one soda pop would be costing him ten dollars.

"You don't want to know," she mouthed back.

"Will ya stay with Grace at the Duval house t'night?" she asked Angel. "I doan want any more unexpected visitors worryin' Lena."

Angel hesitated, looked at Grace for a long moment, sighed in resignation, then nodded.

"And Grace, ya need ta buy some clothes and makeup and stuff fer yer little girl. Lena tol' me that all she had was in a backpack. A gal cain't live from a backpack. Or mebbe Charmaine could take her shoppin'."

"No!" Her reply was more vehement than she'd intended, but, really, she didn't want Charmaine dressing her daughter as a bimbo.

"Face it, girlie, Charmaine has better taste than all the wimmen in Loo-zee-anna. She was Miss Loo-zee-anna, after all, even it if was a bit ago."

Like twenty-five years? "I can handle it myself."

"You ain't got time fer nothin' with all yer worries, bless yer heart."

Grace raised her chin with affront. Like she wouldn't know how to take care of her daughter or make time now that she was here. Actually, she had to be honest, with all that was happening, maybe she would have been a bit remiss, without Tante Lulu's reminder.

"Mebbe we should have a welcome party fer the girl. What-daya think? We could do it in both our back yards, combined, iffen we take out the divider hedge."

Take out a twenty-foot hedge? Like that's an easy job! Is she crazy? Oops, stupid question.

"Wait 'til I get outta the slammer. I gots a power chainsaw what kin take down a telephone pole. We kin use it ta take care of the job lickety-split."

Grace exchanged a glance of horror with Angel at the prospect of this ninety-three-year-old dingbat wielding a sharp electric tool.

"And Angel, kin ya go over ta Remy's storage shed and bring out one of them hope chests, the one with yer name on it?"

Angel, who'd finally managed to shake a soda out of the machine and was in the process of lifting a can to his mouth, choked and spurted out Pepsi in five different directions from his mouth and nose.

Grace chuckled. It was a sign of her deteriorating mind that she got her kicks in such a pitiful way.

But then Tante Lulu turned her attention back to her. "And, Gracie, I want ya ta take that box outta the crawl space at my cottage. It has yer name on it."

Angel, who'd finished wiping his face and shirt with a paper napkin, turned a toothy smile on Grace, even as he addressed his question to Tante Lulu. "And what might be in that box?"

"Why, her monogrammed pillowcases and doilies and St. Jude place mats and bride quilt and such. Whatdaja think, honey chile? I was makin' this stuff up a year ago, before you two busted up. Now that yer back t'gether I 'magine we kin get this weddin' on the road again."

Both Grace and Angel dropped their jaws, simultaneously, then clicked them shut with consternation.

"I'm leaving Louisiana as soon as this mess is fixed up," Angel contended.

"And what mess might that be?" Tante Lulu asked him sweetly, but showing a shark-toothed smile.

"Well...well...you know. The Duvals. Grace's kid. You being in jail. All of it."

"Oh, really? Here I was thinkin' ya were stickin' around fer Gracie. Excuuuuuuse me!"

"Yeah, I wanna help Grace, too." His face was a telling shade of pink as he avoided looking at Grace.

"Also, I have too much on my plate right now, with Andrea and everything," Grace added, trying to help Angel out. "Not that I was thinking about getting married."

"Plate, schmate," was Tante Lulu's contribution. Angel, instead of appreciating Grace's help, gave her a dirty look.

"What?" she asked him.

"Nothing. Not a damn thing."

"Well, you aren't thinking about getting married, either, so don't be giving me that look."

"Same old Grace!"

"I beg your pardon. You're the one skipping town."

"Call me crazy, but I didn't hear you ask me to stay!"

"Stay, then, dammit!"

He laughed. "You sweet talker, you."

"Bite me!"

"No, thanks."

They were both glowering at each other by now.

"It's hard ta book a summer weddin' at Our Lady of the Bayou Church when it's this late, so ya better get on it quick-like. Tell Father Pete that Louise Rivard sent ya," Tante Lulu said, as if neither she nor Angel had said a thing.

Grace put her face in her hands, and Angel was banging his head against the soda machine, which began to shoot out cans of soda like bullets. One, two, three...

Grace went over to help him unload the unexpected booty. She lost count at eleven. Some cans were dented. Others were spraying their contents like fountains. And the machine was still popping them out.

A guard rushed in and gave them all a dirty look. "I should have known a LeDeux would be in here causing trouble."

"Hey!" Tante Lulu yelled at the insult. "I resent that."

"We're not LeDeuxs," Grace and Angel said at the same time.

"They're honorary LeDeuxs," Tante Lulu disagreed.

And the guard said, "That figures." Turning to Angel, he surveyed the scene and concluded, "I figure you owe the parish about fifty dollars for this mess."

"I'm not paying fifty dollars for anything," Angel protested. "I put enough money in this frickin' machine to pay for all these cans and then some."

"Ya have proof of that, sonny?" the guard asked.

"Here," Grace said, slamming a fifty-dollar bill down on the table. "That should cover it."

"No way! I want to file a complaint," Angel shouted, picking up the bill and trying to shove it back in Grace's purse.

"You wanna file that complaint from a jail cell?" the guard taunted as other personnel moved into the room to see what the ruckus was about. Some of them had weapons drawn.

Despite Angel's ranting and raving, and Tante Lulu cheering him on, Grace managed to steer him out of the building. Thus it was that Tante Lulu managed to get herself in jail that day, and Grace and Angel barely managed to escape incarceration. Not to mention Grace meeting her daughter for the first time, and Angel trying his best to leave Dodge.

Just another crazy day down on the bayou.

CHAPTER 18

When angels get pushed too far...

Enough was enough!

Angel was not an indecisive person. Hadn't been even when he was a reckless teenager. Hadn't been when he'd made a dumbass decision to pose nude for a national magazine. Hadn't been when he'd straightened his life out and made a good, legitimate living. He was a millionaire, ferchrissake!

So why the hell was he diddling around, wondering what to do with Grace? *Should I, shouldn't I? Will she, won't she? What if this, what if that?* It was clear what he needed to do. Make love to her 'til his eyeballs rolled like cherries on a slot machine, his bones melted into a puddle of testosterone glue, and his heart got rid of this perpetual heartburn. Yep, that's what he was gonna do.

Okay, it was true, he had decided last night that making love with Grace again would be a mistake. Fuck mistakes! In fact, fuck, period! Time he pleased himself and not the whole damn world.

And then, like some celestial sign from above, the bedroom door opened and Grace walked out. He could swear he heard harps and choirs singing, not hymns, but love songs. In fact, some Motown make-out music. St. Jude had a weird sense of humor.

It was only nine o'clock, but Lena and Andrea, exhausted mentally by the day's events, were presumably asleep behind the closed doors of the other two bedrooms.

Grace's emerging might have seemed to Angel like a sign of approval from above; however, she wore not some angelic robe, but a neon pink sleep outfit that belonged to Lena, a silk tank top and tap pants. She'd told Grace that she purchased it at the local thrift shop, practically new.

"Grace?" he said, rising from the couch where his bed had been made up. He wore nothing but his lucky Aces boxer shorts. Not that he was going to need any luck tonight.

"I can't sleep."

Tell me about it. "I can fix that."

"Too much has happened today, and—you can?"

"Definitely."

He watched, via the dim light from the kitchen stove and by the moonlight shining through the window shades, as she stopped in the middle of the living room, as if there were some invisible line drawn. There was a line all right, and it was gonna disappear any second now.

"I just wanted to thank you"—

Don't thank me yet, sweetheart.

—"for sticking around to help me today. I really appreciate it."

"How much?"

"Huh?"

"How much do you appreciate it?"

She tilted her head to the side. "You're wearing your lucky boxers. You planning on getting lucky?"

"Oh, yeah. And you're gonna be the good-luck fairy. Come here, Tinkerbell. Peter Pan is gonna show you how to...fly."

She laughed. "Don't you think we should talk about this?"

"No, no, no! I'm sick to death of thinking and talking. Action time. Let's just do what feels good and let all the not-to reasons be damned."

"You're being awfully pushy."

"I am alpha male, hear me roar." Stepping over the "line," he yanked her into his arms and leaned down to kiss her. "Ummm, you taste like bubblegum."

"Miles's toothpaste."

"What do I taste like?"

She smiled against his lips. "Sex."

"That's what I like to hear." He kissed her seriously then, deep and hungry. While he was still kissing her, he put both hands under her butt and lifted her off the floor, walking her into the bedroom. Tossing her onto the single bed, he walked over and shut the door, locking it with deliberate care.

"Honey, I'm home," he said then and came down over her with a smile.

"About time, too. I'm so hungry, I could eat a—"

"Me, too."

Burying his tongue deep in her mouth, he began the in-and-out rhythm that his lower body yearned to launch. Then she reciprocated, by dipping her tongue into the hot depths of his mouth. The whole time, his calloused palms moved the sexy, soft fabric over her body. *Silk caresses.* And her hands moved over his back, from shoulders to waist. *Skin talk.* Then her hands slipped under the waistband of his boxers, cupping his ass.

He bucked against her, at just the right spot. Then he caught her cry in his mouth, knowing they needed to maintain at least a modicum of silence, lest they wake up the two girls. Dragging his mouth from hers, he panted for breath.

She moaned and tried to pull his head back for more kisses.

"Wait," he urged.

"No," she gasped out. "I. Can't. Wait."

"Oh, baby!" Her words caused his cock to about double in size, if that was possible. But he needed to slow this sex train down for maximum enjoyment, for both of them. Rearing back, he sat on his knees, then pulled her up to straddle him with her knees on either side of his thighs, her crotch smack dab against his crotch.

He saw fireworks behind his closed lids before he opened his eyes and urged her, "Now show me what you like."

She undulated against him with sweet swaying hips. She moved her silk-covered breasts across his chest hairs and nipples. She tunneled her fingers in his hair and kissed him with gentle coaxing laps of her tongue. "That's what I like," she told him saucily. "Now show me what you like."

He didn't need a second invitation. He lowered his boxers carefully over his huge erection, then lifted her tank top over her head and ripped the tap pants down the center, showing him in damp curly splendor what a true redhead she was.

Grace gasped. "You tore Lena's sleep outfit."

"I'll give her a gift certificate to Victoria's Secret," he replied in a sex-gravelly voice as he feasted his eyes on the woman he loved. And, yeah, no question about it. He still loved Grace, dumb twit that he was. The question was—no, he wasn't going to go there. Not now. Not yet.

"Touch me," he urged, and showed her exactly the grasp and movement he liked, almost immediately followed by, "Take me inside."

And she did. Oh, man, did she ever!

Impaled to the hilt, he moved her thighs so she was spread wider. And he began to strum her right where she was joined to him. Without warning, except for a low keening, she began to convulse around him.

Too soon.

He took her by the waist and forced her to remain still.

"Wha-what?"

"Slow down, honey."

"I want..." She tried to move against him.

He wouldn't let her.

Once he had her spasms halted, temporarily, and her eyes were hazy with arousal, he leaned down and took one of her little nipples into his mouth, sucking deeply.

Immediately, she began to spasm around him, again.

He forced her to remain still.

The spasms got softer, then stopped. She stared at him as if in a daze—a daze of wanting. Just the way he wanted her.

"Sweetie?"

At first she didn't register that he was talking to her.

"Sweetie?"

She began to tremble. All over. "I need—"

"Shhhh." He put a fingertip to her mouth. Then he guided both of her hands to her breasts and said, "Touch yourself. The way you do when I'm not there. The way you fantasize."

At any other time she probably would have rebelled, if only faintly, like she had that night in the shower, but she was too far gone. She lifted both breasts, then massaged the centers with her palms.

"Look at me."

Holding his gaze, she used just her fingertips to circle the pearly tips, over and over and over, biting her bottom lip to keep from crying out. When her inner muscles started to milk him once again, he forced her back so that her knees still straddled him and his cock was still inside, but her shoulders were on the mattress. He could see that she was almost in physical pain with wanting.

"Will you do whatever I want you to, Grace?"

She blinked with surprise. "I don't kn—"

"Do you trust me, Grace?" A loaded question in light of everything that had happened the last few days.

She nodded hesitantly, then more resolutely.

"Good girl." He pulled out with painful slowness, then said, "Over on all fours, sweetheart."

Without reservation, she scrambled to do as he asked. He

pressed her face to the mattress and raised her butt even higher by spreading her thighs with his knees. Only then did he enter her again and begin the long strokes that would carry him home.

Way too soon, with neck arched back, he thrust hard into her. Her orgasm came with his in long, almost violent waves 'til she shattered with a harsh whimper, digging her nails into the sheets, and he joined her with a guttural grunt of satisfaction.

A while later, he lay over her, caressing her arms and shoulders and hair as she cried—happy tears, she told him—and shuddered into a sated sleep.

The sex had been phenomenal, better than he'd ever had, and Grace would share his wonder, guaranteed, if she was honest. But, frankly, he had other problems. He was concerned about how she would berate him for the itty-bitty misstep in their sex play.

He'd forgotten to use a condom.

~

Their playground was not for kids...

"HEY, GRACIE, WANNA PLAY?"

Grace emerged from the most delicious sleep, her body aching in some special, and not so special, places. *Play?* Her eyes shot open.

Angel was leaning over her, tickling her breasts with the tassel ties from the living-room drapes. She recognized them because she'd helped Tante Lulu put them on last week.

"Play? What kind of play?" she inquired as she stretched the kinks from her body, which reminded her of something...kinky. As memory returned, she sat up and smacked him on the chest, several times.

"Hey!" He wrestled her back down, linking his hands with hers above her head. "What was that for?"

"You know exactly what, you...you pervert. What do you think I am? Some kind of a dog?"

"Oh, *that*. Honey, doggie sex isn't perverted." He grinned at her, unrepentantly. "I thought you'd like it. You *did* like it."

"I did not."

"Coulda fooled me. You were going 'Oooh, oooh, oooh' in that squeaky little orgasm voice of yours."

"That's because you tricked me."

"How so?"

"By getting me so aroused I couldn't think straight."

"And you're complaining about that?"

"I don't like being—" She searched for the right words.

"Out of control?"

"Exactly."

"Sweetie! That's the point of good sex."

"Oh, yeah? How 'bout I'm the one who gets you out of control this time?"

"I thought you'd never ask." Releasing her hands, he rolled over onto his back and handed her the tassel ties. Then he flashed her an I-dare-you grin.

It wasn't long before Angel changed his tune. With his wrists tied to the headboard, tightly, she'd examined every inch of his body, toes to the tops of ears with kisses, and licks of her tongue and nips of her teeth, commenting at each step on what she saw and was about to do, in explicit detail.

"Oh, I do like your belly button, Angel. I really do."

"Did you like what I did to your nipples? You did? Harder? Okay."

"Can I touch you here? Oooh, ticklish, are you?"

"I can't tell you what it does to me when you make that rough sound."

"Did I ever tell you how I like to play bouncy balls?"

"Can I taste you here? And here? And, oh, my goodness, yes, here."

"Are you ready to say please?"

"Please."

"Please what?"

"Pretty damn please, will you put me out of my misery?"

"Okay." Truth to tell, she was as worked up by then as he was. She was about to climb on for a ride when he said, "Wait," and motioned with his head toward a foil-wrapped item on the bedside table. Something niggled at the back of her mind as she slowly, very slowly, suited him up, but then she had no time to think as she undid his ties and he showed her the best way to play rodeo.

As she drifted off to sleep a short time later, in Angel's arms, she murmured, "What should I do about Andrea?" He kissed the top of her head. "Just be yourself. She'll come around."

"She's nice, isn't she?"

"Yep. Like her mother."

"You're just saying that because I let you have your way with me."

"Ya think?"

"I'm worried about Tante Lulu and the Duval kids."

"I'm not."

She raised her head to look at him.

"The LeDeuxs have a way of always landing on their feet. Cajuns stick together. Besides, they have St. Jude on their side."

"You're beginning to sound a little Cajun yourself."

"*Mais oui, chère.*" He traced her lips gently with a forefinger, then smiled at her. "A month from now, things will be back to normal, or as normal as they can be on the bayou."

"I suppose you're right."

He tucked her face into the crook of his neck and arranged her one leg over his thighs. "Take a little nap, Grace, and then..."

She waited, sensing that he was going to zap her with something.

And he did.

"And then?" she prodded.

"I have another game I'd like to play with you."

They wanted them to play house, literally...

ANGEL WAS HAVING breakfast out on the deck the next morning, having left Grace in the bedroom, alone, before dawn in order to protect her reputation with the girls. Himself, he couldn't have cared less. In fact, he'd like to shout to the world what a great night he'd had.

Instead, he'd made Lena and Andrea his special Spanish omelette with toasted Italian bread and broiled cheese tomatoes. They were now on second helpings.

"Shouldn't we wake Grace?" Lena asked.

"Let her rest. Yesterday was very stressful for her."

Andrea made a grunting sound of disparagement. "Yeah, I guess I've ruffled her perfect life by showing up like this."

"Cut it out, Andrea. Grace is a good woman, and she loves you. I know she does. Just give her a chance."

"If you only knew how bad it's been living with my stepfather, you wouldn't—"

"Hey, my life hasn't been a bed of roses, either," Lena interjected. "And, by the way, Grace told me one time about how mean her parents were. Betcha they made her life hell when they found how she was preggers."

"Lena's right," Angel said, taking one of Andrea's hands in his, to soften his criticism. "You have a right to your own feelings, no matter what they are, but I wish you'd reserve judgment until you get the whole story."

"Why don't *you* tell me?" she said, yanking her hand away.

"I don't know myself."

The gloating look of satisfaction on her face pricked at him, but he cautioned himself that she was just a kid. He needed to be tolerant. For now, anyhow. "I may not know the whole story, kiddo, but I know Grace. You should trust her."

Just then his cell phone rang, sparing him further discourse on a subject that was uncomfortable for him. He was still mad at Grace for keeping all her secrets from him.

"Sabato here."

"Hey, Angel! Luc LeDeux."

"What's up?"

"I just came from Judge Wilkins's chambers. He's waiting for me to return. I have a proposition for you...and Grace."

"Uh-oh."

"The judge might be amenable to releasing the kids today provided there's suitable adult guardianship until the official hearing on Wednesday."

"And Lena won't do?"

"Nope. Not for now, anyhow, considering the role she played in hiding the kids from CPS. Her suitability has to be determined by the courts and protective services."

"So what do you suggest?"

"Could you and Grace offer temporary guardianship for the three kids?"

"I was supposed to be leaving town today."

"So I heard. I realize I'm asking a big favor, but can your departure be delayed?"

He glanced over at a clearly worried Lena, who had tears in her eyes. Her clenched hands were held against her heart in a prayer-like attitude. "I suppose so."

"There's something else."

"Uh-oh," he said again.

"Could you two pretend to be, like, engaged?"

"Oh, boy!"

"It would only be temporary."

"Oh, boy!"

"It's just that the judge would be more likely to grant guardianship if you presented yourselves as a couple."

"I'll see what I can do. Grace is still asleep."

"There's a Walmart on the way. Maybe you could stop and buy a cheap ring."

He laughed. Somehow he couldn't picture it happening without dragging Grace bodily to the jewelry counter. And Walmart? That would be the day!

"If there's a problem, call me back. Otherwise, meet me in two hours." He gave him the address and room number for the judge's chambers.

"How about Tante Lulu?"

Luc laughed. "The district attorney is insisting on keeping her until Monday, while the cops on guard duty at the jail are begging for her release. Needless to say she's causing all kinds of problems. Wants to teach the cook how to make gumbo *the right way*. Has been giving St. Jude statues to the inmates. Wants the right to play Cajun music in the corridors. Won't take a shower 'til they let her disinfect the tiles. Wants to know who's in charge of toilet cleaning. That's for a start."

Angel was laughing by the time he hung up. Then he noticed Lena and Andrea staring at him as if he'd lost his mind.

"Well, Lena, looks like Grace and I are going to be your mommy and daddy." Not the smartest thing for him to say, he soon found out.

Andrea let out a sob of distress and ran into the house, slamming Ella's bedroom door behind her.

He sighed deeply. Time to go propose to Grace.

He couldn't wait.

CHAPTER 19

Sometimes the wheels of justice get a push...

Grace sat in the small auxiliary courtroom, but did she focus her attention on the judge, whose voice droned on and on and on about family responsibility and children's needs; or on the two scowling CPS personnel, Merrill Olsen and Jancie Pitot; or Luc; or even Angel?

Nope.

Her gaze kept going down to the ring on the third finger of her left hand. A two-carat Diamonique ring from Walmart, where Angel had dragged her against her will. It was the most beautiful, garish piece of jewelry she'd ever seen.

She'd been worried that Angel would consider it a real engagement, that he would extrapolate their amazing lovemaking into a commitment of sorts. But he'd been the one to put her in her place, in the shopping mall parking lot. "Chill out, Grace, and stop thinking only of yourself. This is a pretense, for the good of the Duval kids."

Still, she got a thrill just looking at the ring...and thinking of what it might have symbolized, in different circumstances. And she had to admit, the lovemaking had been extraordinary. Beyond that, she didn't want to think.

Looking up, she saw Angel watching her. He winked.

Good heavens! How could a mere wink turn her on, after everything she'd done with this man last night? She must have blushed, because a smile tugged at Angel's lips, which were swollen from her kisses and nips of her teeth. She imagined her mouth was in the same condition.

"I beg your pardon," the judge said. "I hate to interrupt."

Both their heads shot to the right.

"If you two lovebirds don't mind, we're conducting a serious hearing."

"Sorry," they said, as one.

Even so, Angel reached over, linked her fingers with his, raised the fist to his mouth, and kissed the ring, maintaining eye contact the whole time.

Luc surreptitiously flashed a thumbs-up at them, thinking this was a deliberate act in line with his advice to act like a soon-to-be married couple.

Grace's heart ached then, realizing that it must have been just a planned gesture on Angel's part.

She gave herself a mental shake. *Stop it, Grace! You and Angel are not going to happen. He'll be leaving soon. Andrea is here, needing you. Tante Lulu and the Duval family need you, too. You cannot handle any distractions if you want to straighten out the chaos that has become your life. Stop dreaming!*

"Where would these children be living if I release them into your temporary care?" the judge asked.

"In the home that was built for them on Live Oak Lane," Luc answered.

"Where do you two live?" the judge asked her and Angel.

"In the new Duval house," Grace replied.

"For the time being," Angel added. "I own a home in New Jersey, which I plan to sell, and Grace has a cottage on Bayou

Black, which we're going to enlarge and remodel once I purchase an adjoining lot. I can show you the plans, if you'd like."

Whaaaat? Grace stared at him with shock. Was he serious? Or just that good an actor?

"When's the wedding?" the judge inquired.

"Next year," Grace said.

"Next month," Angel said.

She refused to look at him.

"Grace means that she'd like to wait 'til next year and have a big wedding with all the works, but we just can't wait that long. Her old clock is ticking, if you know what I mean. Grace is almost thirty-five years old. Oops. I forgot you're sensitive about your age, hon."

"That's okay, *hon.*" Grace would have gleefully smacked him upside the head if it wouldn't jeopardize their case. Instead, she squeezed the fingers of the hand that still held hers, real hard. She hoped the ring left a mark.

"You can't put those kids in their hands," Mr. Tums from CPS spat out. Saliva pooled in the corners of his chalky lips. "Mr. Sabato and Ms. O'Brien are practically in bed with that dangerous Louise Rivard, who I might note is in jail right now for several felonies, including illegal gun possession, resisting arrest, and assaulting a police officer."

"Whoa, whoa, whoa!" Luc said, rising from his seat and leaning across the table, putting himself in Mr. Tums's face. "My aunt, who is no more dangerous than a kitten, has been charged but not convicted of anything, Mr. Olsen. She would be out on bail right now if she hadn't *chosen* to take a stand against government ineptness and tyranny. Furthermore, one of those charges has been dropped, and the remaining two are misdemeanors, not felonies. As for 'being in bed,' maybe your wife would like to know whether your initials are monogrammed on Ms. Pitot's pillowcases."

Mr. Olsen started hyperventilating and popped a Turns in his

SANDRA HILL

mouth. Ms. Pitot turned beet red and sputtered her outrage, her cheeks going in and out like a blowfish.

Judge Wilkins hammered the desk with his gavel. "That will be enough. LeDeux, if I didn't know your aunt so well and realize you spoke out of fond protectiveness, I would charge you with contempt of court, and you'd be joining her in a jail cell." He turned then to the two CPS people, who were muttering about unfairness in the court system. "Where are the three children now?"

Ms. Pitot told him, reluctantly.

"You've separated them? Already?" The judge was clearly displeased.

"We couldn't find anyone to take three of them on such short notice," Mr. Olsen explained.

"Maybe you should have thought of that before charging in like a SWAT team," the judge remarked, then raised a halting hand when they were about to protest. "Have the children here"—he checked his watch—"in one hour and turn them over to Mr. Sabato and Ms. O'Brien. Since the children have temporary guardians, we can postpone the case scheduled for Wednesday." He told the court reporter, "Reschedule for two weeks. That should give us sufficient time to evaluate the situation."

Then he got up and left the stunned-silent courtroom, removing his robe as he walked out, *click, click, click.* Underneath was a white golf shirt, green slacks, and spiked golf shoes. Just before he left the courtroom for his chamber, he turned and told Luc, "Tell your aunt that the hair-growing salve she sent me is workin' just fine." He did have a full head of Phil Donohue white hair.

Angel leaned down to whisper in Grace's ear. She almost swooned under the onslaught of his breath, which was hot and stimulating. She thought he'd ask something about whether she was okay with the judge's decision, or whether she wanted to go to lunch while waiting for delivery of the kids, or whether she needed to stop at her cottage for extra clothes. Something mundane.

Instead, he licked her ear, and, with a smile in his voice, said, low and soft, "Darlin', I was just wonderin'—how soon can we make love again? I just got a great idea for a new game. Have you ever heard of nude golf?"

~

The cure for all female complaints: shopping...

ANDREA WAS at the mall with Grace and hating every minute of it.

Yeah, Grace had dropped a bundle on her. Andrea now had some new clothes—jeans, shorts, tops, shoes, not to mention a shopping bag loaded with personal products, like deodorant and shampoo, along with high-end cosmetics, purchased at a department store she would have never dared enter in the past. Too expensive.

But it was only money, which Grace apparently had plenty of, and present-day generosity didn't make up for eighteen years of neglect after giving her away.

"Let's stop here at the Pizza Buffet," Grace suggested. "I'm hungry."

"Don't you need to get back to your *fiancé* and your little family?"

"Don't be snide. You know that I'm not really engaged to Angel, and the situation with the Duvals is a temporary legal situation."

"I don't know about that. Angel is awful quick to come to your defense." And, boy, was that the truth! This morning, when she'd declined Grace's offer to take her shopping, he'd taken her aside and read her the riot act. "Either start acting like an adult, which you are at almost eighteen, or go home and live with your scuzzball stepfather. Stop punishing Grace." When she'd tried to defend herself, he stopped her short, adding, "Everyone makes mistakes. Live with it!"

Angel had also forced her, when Grace's pleas hadn't worked, to call her adoptive mother and tell her she was all right. What a joyful call that had been! Not! Her stepfather had been prodding Ruth in the background to encourage Andrea to come home, telling her that they missed her, and her friends had called, and maybe they could take a vacation together, yada, yada, yada. Yeah, right. Even she recognized a ploy for George to retrench and come after Grace's money from another angle. The call ended badly when Andrea mentioned that the police were asking questions about George.

So, here she was, playing the Mommy/daughter act at the mall restaurant, and, holy cow! Did they really both pick up the same type pizzas—dried tomatoes and basil with extra cheese? They both reached for the same diet soda, as well. There were way too many similarities between them for Andrea to ignore.

Sitting down in a booth, they ate silently for a few moments.

"Andrea, I need to discuss something with you."

Andrea was immediately wary. Grace had already filled her in on the conditions surrounding her birth and adoption. Down deep, Andrea understood. Heck, she was three years older and wasn't sure what she would do if she suddenly found herself pregnant with no family to help her, although there were a lot of agencies for pregnant teenagers today that might not have been around then. It was all the years since then that bothered her. Why hadn't Grace checked up on her to see what conditions she was living in? For all Grace knew, she could have been living with monsters.

"Despite what others might think, like your stepfather, I don't have a lot of money," Grace was telling her. "I've donated a lot to, um, charities, but there is this." Grace opened her purse and took out an envelope, which she slid across the table toward her.

"What?"

"Open it. It's yours."

Feigning disinterest, Andrea slid a finger under the flap and peeked inside. Then did a double take. "I don't understand. It's a cashier's check for a hundred thousand dollars."

Grace nodded. "It's half what I would have given your stepfather for information about you, but now it's yours, hopefully for your college education."

All kinds of emotions hit her at once. First, she would be able to go to college, after all. Second, she could definitely cut her ties with the scuzzball. Third, and most important, maybe Grace really did care for her. But, no, that's not what this was. Hard as it was to do, she shoved the envelope back across the table. "Guilt money, Grace?"

Grace shook her head. "I've given most of what amounts to a fortune away, but I set this aside for you. I didn't know your name or where you were, or even if I would ever be able to connect with you, but it was always for you."

Tears began to well in her eyes, to match those in Grace's, green eyes that matched her own. Hers were tears of hope. She suspected the same of Grace.

"Honey," Grace said, taking both her hands in hers.

For once, she didn't resist.

"Money really is not that important, once you have the essentials for living. If I run out, I can go back to playing poker, or join a Jinx treasure-hunting excursion again, or start being a paid folk healer. Right now, all I want is to make you happy."

"I don't know what you mean."

"I'm hoping that you'll stay here in Louisiana with me—make it your home. I'm hoping you'll go to college, if that's what you want. But even if you decide to go back to Atlanta and live with your adoptive parents, that won't alter my wanting to help you, or be with you occasionally."

"What do you want from me?"

"Forgiveness? Compassion?" She paused. "Love?"

"Why are you being so nice, when I haven't been very, well, nice?"

"Because I love you." They were both about to burst out crying by now. Sensing that, Grace said, "Let's get out of here."

Gathering their numerous bags, they were about to exit the restaurant when an elderly couple sitting nearby stopped them. A gray-haired lady, who had to be as old as Tante Lulu, said, "My husband and I have been admiring you two. Are you sisters?"

Andrea's heart started beating so fast she could barely breathe. But then she looked at Grace. In fact, she looped an arm over her shoulder. And said, "This is my mother."

~

Who says the legal process has to be dull?...

ANGEL WAS one of more than twenty people in the courtroom to support Tante Lulu, and, yes, she had somehow managed to find a pint-sized prison coverall, although hers was pink, not the traditional orange. With her hair, which was light brown and flat today, cupping her small head, sans jailhouse beauty salon, she resembled an upside-down cone of teaberry ice cream.

Grace sat next to him. That was the closest they'd been since this whole LeDeux/Duval fiasco had begun. Hard to have wild monkey sex with five other people in a tiny house.

On a positive note, Andrea sat on Grace's other side. Ever since their shopping trip yesterday, they seemed to have come to an understanding. They weren't exactly kissing cousins, or kissing mother/daughter, but they were actually nice to each other. That was a huge beginning.

Just then a lewd-and-lascivious-behavior court case was ending with fines and community service being levied. It involved a college student who had flashed some coeds during a keg party, which happened to show up on YouTube.

"I did that once when I was in college, except I managed to show my butt to a whole squad of cheerleaders who happened to be walking by," whispered John LeDeux, who sat on his other side. "The cheerleaders wouldn't have minded. In fact, they cheered, but their coach wasn't a connoisseur of fine Cajun ass."

"Why am I not surprised?"

"Hey, at least I didn't bare it all for *Playgirl* magazine."

"It had its compensations."

"Bet it did."

They grinned at each other.

"Oh, spare me, Lord, is that John LeDeux I see sitting there in the front row?" Judge Lightley said then. "What's a Fontaine cop doing here?" He glanced down at some papers in front of them. "Hmpfh! This oughta be good," he muttered.

While the judge read, John told him, "I've known Judge Lightley for years, way before he became a judge. I used to run around with his son Fred, aka Zippo."

Why was he not surprised?

The bailiff stepped forward and called out, "This is the case of Houma versus Louise Rivard. The charges are resisting arrest and assaulting a police officer. The charge of illegal possession of a weapon has been dropped since Ms. Rivard produced a license."

Judge Lightley put his chin in both hands, elbows propped before him on the desk. "Hello, Louise."

Tante Lulu did a little wave. "Hi, Bob."

Apparently, the two were acquainted.

Why was he not surprised?

Luc stood up and addressed the judge. "Lucien LeDeux here, representing the defendant."

"John and Luc LeDeux in one courtroom! Spare me, Lord! Why couldn't I have taken my vacation this week?"

"Your honor, I believe that we may be able to come up with a plea deal, provided the prosecution agrees," Luc said, not at all embarrassed by the judge's remark.

The assistant DA, discomforted by the clear association of the judge with the LeDeux family, nodded.

"No, no, no!" Tante Lulu stood, despite Luc's attempt to make her sit, reminding her that she'd promised to be quiet and say nothing. "I wanna take the stand. I ain't takin' no deals. I know my rights. I watch *Law and Order*."

Luc groaned.

"Besides, all my family and friends came all this way ta be my character witnesses, bless their hearts." She motioned toward the rows of filled benches behind her and blew a kiss toward a white-suited Stanley Starr, who could be the ice cream man to her ice cream cone.

The judge's eyes went wide. "All these are character witnesses? How many?" the judge demanded of Luc.

He said something.

"What? I can't hear you."

"Twenty-three."

"Case dismissed," the judge said, pounding his gavel, to the cheers on Tante Lulu's side and the sputtered chagrin from the other side of the aisle. "One thing, though, Ms. Rivard. The next time you want to go on a rampage, please do it while I'm out fishing on the Gulf."

"Sure thing, Judge," Tante Lulu replied, doing a little Snoopy dance in front of the chief witness for the prosecution, the red-faced, furious police officer she had "attacked." Then she added, for the judge, "By the way, Bob, how's yer mama?"

Sins of omission sometimes have consequences...

HE WAS TOAST.

But he couldn't put it off any longer. Grace had to be told.

For the past week, he and Grace hadn't had much chance to

talk, let alone have some privacy for more than five minutes. Four teenagers and a kid in the house were an erotic buzzkill, for sure.

Still, Luc was building a good, solid case for Lena to get complete, official guardianship over her siblings. Things were going well with Grace and Andrea, too. In fact, Andrea was going to move in with Grace once the Duval case was settled. Then Andrea and Lena would both be attending LSU in the fall, Andrea as a resident at the main campus in Baton Rouge, and Lena commuting to a branch campus in Alexandria. There had been lots of busy bees at work these past seven days.

"Gracie, I need to talk to you," he said, coming up to her on the back deck, where she was listening to some CDs with Lena. Jazz blues performed by Lena's parents.

Alarm crossed Grace's face, but she got up immediately.

"Let's walk," he said, steering her off the deck and onto a wooded path.

"You look so serious," she tried to tease, but her voice was wobbly. "Andrea told me that you talked with Ronnie today. Are you leaving? Is that what you wanted to talk about? Are you going back before the hearing next week?"

First, her question surprised him. "No, that's not what I wanted to discuss. I promised to stay 'til the hearing, and I will." Then her question irked him. "Would you care that I'm leaving?"

"Of course I would care, Angel." She put a hand on his forearm. "I truly appreciate everything you've done to help me here."

"I'm not looking for appreciation." Ask me to stay, Grace. Oh, God! Please ask me to stay.

She blinked back tears. "Andrea—and the Duval kids—have grown very fond of you."

And you?

"They'll miss you." She gulped. "I'll miss you."

Then ask me to stay, dammit.

When she didn't, he shrugged her hand off his arm and moved forward down the path 'til he came to the fallen tree where they'd sat weeks ago. Kicking it several times for snakes, he sank down.

"Now that Andrea is accepting you as her mother, and your big bad secret is out, will your life change?" He hated the surly tone in his voice.

"How?"

"Will you marry, have kids, live a normal life?"

"I don't consider my life abnormal."

"Don't get your hackles in an uproar."

"There are still a ton of loose ends in my life, Angel. I can't predict what my future will hold."

Well, that pretty much told him where he fit in. Not at all. "Okay, here's the deal, babe. When do you get your next period?"

"What?" she squawked.

"Shhh. You'll wake every bird in the bayou."

"Why are you asking that question? You can't mean...it's not as if you didn't use a condom every time. Right?"

His face heated up. "There was one time...the first night I stayed over at the Duval house. Don't get angry with me, Grace. It was a mistake. I was so worked up...hell, all I want to know is whether you're pregnant."

She sank down next to him, clearly in shock. "I'm due any day now. And I don't blame you, Angel. I was just as worked up. But pregnant? I couldn't be pregnant, could I?"

Do I have to explain the facts of life to you? Bad enough that Miles is asking so many questions. I mean, how do I explain wet dreams to a ten-year-old? "Would it be such an awful thing?"

"It would be the worst thing of all."

And all his hidden hopes crashed. Having his baby would be "the worst thing."

Sensing his disappointment, she said, "Think about it, Angel. With Andrea just coming into my life, it couldn't be a more incon-venient time."

"Since when are babies convenient?"

"You know what I mean."

"No, I don't, actually. You will let me know if you're pregnant, won't you?"

"Of course, but what would you want..." Her words trailed off.

"I wouldn't be dumb enough to ask you to marry me again, if that's what's worrying you, but I would want to be involved in my child's life."

She winced as if he'd sucker-punched her. Hell, that's exactly how he felt.

Too upset and angry to say any more, he rose to his feet and glared down at her. "Just for the record, if you were pregnant, I would be the happiest man alive. Too bad you'd feel just the opposite."

He was too far away to hear when she said, "I would be happy, too, Angel. I really, really would."

CHAPTER 20

She was the Ann Landers of the bayou...

*A*s an indication of how messed up she was, Grace was thinking of asking Tante Lulu for advice.

Driving the old lady on her rounds of *traiteur* clients gave Grace the opportunity to learn more about Tante Lulu's healing arts, but also to benefit from her wacky wisdom. Angel and René LeDeux—bless their hearts, as Tante Lulu would say—had taken all the kids to a bayou fishing camp, mudbugs being the catch of the day. Andrea, the Duvals, René's son and daughter, and John LeDeux's rascal son, Etienne. Mudbugs was another name for the Cajun favorite, crawfish. Hopefully they would feast tonight.

"Who are we visiting today?" Grace asked.

"Elvira Benoit. I wanna give her some of that special tea marked 'Baby Blues.' She's seein' a doctor, but nothin' seems ta be workin'."

"Postpartum depression can be serious business. Maybe instead of tea, we ought to be giving her husband a gross of condoms."

"Or cut off his wee-wee." The old lady grinned at her. "Elvira will be all right. She's got her Aunt Celie helpin' her. And my tea should raise her spirits a bit an' give her some energy. Didja remember ta bring that mess of collard greens from the garden?"

She nodded. "It's beyond me how one little garden can produce so many greens, okra, beefsteak and plum tomatoes, green beans, beets, and corn."

"The secret is in the gator poop. No, seriously, doan be shakin' yer head at me. Farmers swear by cow manure, I swear by gator poop. Of course, squirrel poop is better fer my roses. But chicken poop, phew, it ain't good fer nuthin', if ya ask me."

"If you say so."

"Besides, I plant the Indian way. Three different vegetables kin flourish in one spot—those that root, those that grow upward, and those that spread."

Grace was continually amazed by this woman. She was a treasure in so many ways. "Who else will we visit today?"

"Leroy Daigle needs some strengthenin' tonic ta help him gain weight from the cancer treatments. I got some of that condensed moose marrow, but the bes' thing is ta boil up some beef-shin meat with lotsa marrow bones 'til it's all shredded like a thick broth what gels when it cools. It tastes better than that vile condensed stuff. My mother usta serve shin-meat soup ta us young'uns at least once a week. Yum! Mebbe I'll make a batch when we get home. We kin stop at the butcher on the way back. Oh, 'nother thing. Mebbe Leroy would like ta try some of that tea fer fightin' prostate cancer."

"The saw palmetto and yarrow one?"

She nodded. "Toss in some licorice root, too."

"Okay." Grace took more notes. "Don't forget that we were supposed to take some diaper-rash salve for those Comeaux twins, too."

"I swear, their mama is thick as the bark on a live oak tree. I tol' her and I tol' her ta jist use Vaseline on them little butts, but she insists on buyin' that highfalutin nonsense what smells purty but irritates the skin."

Then they talked about the Duvals, plans for the foundation, and Andrea before Tante Lulu turned to her and said, "Out with it, girl. Whass really botherin' ya?"

"Angel."

"I figgered."

"I'm afraid that when he leaves this time he'll never come back."

"Yer prob'ly right."

"Thanks a bunch. You're no help."

"I cain't help ya iffen ya doan know what ya want."

"I want..."

Tante Lulu quirked one of her little brows at her.

"I want him to stay. I think. Except I'm not sure under what conditions. Do you know what I mean?"

Tante Lulu nodded. "Friend, lover, or husband, or all three?"

"Exactly."

"I'm guessin' you two been doing the hanky-panky. Hard ta go back ta friendship once ya cross that line."

Crossed, and crossed again.

"He might stay and be yer sometimes lover, but I cain't see him acceptin' that fer long. Besides, God doan approve of all that sinnin'."

"Are you saying that God wants me to marry him?" She tried to laugh it off.

But Tante Lulu wasn't even breaking a smile. "God doan like sex outside of marriage, but he's willin' ta put up with it a little iffen there's a good end in sight. Otherwise, it's jist lust, pure and simple."

"And that's a bad thing?"

"You know the answer ta that, dearie."

"Angel would want the whole works, I suspect. Marriage,

home, and kids." She wasn't about to mention the possibility that she might be pregnant.

"Would that be such a bad thing, havin' Angel's baby?"

"Angel asked me the same thing."

"And yer answer was...?"

"I didn't answer."

"Oh, Grace, ya musta hurt him bad."

"It's all a moot point, anyway. He hasn't asked me to marry him —not since last year."

"He never will."

"What?" It shocked her to have Tante Lulu be so blunt...and hurtful.

"That boy has laid his feelin's on the line too many times. It's up ta you ta propose now. Iffen thass what ya want."

That's what she was afraid of. The cards had been dealt, the game was in play, and it was her turn to either go for the jackpot or fold. She wasn't sure she had the courage, either way, and, let's face it, she was a hopeless basket case. Why would any man want her?

Suddenly, she heard something. Glancing sideways, she saw that Tante Lulu was staring ahead. "Did you hear that?"

"What?"

"Thunder?"

"No, I dint." She narrowed her eyes at Grace, then grinned. "Hallelujah, it's a sign from above. St. Jude is in the buildin'."

PMS is worse some times than others...

GRACE WAS CELEBRATING by cleaning out the refrigerator in her cottage, still wearing that stupid engagement ring. And weeping buckets of tears.

Not the big celebration one would expect after this morning's hearing, where Lena had been granted guardianship. One year provisionally, then final if there were no problems. That Luc LeDeux was some super lawyer, every bit as good as his wild reputation. He'd even got Judge Wilkins to smile a time or two.

The young folks had vetoed a party at Tante Lulu's, and instead all thirty-six of the LeDeux family and friends and some of the Starrs had gone to the Cagey Cajun, a restaurant in Houma that featured a live Zydeco band. Afterward, a bunch of them, including Andrea, had decided to go to a movie. Grace had slipped out before dessert.

Angel had asked her one too many times today if she was pregnant, to which she had finally snapped, "Ask me one more time and you are going to be a fallen angel, as in me walloping you a good one."

To which he had muttered, "Someone is having a bad day."

More like a bad month.

She hadn't asked him to stay here in Louisiana with her, as Tante Lulu had recommended. Lack of nerve. And besides, she wanted him to stay for her, not because of a parental obligation.

To make matters worse, Angel had spent a lot of time chitchatting with a beautiful blonde at the next table whom René's wife Val had introduced to them all. A realtor who worked with the hotshot development company owned by Val's mother, Simone Fontenot Breaux. "You should come talk to her," he had told Grace at one point.

Yeah, right.

"Seriously. She's very interesting."

"And I have a dumb-blonde joke I could tell you. Or a hundred."

"Gracie!" He had smiled with irritating satisfaction at her apparent jealousy.

The zinger of all zingers had hit when she arrived back at her cottage to find that her monthly present had finally arrived, along with a super case of the cramps and PMS oozing out every pore in her body. Her moods kept swinging from one end of the spectrum to the other.

That's why she was on an hour-long crying/cleaning jag. Who knew she would be so upset over *not* being pregnant? Who knew that deep down she'd been praying it would be true? Who knew that all these years of denying she wanted love and marriage and babies were a total crock?

What to do now?

She honestly didn't know.

∼

Oh, baby!...

ANGEL WAS SHOCKED when he arrived at Grace's cottage to see her on the floor, half her body stuck inside an open refrigerator, her shoulders shaking with her sobs.

He'd heard of people sticking their heads in a gas oven, but a fridge? Besides, Grace had never been suicidal. This was nuts.

"Grace?"

Her head shot up, hitting one of the metal shelves. "Ouch!" Standing, she rubbed her scalp and tried to swipe surreptitiously at the tear tracks on her face. He couldn't help but notice she was still wearing the Walmart engagement ring, even though the need for it was gone. That was probably a pathetic straw to grasp at, but he was a strawless man.

"Why are you crying?"

"I'm not crying. It's the ammonia fumes from the cleaner I'm using," she lied. "What do you want?"

"Nice welcome."

"Where's your girlfriend?"

"What girlfriend?"

"Ms. Blonde Bimbo realtor."

"Oh, *that* girlfriend." He smiled.

He could tell she'd have liked to smack the smile off his face, especially when her eyes lit on the package in his hands. *Uh-oh!* Before he had a chance to explain, she planted both hands on her hips. "You bought an early pregnancy kit? Idiot! What did I tell you back at the restaurant about continuing to bug me about—you know? You are a certifiable cement brain."

"Whatever you say, honey. But I thought it would ease your mind to know for sure."

"Hah! More like your mind you want to ease so you can then hop, skip, and jump out of town, like—like a freakin' Dorothy down the yellow brick bayou road."

"Are you crazy?"

"No. Just *not* pregnant." She burst out crying again and tried to run past him into the other room.

He dropped the box and caught her by the upper arm, swinging her to face him. She wouldn't meet his imploring gaze.

"What the hell's going on?"

"I got my period."

"And that's why you're crying?" In that instant, he realized that Grace did care about having his baby. "Oh, Gracie." He picked her up and carried her into the living room, where he sank down into a rocking chair with her on his lap, her wet face tucked into his neck. Then he rocked her, murmuring nonsense words of comfort, for both of them. And, truth to tell, he cried, too. It wasn't only Grace who was realizing how much the baby had been wanted.

When Grace was cried out and exhausted, he carried her into the bedroom, where he pulled off her sandals and jeans, leaving only a tank top and bikini panties, and laid her down on the bed.

"Don't go."

"I'm just going to the bathroom. Be right back." When he returned, he handed her a paper cup of water, a Midol, and an aspirin. He knew from past experience being around Grace that the combination usually helped.

"Thanks." She looked so lost and unhappy.

Taking off his own clothes down to his boxers, he slipped into the bed with her, pulling the sheet up over them both. Tugging her over to rest her face on his chest, with his arms encircling her, he encouraged, "Sleep, honey. You'll feel better later."

"Thank you for staying," she murmured again.

"Where else would I be?"

Around midnight, Andrea came home and popped her head in the bedroom door. He was surprised that she wasn't surprised to see him there. "Is she okay?" Andrea whispered.

"Yeah," he whispered back. "Just delayed reaction to all the stress of the past few weeks."

Andrea nodded. "Not least of all caused by me."

"She wouldn't have it any other way."

Andrea nodded again. "Good night."

"Good night, sweetie."

For hours after that, he lay on his back, staring at the whirring ceiling fan while Grace slept soundly, although she whimpered and grew restless on occasion. At those times, he kissed the top of her head, caressed her back, and crooned soothing words to her. There was a closeness between them now that made his heart ache, all the more powerful because it wasn't sexual. He had so much to consider before making a final decision about Grace. And, yes, it was going to be his decision this time.

In the middle of the night, he kissed her one last time, tugged on his jeans and shirt in the living room, then went into the kitchen, where he left Grace a note. There was so much he wanted to say, but he'd say it in person later. Plus, he had a lot of ducks to herd into a row first. So all he said was:

Grace,

Sorry I wasn't here when you woke up. Important business to take care of. Be back soon. We'll talk then.

A.

The cure for female depression? A cowboy!...

WHEN GRACE AWAKENED the next morning, it was with such a sense of peace.

No, she wasn't pregnant, but she had been touched to see that Angel's pain had matched her own over that "loss." And he'd been so sweet about comforting her, all night long.

As she stretched and went to sit up, the first thing she noticed was her engagement ring. She smiled at the gaudy, precious thing. Then she became aware that not only wasn't Angel in her bed, but she didn't hear him moving about. Maybe he'd moved to the couch because of Andrea being in the house and was still asleep.

Her sense of peace was shattered, however, when she read the note left in the kitchen under a St. Jude refrigerator magnet. His cold, impersonal note that wasn't even signed "Love, Angel."

The insensitive clod!

After her initial hurt and anger, she calmed down. He said he'd be back. That was promising. Besides, she had business to take care of, too. And at least he'd had the good sense to toss that pregnancy testing kit in the trash before Andrea—or God forbid, Tante Lulu—saw it.

But then days went by without hearing from him. She had determined not to call him. But what if he were hurt? So, she called Ronnie to ask if she'd seen him.

"Yes," she said, revealing nothing more.

"Is he going back to work for Jinx?"

"Uh, we discussed it, but—"

Grace had known Ronnie for a long time, and she was hurt at the coolness of their conversation. "I'm sorry to have bothered you."

"Oh, Grace, you're not bothering me. It's just that Angel

confided some things in me, and I'm not free to discuss them without his permission."

"That's okay." Which it wasn't.

"He has some things to work out."

Don't we all?

"Give him a chance, Grace. Please. He's a great guy."

"I was afraid something might have happened to him. An accident, maybe. Wouldn't a 'great guy' have at least let me know he was okay?"

"I'll talk to him."

That must mean he was still in Jersey. "Don't bother." By the fifth day, she gave in and called his cell phone herself. In fact, she tried three times and left a message, "Call me," on the third try. Same was true of the sixth, seventh, and eighth day. Then she gave up. He wasn't calling her back.

She was crushed.

On the ninth day, she met Tante Lulu at Charmaine's ranch spa, an early birthday gift from the old lady to lift her spirits, over Angel and her upcoming thirty-fifth birthday. At her age, the best way to celebrate a birthday was to ignore it. Impossible around Tante Lulu.

Grace was going to get the works. Facial, manicure, pedicure, sluffing—whatever that was—cellulite exfoliation, massage, and a rinse to cover a few gray hairs she'd discovered recently. And, no, she was not going to celebrate her gray hairs, as one magazine had suggested.

"Heard from the idjit yet?" Tante Lulu asked as they lay tummy down on rolling massage tables, wearing nothing but sheets, waiting for their masseuses.

She shook her head.

"Don'tja be worryin' none. He'll be back. In the meantime, I heard sumpin'."

"Oh?"

"Iffen I was you, I would call Ardith Smith over Houma way."

She frowned. "Who's Ardith Smith?"

"She's that realtor gal we met a couple weeks back at the Cagey Cajun. Remember?"

"Oh, yeah. The blonde. Why would I want to call her?"

"Well, I heard from Charmaine, who heard from one of her beauty-salon clients, who heard from Val's mother that Angel has been in touch with her. A lot."

Grace blinked away tears. The lout! The two-timing lout! Not that they were married or anything. She glanced down at her ring. Not even engaged, really.

A middle-aged woman walked in then, wearing white ortho-pedic shoes, slacks, and a medical-type jacket, offset by bottle-black hair and the reddest lipstick she'd ever seen. "Well, Mz. Rivard, good to see you again, *chère*. Ain't you jist the prettiest thing with that green hair?"

Grace wouldn't exactly call it pretty, but it did make Tante Lulu stand out in a crowd, and that was the point with her.

"It weren't supposed ta be green. I was aimin' fer champagne blonde, but instead I got elfin lime. Ha, ha, ha. Jist overdyed, accordin' ta Charmaine. But I like it."

Oh, yeah. Elf is about right. The Jolly Green Elf.

"It does give ya pizzazz."

Tante Lulu motioned with her head toward her table. "We're gonna give Grace here some pizzazz, too."

Not if I can help it.

"This is my friend and associate Grace O'Brien. She's prob'ly gonna be gettin' hitched soon. So we gotta get her in good shape ta handle a real hottie of a guy."

Oh, good Lord!

"And Gracie, this is Erline Vincent. Her momma was one of my bestest friends, bless her heart, before her recent departure."

Grace nodded to Erline. "My sympathies on your mother's passing."

"Oh, she didn't pass. She jist went ta one of them active-senior casino communities up north of Baton Rouge."

On that happy note, Erline wheeled out Tante Lulu. The last thing she heard was Tante Lulu saying, "See if ya kin pound some of them golf-ball dimples outta my butt. I got a date t'night."

Grace must have dozed slightly then, trying her best not to think about Angel and the blonde. Until she heard a deep voice say, "Hi! I'm Roy."

Oh, my God! They sent me a male. Not a masseuse, but a masseur? A male who is going to get up close and personal with my cellulite. I'm going to kill someone.

When she opened her eyes, she about fell off the table. Roy was indeed a "Roy," as in Roy Rogers. Honestly, what kind of masseur wore low-riding jeans, a cowboy hat and boots, and no shirt, just one of those handkerchiefs tied around his neck? Charmaine's kind, she immediately answered herself.

"Is this a joke? Like one of those stripper surprise-party thingees?"

He laughed as he began to lay out his goods—oils, loofas, and other scary things, including something that resembled a vibrator with pointy, fat rubber bristles. "No, I'm not a stripper. I'm a licensed massage therapist, working on my doctorate in sports medicine at Tulane."

"Are you sure you're not a Chippendale dancer?"

"I can barely do a line dance."

Like dancing is the most important asset for a Chippendale!

"One of the Village People?"

"I'm not gay." His chin went up with pride. "Do you want to request a different therapist? I often get your reaction. People tend to judge by appearances."

Oh, that was a neat verbal maneuver. Perfect way of backing her into a corner. "Of course not. Let's get on with it." *But if you call me ma'am even one time, I'm outta here.*

She barely squeaked when he flicked on the tape deck, not to soothing ocean sounds, but a country music CD, Rascal Flatts singing "I Melt." Just a coincidence, she was sure.

As he began to work her shoulders with oily fingers, humming along to the music, she did squeak and gasp out, "I don't suppose we could get a picture of you giving me a massage."

"That's some turnaround." He chuckled. "I don't know. Why?"

"There's someone I'd like to send it to."

CHAPTER 21

Everything was turning out just ducky...

*A*ngel was returning to Louisiana for the second time since he'd left Grace's cottage two weeks ago.

When he'd been back last week, he'd met with a realtor and an architect. Just one of the ducks he'd needed to put in a row.

Another duck had been the sale of his Jersey condo. He'd expected to just list it, with most of the furnishings, but because of its prime oceanfront location, it sold in two days. For a cool million. A clean cut from all his East Coast ties.

He was driving his pickup truck, loaded with clothes and personal belongings he wanted to keep, towing his Harley. He'd sold his vintage Corvette. A very expensive "duck."

Nesting in his glove compartment was another duck, this one bearing the name of Cartier. Though he would always have a fondness for Walmart.

He'd even checked on Grace's parents and found they were both dead, for more than five years now. Sad to say, no great loss.

He'd made a stop in Philly before beginning this final road trip to take care of the Greek duck, who'd been very interested to learn he had a daughter. Angel hadn't been sure how he would react, and he'd wanted to spare Grace and Andrea the hurt if there was to be a rejection.

Angel was making sure that all of Grace's loose ends were tied up before he hit her with his agenda. But that had been one duck that might very well waddle back to bite him in the butt. Alexander Pappas was divorced, good-looking, if you liked Greek gods, and wanted to know way too much about Grace. When Angel turned a bit uncooperative—okay, surly—Alex asked what his connection was to Grace. And Angel had answered unabashedly, "Fiancé." That wasn't really a lie. *Quack, quack!*

So he was finally, finally back in Louisiana, about to put all his cards on the table and hopefully hit the jackpot. He passed Tante Lulu and Grace's cottages on Bayou Black. No cars in either driveway, but then, he hadn't expected any. There was a foundation board meeting in New Orleans today. Continuing about a half mile past Grace's place but not as far as Remy's, he pulled a hard left onto an overgrown dirt road that led to Sweetland, a decrepit, falling-down Creole mansion that had once belonged to a sugar planter—before the Civil War, no doubt. In the bayou tropical climate, it hadn't taken much to make a once-beautiful setting look like a jungle, but it was still possible to see its underlying beauty. In fact, he had pictures of the way it had been back then. Once cleared there would be a wide *alleé* leading down to Bayou Black under the canopy of twenty enormous live oak trees, probably two hundred years old, which formed once majestic columns on either side. The house itself was white under all the grime, with intricate fretwork, broken in places, and an ornate slate roof in remarkably good condition. It was three-storied with two wide staircases on either side of the front, meeting in the center of the second, or main, floor of the house. There were many outbuildings, including some that had been slave quarters at one time.

Angel had passed this fallen monument to the Old South

every time he'd gone back and forth to Remy's houseboat. He had to admit, the house and surrounding land gave the term *fixer-upper* a laughable new meaning. And snakes...man, oh, man, reptiles had a regular commune going here. Still, something about the property pulled at him. He wondered if it would pull at Grace, too. He hoped so, because as of today, he was the proud owner.

He undid the hitch and put the motorcycle in one of the sturdier sheds. It would probably be covered with snakes by the time he got back. *Note to self: Buy a machete—or snake mace.* He was going to stop at Grace's cottage to take a quick shower and change his clothes. He knew where the key was hidden.

Then: *Time to go tell Grace a story about ducks.*

∿

He had something sweet to show her...

Two weeks had gone by, and Grace was entering the Starr building in New Orleans for a foundation meeting. Andrea had dropped her off before going to the LSU campus in Baton Rouge for some advanced freshman placement testing. Andrea and Andy LeDeux were going out to eat somewhere afterward before heading back to Bayou Black. Tante Lulu and Remy had offered Grace a ride back.

In fact, Tante Lulu had advised her to wear a "party dress," since they would be going to Remy's house for cocktails and a buffet dinner to celebrate something or other. Tante Lulu wasn't exactly clear what.

So, Grace was wearing her white halter sundress with the red peonies, despite the memories associated with it. Maybe she would meet some new guy tonight and make new memories for the dress. Maybe even Tank. On the other hand, maybe not. The thought of making love with anyone other than Angel, or even going to the trouble of starting a new relationship, was oddly repugnant. Still, she had to start somewhere. Just not yet.

Grace took a seat at the table next to Tante Lulu, who squeezed her forearm in greeting. Luckily, the meeting was just starting.

There were only nine people here today, and Grace suspected that Samantha was disappointed at Daniel's absence, even if only because she liked to needle him. Aside from Grace and Tante Lulu, on their side of the table were Luc, René, and Remy. On the Starr side were Samantha, Stanley, Aunt Dot, and Angus.

After reading the minutes from the last meeting, Aunt Dot called on the treasurer. Angus, the computer techie, gave them figures on how much had been earned from various sources—donations, the Swamp Tavern auction, the poker tournament, bank interest—offset by expenditures, mostly for Starr Wishes at this point. Samantha asked Tante Lulu to report on the Duval children, even though they weren't specifically a project of the Hope Foundation.

Tante Lulu stood, her proud little figure adorned in her very own version of party attire—a dressy lavender pantsuit with matching low-heeled pumps and, yes, lavender-tinted gray hair. Lavender enamel covered her fingernails, which had little painted violets on them. She must have spent the entire morning in Charmaine's beauty salon.

Stanley's white suit had a lavender-sprayed carnation in the lapel. That must mean he would be coming with them to the party. To her chagrin, she had to admit these two senior citizens were having more luck in the love department than she was, though that image didn't bear much deliberation.

"The chillen are fine," Tante Lulu concluded after telling them all that had been done, highlighting with glee her jail stint for justice. "We learned lots of stuff from this project," she said. "Mostly that we gotta do more ta keep families t'gether before it reaches a crisis like the Duvals. We're workin' on ideas." She beamed as everyone applauded her efforts before she sat down.

Then came a discussion of the Arnaud family and what the foundation might be able to do for them. They were going to be so pleased.

Samantha reported on wishes that had been granted that month, and date-important ones—as in, terminal illnesses—that were coming up. Aunt Dot told them about her efforts to create a database of families with critical needs.

"What we need is a house or sumpin' where families kin go 'til somethin' permanent is available," Tante Lulu interjected. "Sorta like a halfway house." The strange thing was that Tante Lulu stared at Grace meaningfully as she made this statement.

Grace was so bemused by that prospect that at first she didn't realize someone had slipped into the chair next to her. She smelled his aftershave before she realized who it was.

"Hi, honey. I'm back."

Slowly, inch by inch, she turned to see Angel sitting there, a clean-shaven, hair-trimmed, neatly-dressed-in-golf-shirt-and-khakis Angel, who had the nerve to wink at her. The jerk! To the others at the table he said, "Sorry I'm late," even as he was reaching for Grace's hand.

Without thinking, she smacked him on the chest, so hard he was knocked back and his chair tipped over, landing him on the floor. As he stood, adjusting his chair, the fool grinned at her. "I missed you, too, baby."

Everyone in the room was staring at them as if they were crazy.

They were. At least, she felt crazy.

"Guess you're not gonna pucker up."

"Get lost," she hissed under her breath, turning her attention back to the table. "Get on with the meeting," she directed Aunt Dot.

"Uh...well, uh, as I was saying—" Aunt Dot sputtered.

"Let's get out of here." Angel was leaning close to her ear, a hand on her shoulder.

She pointedly removed his hand. "Touch me again and I'll bite off your fingers, one by one."

"Maybe we should adjourn 'til later," Samantha suggested.

"No, that's okay." Grace was mortified to be causing so much distraction, but she couldn't stop herself.

"Grace and I will step outside for a minute," Angel said.

"Over my dead body. Hey! Stop it." He had lifted her bodily from her chair and tossed her over his shoulder, her dress having ridden up so high her butt was practically exposed.

"Dare I hope you're not wearing underwear?" Angel said to her butt.

They created quite a scene as she yelled and kicked the whole way down in the elevator, through the lobby, and out to the parking lot. "I'm going to kill you," she warned when he opened the passenger door on his truck, the bed of which was loaded and covered with a tarp. Before she could escape, he shut the door and clicked the child-lock mechanism, which precluded her jumping out.

Once he came around the driver's side and was behind the steering wheel, he inhaled and exhaled several times before turning in the seat to stare at her. "I'm back."

"Big deal!"

He laughed. The jerk laughed, then pulled her into his arms and kissed her hungrily, then set her back, before she could whack him a good one.

Turning on the motor, he pulled out of the parking lot. "Put on your seat belt, honey."

"Where are we going?"

"Bayou Black. I have something to show you."

"You have nothing that I want to see."

"You sure about that?"

"Positive. Where the hell have you been?"

"Jersey, Philly, other places. I had lots to do."

What had he been doing—especially in Philly? But she was too proud to ask.

"I sold my condo, most of the furnishings, my Corvette, and my fishing boat."

"You sold your Corvette? You love that Corvette."

"I love other things more."

That was such a loaded remark she didn't dare ask what he meant.

"I'm sorry if I hurt you by staying away so long."

"Were you punishing me?"

He frowned his confusion.

"For turning you down last year?"

"I didn't think of that. If I had—no, I needed to make a complete break with my East Coast life."

"Did you get my messages?"

"Yeah, but I couldn't call you back. I was afraid you would try to talk me out of what I was doing. I had to get my"—he grinned at her—"ducks in a row."

With a killing glower, she told him what he could do with his duck, and it rhymed. After that, she refused to talk to him for the long drive back to Houma, then on to Bayou Black. When they passed Tante Lulu's cottage, and hers, too, Grace looked at him. "Where are we going?"

"Decided to talk to me again, huh?"

"You are really annoying me."

"In a good way, or a bad way?"

"Aaarrgh!"

"I love it when you growl." He pulled onto a dirt road that had a broken-down sign saying "Sweetland." When he was up to the small clearing in front of a mansion, he stopped the motor. "We're here."

"Here where?"

"Home."

"Whaaat?"

"I bought this place."

"Are you crazy?"

"Can't you see the potential?"

"What I see is a million-dollar redo. In fact, a complete teardown."

His shoulders drooped.

Grace stared at him. She was so angry, and so glad, to have him back. She could tell that her lack of enthusiasm hurt him, but why was it so important to him that she like this dump?

With a deep sigh, he got out of the truck and came around to open her door. "I'll show you around."

"Is it safe?"

He grinned at her. "Mostly, except for the snakes. I've given names to some of the bigger ones. Wait 'til you meet Wilbur."

"You're not kidding, are you?"

"Nope. Now, first, look at the house. Really look at it." He pulled a photograph out of his pocket and handed it to her. "This is the way it will look when I'm done."

Okay, it had been a charming mansion in its day. "When? Twenty years from now?"

"Oh, you of little faith!"

"And you have so much faith all of a sudden?"

"I got religion, thanks to Tante Lulu."

"Does she know about this?"

"As of this morning she does."

Something occurred to her suddenly. "Is this why you've been in contact with Realtor Barbie?"

"Yeah."

She smacked him on the shoulder.

He pretended that it hurt. "What was that for?"

"For making me think you were a two-timing son of a—"

"You were jealous?" He kissed her, short and quick, jumping back before she could slap him again. "Anyhow, be careful on the steps. If you walk over here, closer to the house, they're more sturdy." When they got to the top and what would be a wide covered verandah or galleria that went all around the house, repeated on the third floor, he told her, "This is the main floor," he said, after they entered the double front doors. "Down below on ground level are the kitchens, storerooms, servants' quarters, and so on. Up here are a ballroom, salons or living rooms, and a dining room. The next floor has six bedrooms." Grace looked around the foyer and had to admit, the house had some merits. Though painted over, the carved woodwork and the banister leading to the second floor were magnificent.

"Some famous furniture maker, when he was down and out, did all the interior woodwork and the fancy fretwork outside."

"They could be restored," she murmured as she continued the tour.

The random plank cypress flooring was also battered and stained but intact. Walking around slowly, she noticed the ceiling medallions and crown molding. The marble fireplaces. The old windows, in some cases ten feet high, with wavy glass, but beautiful, looking out onto what had once been gardens, overgrown now, but showing color here and there, especially the various roses.

"There's a bunch of interesting stuff in the attic. I decided to wait to open it with you."

She nodded.

He took that for another positive sign. *Please God!* When they were standing in a back bedroom, he pointed to a bunch of buildings some distance from the house. "The old slave quarters," he said. "I'm thinking about making them into bungalows, complete with little kitchens and bathrooms."

"I don't understand any of this." She turned to look at him.

He inhaled deeply, for courage. This was do-or-die time for him. He had to get the words just right. He took both her hands in his and was encouraged by the fact that she didn't draw away. "I want you, Gracie. I've wanted you for as long as I can remember. But I knew as long as I had the fallback position of a home and job back in Jersey I would never be committed to moving forward. With you."

She said nothing, but at least she hadn't shot him down. Yet.

"I tried to think what I could do if I moved here. I knew you wouldn't want to leave Tante Lulu and the *traiteur* work, not to mention your daughter. You need a stable home base. I do, too, by the way. Anyhow, I decided I like working on houses, and I think I would have a talent for restoration. What I don't know, I could learn."

"But why such a big place?"

He saw the fear in her eyes. "I want kids, Grace, but they're not a necessity. Andrea would be enough. Still, I have to tell you, I would do my best to convince you that one—okay, two—more babies would make a great family for us."

Tears pooled in her eyes, and fear. So he barreled ahead, to get to the good stuff.

"How would you feel about us providing temporary homes"—he waved to the slave quarters—"to families in crisis?"

"Like halfway houses?" she asked, eyebrows raised with suspicion. Tante Lulu must have hinted at something. The old busybody.

"Exactly. And, really, this house isn't as big as it appears at first."

She made a scoffing noise. "It's a mansion."

"A mini-mansion."

"And the grounds! You would have to hire a full-time gardener."

"Gracie! I sold my condo for a million and my Corvette for two hundred thousand, and I have two million in stocks and CDs. I can afford a frickin' gardener. Unlike you, I was selfish and didn't give my money away."

"So now you're trying to entice me with money."

"No, Gracie, I'm not." He glanced down at their hands, which were still joined. "You're still wearing my engagement ring."

She laughed. "My fingers are swollen and it won't come off."

Giving lie to her words, he slipped it off easily.

"Hey! Give that back."

He shook his head, released her hands, went down on one knee, then took a small velvet box out of his back pocket.

She put her fingertips to her parted lips where a small sob escaped.

"Gracie, will you marry me?" He blinked away the tears in his eyes. God, he hoped he didn't embarrass himself.

"Oh, Angel," she said. There were tears in her eyes, too, as she opened the box. It was a replica of the Walmart ring, but not quite so big and garish.

Before she could object, he slipped the ring on her finger. "Look at that, Gracie. It fits perfectly." He folded her fingers so she couldn't take it off, then kissed her knuckles.

"You would accept Andrea as your stepdaughter?" she asked.

Angel nodded, and his hopes soared.

"And you'd be satisfied with one child of your own?"

Actually, no. I really, really want two. A boy and a girl. "Sure."

"I do like the house. It has an aura. I can sense the people who lived here before. It was a happy home, I believe."

"What about me? Do you like me, Gracie?"

"You are such a fool." She sank down to her knees in front of him. "No, I don't like you, Angel."

His heart stopped.

"I love you."

They both wept then, for this was a long time coming.

Then they made love on the floor, which they covered with his shirt and her dress. The words "I love you" were repeated over and over, by both of them. And it was sweet, sweet loving in their new home, which they later decided had been appropriately named Sweetland.

CHAPTER 22

Their first "houseguest" had to be...guess who...?

*I*t was several hours before they left Sweetland, and Grace was ecstatic, happier than she could ever remember being.

After making love on the floor, they explored the house and property in more detail. Almost everywhere they went, they found something new and exciting to exclaim over.

First the kitchen. "Honey, look at all these signed crocks," he said.

"How can you tell they're signed under all that crud? But the fireplace! My goodness, you could cook a whole cow in there."

"We'll cook a cow for our first housewarming party."

"Eeew!"

Angel grinned at her.

"I love your grin."

"Yeah?"

"It makes me all tingly inside."

"Tingle, tingle." He grinned some more, then tucked her in

closer to his side. "I love you so much, Gracie. It feels like a dream."

She nodded. "But we're never going to wake up. Forever, Angel. I'll love you forever."

"Forever," he repeated.

They were both overwhelmed and so, so happy over this newly declared love. And they couldn't keep their hands off each other as they walked the grounds.

"It's as if a dam of emotions has been let loose," she told him. "How could it have been there, possibly for years, while I held it back?"

"Because you're a stubborn wench?" He ducked her punch, then pulled her back into his embrace again.

"If you hadn't left the morning after...after I discovered I wasn't pregnant, I would have told you then."

"Maybe it wasn't supposed to happen until now. Maybe God"—he laughed—"correction. Maybe God *and* St. Jude work at their own pace."

"Your born-again faith?"

"Yep."

In one of the sheds close to the house, they discovered an armoire. Then antique tools in the barn. Primitive furniture in the slave quarters. The place was an unending treasure trove, better than any Jinx bonanza, in her opinion. Sweetland was an unpolished jewel that they would work on for a lifetime, she suspected.

While they walked, and stopped often to kiss or just stare at each other in wonder, they talked about where Angel had been the past two weeks.

"You didn't! You had no right, Angel," she said when he told her about contacting Alexander Pappas.

"I did it to spare Andrea pain, and you, too, in case the jerk wasn't interested in having a kid at this late date."

"And was he a jerk?"

"I wish! No, he was actually a pretty nice guy, but he exhibited way too much interest in you. He'll probably come strolling down to Loo-zee-anna trying to hook up with you again."

"You're jealous," she hooted, then smiled with satisfaction.

"Damn straight! Just like you were over 'Realtor Barbie.'"

"Don't remind me."

"I did something else you might not like."

"Uh-oh!" She stopped in her tracks, forcing him to stop, as well.

"I checked up on your parents. No easy way to say this, but they're both dead. Her of cancer six years ago, and him of a heart attack five years ago."

She pondered his news for a long moment "The sad thing is that I feel nothing."

They discussed wedding plans then.

"Let's do it as soon as possible," Angel said. "I've waited too long already."

"You know Tante Lulu will want to be involved."

He groaned. "A church wedding?"

"Definitely."

"I wish it could be here at Sweetland."

"Are you kidding? That would take at least a year. How about one month?"

"Okay, but try to rein in the Cajun tornado."

"How 'bout you try to rein her in? You're her favorite Yankee man."

"We'll both work on her."

"Where will we live while we get started on Sweetland?"

"How 'bout we stay at your cottage? It'll be cramped, up close and personal to the max, but an incentive to get the property cleared and plumbing and electricity brought up to code before winter. Besides, Andrea will be leaving for college."

"I kinda like the idea of up close and personal with you."

"I noticed."

"It's nice to think that we'll be having all our future memories here. Even weddings. Maybe Andrea's," she mused.

"Or our future children's weddings someday." He hesitated before asking, "Do you think we made a baby already?"

She raised her eyebrows in surprise. That hadn't occurred to her, in the heat of the moment. So she paused to think.

"Grace?"

She was touched by the vulnerability in his voice over her hesitation and the worry that she wasn't committed to another child. "I don't know. It sure would be a great way to christen our new home. And, yes, in answer to your hidden question. I do want to have your baby. As soon as possible. Like you told the judge that day, my old clock is ticking."

He rewarded her with a scorching kiss. "I have great affection for your old clock. Wanna make love again?"

She laughed. "Out here with the snakes?" They were near some statuary that marked the edge of the onetime flower gardens. "I. Don't. Think. So."

"Can't blame a guy for trying." He let out an exaggerated sigh. "Guess we'll have to settle for the back seat of my truck."

By the time they finally arrived at Remy's house, the party was already in progress. No surprise there. The surprise was in the number of people, the big tent in the back yard, and the banner that read: "Congratulations Angel and Grace."

Grace immediately turned on him. "You were awfully sure of me."

"I swear, I didn't say a word."

"Not even to Tante Lulu?"

"Most especially not to Tante Lulu."

"I better go in the bathroom and check my hair and makeup. How do I look?"

"Great."

"What's the grin for?"

"Okay, here's the truth. You look like you just got laid."

"Oh, that's just great."

"That's what I said."

She stopped and faced him. "Before we get swallowed by the crowd, I just want to say again: I love you."

"I love you, too, babe."

"I am so blessed that you hung in there and waited for me to make up my mixed-up, hopeless mind."

He hugged her tight, then chuckled. "Bet I know what the first purchase will be for our new house."

"A St. Jude statue," they said as one.

~

The Cajun matchmaker always wins in the end...

TANTE LULU SAT in a lawn chair on a small rise of Remy's back lawn, pretty much like a queen overseeing her domain. She liked that image.

Remy had a huge house here that led down a distance to the bayou where his old houseboat was anchored. The boat had been his home at one time before he married Rachel and gathered a passel of young'uns about him, natural and adopted.

"Whatcha smilin' 'bout, Auntie?" Tee-John asked as he folded his long legs to sit down on the grass beside her.

"I'm allus happy when we get into the short rows. Means mah job is almos' done."

"With Grace and Angel?"

She nodded. "I swear, those two were slower comin' t'gether than cats eatin' a grindstone. When're you and Celine gonna have another baby?"

He was used to his aunt dropping bombs like that in the middle of a conversation. "What? Etienne's not enough for you?"

"The boy needs a brother or sister to tame him down. Only childs are so lonely."

"Soon," he conceded. Then he changed the subject. "How'd you arrange this *fais do do* so quick? No one else even knew about the engagement. In fact, Angel says he only proposed today."

Tante Lulu smiled her little cat smirk. "It's the bayou, honey. I learned from someone at Charmaine's beauty shop, who learned from Val's mother, that Angel was lookin' ta buy real estate here on Bayou Black, and Lawdy, Lawdy, that boy's biscuits ain't all done ta be buyin' that Sweetland place. Then Angel asked Lena ta take a picture, sneaky-like, of Grace's Walmart ring. And Ronnie called ta tell me Angel was sellin' up all his stuff back in Yankee land."

After Tee-John left, she noticed Daniel trying to sneak by her. "C'mere."

He balked, and she gave him one of her best dirty looks.

With a sigh of surrender, he walked over.

"Where ya goin'?"

"Home."

"What for? To drown yer sorrows agin?"

"What do you know about my sorrows, old lady?"

"I know ya seen a lot of chillen dyin' and yer all burned up."

"Burned out," he corrected her.

"Thass what I said. Ya got any lady friends?"

"No. And I don't want any."

"If dumb was dirt, you'd cover an acre. Ah, well, even a blind hog finds an acorn now and then."

"Thanks a bunch."

"I saw ya makin' googly eyes at Samantha a bit ago."

"I wouldn't know how to make a googly eye if I tried."

"I know googly when I see it. Besides, it comes natch'ral ta some men, especially you LeDeuxs. Yer next, boy. I kin smell the thunder rollin' yer way."

He didn't even bother to ask what she meant. He must have been told about her theory of love and thunderbolts and such.

Instead he said, "Oh, no! Concentrate on my brother Aaron if you want. Not me!"

They both looked toward the makeshift dance floor, where Aaron was talking flirty with Samantha. The two men looked almost identical, except for their haircuts and style of clothes.

"Actually, I think it'll be a package deal. St. Jude ain't done twins in a long while."

"I'm sorry, but I lost any religion I might have had a long time ago. I no longer believe."

"What a load of hooey! My, oh, my, St. Jude is gonna love you ta pieces, I do declare."

"I'm outta here," he said, but then he did an about-face and stomped back to the dance floor, where he tapped his brother on the shoulder, then pushed him aside to dance with Samantha. Yep, everything had a way of working out in the end. Daniel and Samantha looked like they was spitting fire at each other. She wouldn't be surprised if they were married before the end of the year. Another notch on St. Jude's holy belt.

Grace and Angel, at the same time, noticed Tante Lulu sitting alone.

"Should we?" Grace asked.

"I guess so."

"Thanks for all your help," Angel told the old lady.

"Ya finally got her—thass the most important thing." Turning to Grace, she added, "Sometimes you were dumber'n a toad sittin' on a bullfrog when it come ta lovin' this boy."

"Ribet, ribet," Grace said, squeezing her arm lovingly. "How did you manage to pull together this party on such short notice?"

"It's easy when ya got family and friends. Thass what you two have, now that yer settlin' here on the bayou." Both Grace and Angel got misty over that, family being something important that they wanted to build together.

A short time later, after some of the partygoers left, while a good number were still hanging around, Angel looked at Grace and said, "Wanna dance?"

"Okay." She stepped onto the portable dance floor. Angel shook his head. "Not here."

She tilted her head to the side.

"You remember that fancy shower in the houseboat?"

"The Playmate shower? How could I ever forget?"

"Well, I was just wondering." He examined his fingernails, pretending to be giving something a great deal of thought. "Would you consider shower dancing?"

"In the nude?"

"Is there any other way?"

One month later, they were married in Our Lady of the Bayou Church. Andrea gave her mother away. Tante Lulu prepared a wedding feast, Cajun style, in the church hall. Much food, rowdy music, and a good time were had by all.

Thanks to Tante Lulu's intervention, Andrea had made peace with her adoptive mother, Ruth, who'd finally got disgusted with George and kicked him out. Luc was filing papers for Angel to adopt Andrea, with Ruth's blessing. And Angel was gritting his teeth over the budding relationship between Andrea and Alexander Pappas. In all the ways that counted, Andrea had been and always would be Grace's child...and now his.

Not surprisingly, Grace was pregnant.

And up above—high up above—God and St. Jude gave each other high fives.

TANTE LULU'S SEAFOOD ÉTOUFFÉE

*1 1/2 lb. crawfish (or 1 lb. peeled and deveined shrimp, cooked, with one
8 oz. can lump crab meat), or any preferred combination)
2 cups chopped onions (regular and green scallions, if possible)
1 medium size chopped bell pepper
1/2 cup celery
2-3 cloves finely chopped garlic
1-2 bay leaves
1 pinch Old Bay seasoning (optional)
1/4 tsp thyme
1/2 tsp dried basil or two leaves fresh basil
1/4 cup chopped parsley for garnish*

*1/2 cup butter
1/4 cup flour*

*8 oz. can tomato sauce or finely chopped fresh tomatoes
1 cup white wine, dry preferred
8 oz. clam juice (or 1 cup shrimp stock if you cooked raw shrimp)
1/2 cup water*

*1 tbsp Worcestershire sauce
1 tsp tabasco or hot sauce
2 tbsp lemon juice, with zest
1/2 tsp pepper*

*salt to taste
1 pinch of cayenne pepper (optional)
1 pinch paprika (optional)*

∼

Listen carefully, y'all. I'm gonna show ya how ta cook Cajun style. First, grab yerself a tall glass of sweet tea ta cool off in the kitchen. Then cook the butter and flour in a large pot, preferably cast iron, stirring often 'til it bubbles and forms a brown roux. Ya know, 'cause I tol' ya many a times, that roux is the heart of any Cajun dish. Stir in all the veggies and spices, startin' with the Holy Trinity: onions, celery and bell peppers. Ya'll kin put some Cajun music on the radio iffen ya want 'cause ya need ta cook this batch over low heat, covered, fer 'bout 20 minutes or 'til the veggies are done ta taste. I likes them a little al dente. Thass French fer a little bit crisp. After raisin' the heat again, add the wet ingredients. Bring ta a boil. Add the shrimp and crab meat. Then reduce heat again and let simmer fer five minutes. Make sure ya stir carefully once the crab is added so ya don't break up the lumps of crab. Serve over cooked rice.

Hints:

Any combination of seafood can be used. If ya have crawfish available and ya like it, by all means use that. I like shrimp 'cause of the chewy texture and crawfish or crab fer the flavor.

Ya kin use other seafood, too. Like scallops or mussels or clams...whatever ya got in yer ice box.

Iffen ya want ta plan ahead, ya kin make this dish and serve the next day.

Enjoy, good friends!

READER LETTER

Dear Readers:

I hope you like this reissue of SO INTO YOU, which was originally published in 2009. Lots of authors cringe when they go back and read their older works, but I must admit to being pleased with Angel and Grace's story. I think it has held up well. What do you think?

Please try the recipe for Seafood Étouffée, as well as those in the back of my other books. Peachy Praline Cobbler Cake in WILD JINX, Red Beans and Rice in SNOW ON THE BAYOU, Shrimp Gumbo in THE CAJUN DOCTOR, and beignets in "Saving Savannah," for example.

Lots of people don't realize that the very first book in this Cajun series, the first appearance of Tante Lulu, was in THE LOVE POTION which was put out by a previous, now defunct, publisher. It has now been reissued, of course. But what I never expected when I first wrote that book was that there would be so many other linked Cajun stories to follow. They are THE LOVE POTION; TALL, DARK, AND CAJUN (*USA Today* bestseller and named by both Amazon and *Booklist* as one of the Top 10 Romances of 2004, as well as getting a starred review by the latter); THE CAJUN COWBOY; THE RED-HOT CAJUN; PINK JINX; PEARL JINX; WILD JINX (a *New York Times* bestseller and one of *Booklist*'s Top 10 Romances of 2008); SO INTO YOU (BAYOU ANGEL); SNOW ON THE BAYOU; THE CAJUN DOCTOR; and, coming soon, CAJUN CRAZY (December, 2017), and CAJUN PERSUASION (July 2018). There are also several Cajun novellas in which Tante Lulu continues with her adventures: "Jinx Christmas" in A DIXIE CHRISTMAS and "Saving Savannah" in HEART CRAVING.

And here's the best news. As so many of you have requested, Tante Lulu will tell you her very own story in a book called WHEN LULU WAS HOT. To be informed of its release date, watch my website at **SandraHill.net**, or my Facebook page at **Sandra Hill Author**, or sign up for my newsletter at:

https://www.sandrahill.net/mailinglist.html.

As always, I wish you smiles in your reading, and Tante Lulu sends along wishes for *joie de vivre* in your life.

Sandra Hill

ABOUT THE AUTHOR

Sandra Hill is the best-selling author of almost fifty novels and the recipient of numerous awards. She has appeared on many bestseller lists, including the *New York Times* and *USA Today*.

Readers love the trademark humor in her books, whether the heroes are Vikings, Cajuns, Navy SEALs, treasure hunters, or vangels (Viking vampire angels), and they tell her so often, sometimes with letters that are laugh-out-loud funny. In addition, her fans feel as if they know the characters in her books on a personal basis, especially the outrageous Tante Lulu.

At home in central Pennsylvania with her husband, four sons, a dog the size of a horse, six dogs belonging to her sons, and three grandchildren, Sandra is always busy. When she is not at their home, so close to the Penn State football stadium that she can hear the Blue Band practicing every night, she can be found relaxing at their Spruce Creek cottage.

Sandra is always on the lookout for new sources of humor. So be careful if you run into Sandra. What you say or do may end up in a book. If you want to take the chance, you can contact her at **SandraHill.net.** She loves to hear from her fans.

ALSO BY SANDRA HILL

Sandra Hill's Cajun Novels (In Order):

The Love Potion

Tall, Dark, and Cajun

The Cajun Cowboy

The Red-Hot Cajun

Pink Jinx

Pearl Jinx

Wild Jinx

So Into You (Bayou Angel)

Snow on the Bayou

The Cajun Doctor

Cajun Crazy

Cajun Persuasion

Novellas

"Jinx Christmas" in *A Dixie Christmas* Anthology

"Saving Savannah" in *Heart Craving* Anthology

"When Lulu was Hot" (Coming Soon)

57783201R00175

Made in the USA
Middletown, DE
17 December 2017